You are enjoying this material
thanks to a generous
appropriation from the
Wyoming State Legislature.

WALKING IN CIRCLES BEFORE LYING DOWN

 This Large Print Book carries the
Seal of Approval of N.A.V.H.

WALKING IN CIRCLES BEFORE LYING DOWN

MERRILL MARKOE

THORNDIKE PRESS

An imprint of Thomson Gale, a part of The Thomson Corporation

THOMSON
™
GALE

Detroit • New York • San Francisco • New Haven, Conn. • Waterville, Maine • London

LIBRARY OF CONGRESS CATALOGING-IN-PUBLICATION DATA

Markoe, Merrill.
    Walking in circles before lying down / by Merrill Markoe.
        p. cm. — (Thorndike press large print laugh lines)
    ISBN-13: 978-0-7862-9284-4 (hardcover : alk. paper)
    ISBN-10: 0-7862-9284-9 (hardcover : alk. paper)
    1. Dogs — Fiction. 2. Large type books. I. Title.
PS3563.A6652W35 2007
813'.54—dc22   2006033228

Published in 2007 by arrangement with Villard Books,
a division of Random House, Inc.

Printed in the United States of America on permanent paper
10 9 8 7 6 5 4 3 2 1

For Lewis

Preface

I probably wouldn't have ever gotten around to writing this book if I hadn't agreed to work with a Life Coach. And I only agreed to that because I was trying to help her feel good about herself.

She started out by telling me not to be held back by my old programming. She said I had "a self-limiting belief structure" and needed to ask myself, "What has kept me from taking action on this goal?" and, "What can I do to overcome this obstacle?" Actually, she didn't "say" those things so much as she hammered me with them. In order to shut her up, I went online and typed "how to write novels" into Google. I had barely begun going through the 13,700,000 entries when my Life Coach started crawling up my ass again.

"What specific plans have you made to move forward?" she badgered, making it clear that she did not consider a Google search a forward move.

After enduring a condescending lecture about self-sabotage, I figured I'd better start doing something fast. Luckily I found some of the online tips from "a respected novel-writing manual" very helpful. For example:

> #5. Even if you're not sure what the plot is going to be or what comes next, you will find that it's a lot easier if you are writing about people, places, and things with which you have already grown familiar.

So I thought: Why not write about women who like serial killers, swingers, regifting, being offered love advice from the most inappropriate source imaginable, learning to identify your instincts, and something called the Every Holiday Tree. In other words, I decided to tell the story of Dawn and Halley. And Chuck.

1
REMEMBER TO WRITE FROM YOUR UNIQUE PERSPECTIVE

I think one of the things that makes me unique is that as far back as I can remember, I have always talked to a lot of things besides people. I found it comforting, a way to prove that I existed. From early childhood on, I was haunted by the feeling that no one could hear me.

I was not without my reasons. My mother, Joyce, demanded and usually got all of whatever attention was available. She was beautiful enough to have stumbled into an accidental modeling career when she was seventeen just by waving at a photographer at the beach. Dressed in her yellow plaid shorts set and a big straw hat, she looked like a cast member of some seldom seen television show greeting smitten fans. A few months later, when her picture turned up in hundreds of inexpensive frames for sale at discount drugstores, it made my mother a local celebrity. Unfortunately, because she'd signed a release and accepted fifty dollars, she never received any more money. But once she realized that people knew who she was, she felt entitled to dominate any gathering, large or small, whether or not she had anything to say. I figured out, early on, that getting a word in edgewise wasn't going to be in the cards for me. So I became a quiet, obedient kid, good at blending in, easy to overlook. I learned to cope with my need for attention by creating my own private personal rituals to make myself feel special.

As early as second grade, I'd take the phone into the closet when I got home from school and call local radio shows so I could dedicate songs to myself. Then I'd spend hours by the radio, switching from station to station in the hope that at least one dee-jay would say, " 'You Light Up My Life' by Debbie Boone goes out to the girl who lights up everybody's life, Dawn Tarnauer." I never did hear anyone say it, but I kept right on hoping. While I waited, I would pretend to host my own TV show. For guests I would interview whatever was available: my plastic horses, my stuffed animals, my mother's cat, my chair, my own reflection.

But The Day Everything Changed was the

first time that anything ever answered me back.

I was born to the prefeminist version of my mother, a woman with a constantly lit cigarette and a perpetually jiggling leg, bored out of her mind but not sure what to do about it. I think she saw her firstborn much the same way she did her never finished pieces of découpage: as something that needed more work than she had time for. By the time I was five, I had figured out that the fastest way to my mother's heart was to fetch her cigarettes and tell her everything was going to be okay.

Halley, my sister, was born when I was six. Sometime during that pregnancy, my mother turned into a feminist. She dropped her découpage work (which consisted mainly of hatboxes shellacked with magazine clippings of female faces that looked like her own) in favor of something called "creative breakthrough parenting," where she learned that she could offset parental neglect through the use of extravagant praise. I remember not quite trusting all her suddenly effusive reinforcement, even finding it kind of embarrassing. But it worked like gangbusters on Halley, who loved hearing that her preschool drawings were "as

11

good as Matisse" and her one-finger piano compositions had the precocious brilliance of a grade school Beethoven. This despite the fact that neither of us really had any idea who those people were.

Of course, now that Halley and I were both effortlessly producing masterworks and our careers in the arts were assured, my mother rationalized that her presence at parent-teacher conferences and school events would be gilding the lily. This was fine with me. I was comfortable living under the radar. But it was different for Halley, who grew up feeling entitled to center stage and wondering why it seemed to elude her. When she auditioned for the seventh-grade play, *Miracle on 34ᵗʰ Street,* and was cast not as the lead but as one of the two dozen Christmas shoppers, it triggered in her an obsessive desire for a persona that everyone noticed. Soon she was dying her curly brown hair blue black, then red, then blond, and then black with orange streaks. She also started dressing more and more theatrically, favoring oversize round sunglasses, a dark head scarf, and a floor-length faux-fur coat — kind of an unintentional homage to Jackie O at Aristotle's funeral. But despite her valiant efforts, Halley never succeeded in gaining the moniker she wanted, which would have been something as simple as "the mysterious girl dressed in black." If the kids remembered to call her anything at all, it was something less mythic and more direct, like "dork."

In that way, Halley was a chip off the old block. Because as we got older, Joyce, our mother, kept searching endlessly, tirelessly, for her true life's calling. A new image was usually the first sign that things were about to change. She bounced from long-haired flamenco dancer to short-haired Scientology acolyte to buzz-cut-wearing animal-rights activist who walked picket lines at pet stores, held fund-raisers for rescue organizations, and chained herself to a five-hundred-pound Galápagos tortoise at Marine World. There was always something more pressing for my mother than paying attention to her daughters. It was clear to us that if we demanded too much of her time, it would have to be unfairly stolen from condemned animals. By taking care of ourselves and asking for nothing, we believed we were helping puppies and kittens stay alive.

On the surface, Halley and I probably looked like nice if slightly eccentric girls. Our grades were okay. We weren't out partying or doing drugs. But on closer inspection, we had constructed a yin and yang of defense mechanisms, neurotic tics, and eating disorders. While I was busy hiding bags of pecan sandies under my bedspread to make sure I was never more than an arm's length from sugar, just a few feet away Halley was diligently dividing a single package of celery into three days' worth of meals.

Fortunately, there was a father in residence to help this teeter-tottering family create some stability: Ted Tarnauer, owner and general manager of a small but popular vintage car repair. Ted was very proud of his history as a rockabilly guy from the days of Levi and the Rockats, a glimpse of which could be gotten by scrutinizing the triptych of dusty warped black-and-white photos in plastic frames that hung on the wall by his desk at the shop. Though taken from below stage level so he appeared to be fifteen feet tall and 50 percent nostril, you could still recognize the young Ted, his big greasy blond hair swooping into his face, his skinny body curled like a question mark over his guitar, looking handsome and arrogant, sporting a curled-lip sneer that spoke of meth and moonshine. This was Dad's real passion. He put a lot of time into perfecting the authentic fifties outfits he wore when his band, the Cheaterslicks, played. Even now he was very pleased when girls under forty got crushes on him and was proud when they sometimes said he looked like Brian Setzer. (Though the older ones more often referenced the mature Conway Twitty, which was also fine, but he liked it less.)

Ted was quite the talker. It didn't take much to launch him into a monologue so impenetrable that his friends worried there might be no bathroom breaks. Yet despite his retro rocker exterior, by middle age Dad had morphed into a right-wing neocon who wrote in Pat Buchanan's name on ballots where once he had written in Duane Eddy.

From early childhood on, Halley and I worshipped our daddy but were constantly worried that he might leave. We knew he was unhappy. It was hard to miss, since he had a tendency to break down and weep after a couple of beers.

To say nothing of the fact that by the time I was in third grade, I was finding him asleep on the couch in the morning when I left for school. The realization that I couldn't remember when I'd last seen him in the bedroom with Mom caused me to lie awake at night, plotting ways to make him happier. As it turned out, homemade greeting cards and blueberry muffins weren't what his life was missing. He left our home for good when I was ten.

Less than a month after he moved out he announced his intention to marry a woman from the neighborhood whose car he'd remodeled. It was unnerving that she looked enough like my mother to be her sister. The nuptials, which took place a few months after that, were a big festive event with a meticulous, if somewhat desperate, retro fifties theme full of hoop skirts, pegged pants, and Jell-O molds. The Cheaterslicks played. Everybody danced the Lindy hop.

The following day at school, I had my first asthma attack.

From that point forward, the only time I could count on seeing my dad was when each of his new romances imploded. Then he'd reappear with bribes for us in exchange for helping him pack. "I got some more cool stuff for you," he'd say, revealing a box of things he took out of the cars he got from salvage: pencils, reading glasses, comic books that were missing a cover, gloves with the fingers stuck together, bobble-headed Dodgers. "You girls take whatever you want," he'd say, "but first do Daddy a favor and stuff those *Road and Track*s into that black gym bag."

By my late teens, I was tall and blond and

tan from swimming, running, surfing, and riding my bike. I was in good enough shape to wear a bikini without flinching. Even though my grades were all B's and A's, I was an insecure mess. When I think back to that period, I see myself as kind of the flip side to the Girl from Ipanema. Because although I was getting my share of attention from the opposite sex, I remember a lot more people saying "Jesus Christ, Dawn! Are you nuts?" than going "Aaaah." Like when I decided to get married right out of high school to someone I barely knew, in an unintentional homage to my parents.

In keeping with the Tarnauer family tradition, my first husband, Neil, was domineering, helpless, and prone to spontaneous bursts of theatrical emotion. Like Dad, Neil was equal parts in love with his own dramas and the selfless way I offered rapt attention.

When I met him, I was working the mid-morning shift at the Lunch Box in Simi Valley, the only job I could find when I graduated from high school. I was feeling anonymous, directionless, and at a loss when Neil and his big, big plans appeared one day like a door to a world of limitless possibilities. Neil was fourteen years my senior and knowledgeable about lots of things: the stock market, the environment, politics, civil law, filmmaking. We got married at City Hall a month after we started dating and moved to a two-room apartment in his hometown of Fresno, where, he claimed, his connections would work to our advantage.

The plan was for us both to get jobs, pool our money, and produce a series of documentaries about the deadly fungus endangering the health of many species of frogs. With Neil's knowledge and my energy and support, we were poised to accomplish great things. Right up until the day Neil got a job tending bar at the Scoreboard, a sports bar downtown. He quickly became so enamored of his new role as the local long-haired authority on absolutely everything that he didn't even notice when our dreams of glory began to die on the vine.

Without them, it became harder for me to ignore the fact that sex with Neil reminded me of being in bed with one of those waving mechanical Santas that department stores put in their Christmas windows: every move, every word, always the same, and in the exact same order. This unfortunate set of associations would have been less distracting if I hadn't noticed one night that his moans of passion sounded a lot like "Ho-ho-ho."

By year three, about the same time I was giving up hope in general, I found a large black-and-white Labrador-Newfoundland mix, abandoned at the market. He was about eight years old, the vet thought, and seemed to be in good health. No one knew why someone had tied him to the shopping cart return and just left him there. He didn't bite. He didn't cry. He didn't pee in the house. He was very affectionate. He knew "sit" and "down." The only other information available was that he was wearing a red collar from which hung a small round silver tag that had been engraved with a single word: Swentzle. Assuming it was his last name, I conducted an exhaustive search through local phone books for his owner. I even put up posters featuring his picture under block letters that read, "FOUND. HEY EVERYBODY! LOOK! IT'S SWENTZLE!!" No one called.

By the fourth day he was following me everywhere, greeting people no matter what their circumstances, like some kind of dazed goodwill ambassador. Just as tickled to meet someone new at the scene of an accident as he would have been if they climbed in through the window in the middle of the night, Swentzle was democracy in action. The most amazing thing was that once

Swentzle arrived, life with Neil seemed to get better. Swentzle distracted me in the best way possible. Right up until the day that Wayne, the manager of the Scoreboard, informed Neil that the Sacramento County Department of Child Support was planning to "assign" 50 percent of his wages after taxes for child support payments. If I hadn't walked in on Wayne explaining the whole thing to him, I still wonder if Neil would have ever mentioned it to me.

"Why didn't you tell me you were married before?" I gasped. "How could you forget to mention you had a kid?"

"Ah, it's one of those things I'm trying to put behind me," he said. "I've got my doubts the kid is even mine."

Turned out Neil had never paid a penny of the thousands of dollars in child support he owed to the mother of a seven-year-old boy in Sacramento. She had a pretty good case against him, since Neil had been married to her for six and a half years. I was thunderstruck.

"How many people do you think are going to listen to what we have to say about endangered frogs once they find out you're a deadbeat dad?" I said.

"Well . . . I figured once our documentary started raking in the bucks, I'd, you know, try to pay her something," he said.

"I thought all the money we made was going toward helping the frogs," I said, immediately feeling bad for stiffing some poor underfinanced little kid.

Neil's solution was for us to buy a school bus and live on the road while we figured out how to raise money.

The next day I took my private stash of ones and fives and the birthday money I'd been wisely hiding in a Tampax box and bought bus tickets back to L.A. for Swentzle and me. At the time, I was filled with shame about running away from a marriage, especially one that everyone warned me wouldn't work. I hated proving all the naysayers right. But what never really occurred to me was that I was finally taking a step toward turning my life around.

2
HALLEY

The five-and-a-half-hour bus ride from Fresno was tedious. I had to flirt with the driver until he gave me permission to let Swentzle sit on the seat beside me. Then I had to pretend to sleep the rest of the ride in order to avoid answering a lot of nosy personal questions. Swentzle was, as always, a very good boy. Whenever I slept, so did he.

After five and a half hours on a bus, it was a great relief to see Halley's dented dusty black Blazer parked in front of the depot. The hour drive to where she was living in Malibu flew by once the car rolled off the freeway heading north on the Pacific Coast Highway. After almost six years of Fresno's heat and squalor, that mesmerizing expanse of glittering mirrored ocean on the left looked to me like a colossal sigh of relief. Its mere presence made everything nearby seem somehow picturesque. Even that twenty-foot-high concrete sombrero-wearing hombre on top of Malibu's ocean-side taco stand struck me as more inspired than all of his twenty-foot-high Paul Bunyan–esque relatives stationed at fast-food establishments across the rest of the state.

Swentzle hung his upper body out the window the whole way up the coast, enjoying the cool wet breeze. I think he also loved the way the ocean smelled like things he might eat.

Halley was living in an extra-large Winnebago, which was parked on a hillside lot that overlooked the ocean. In its heyday, it had been the makeup trailer for the original cast of *Baywatch.* Now all that remained of its glorious past was a fading "Luv ya, David Hasselhoff" written in red Sharpie on the cupboard over the stove. When the show ended, the producers had donated the Winnebago to Dr. Richter, the vet for whom Halley worked, so he could turn it into a mobile spay and neuter clinic. The reason Halley found herself living there, enjoying a million-dollar view while sporting a two-, not an eight-, digit bank account, was that the lot where it was parked held the foundation of a house that had burned to the ground in the Malibu fires of 1993. Outside

Halley's bedroom window, you could still see the living room fireplace. The view from the kitchen included a weed-choked stretch of tile floor and the charred remains of a Jacuzzi. The original owners had sold at a loss to Dr. Richter in gratitude for repairs he did on their badly burned dog. I think they also felt that rebuilding the place from scratch would be painful and risky. So Richter quickly hauled the *Baywatch* Winnebago up there as a placeholder and offered Halley a caretaker position while he drew up plans to build.

In a way, a Winnebago sitting on that expensive lot was kind of a throwback to the old mid-twentieth-century Gidget-beach-house-and-surf-shack Malibu I used to see when I was a kid. Things changed radically in the nineties when the Malibuians began systematically leveling every weathered wood structure and replacing it with clusters of fifteen-thousand-square-foot single-family dwellings. Those beach homes of old that were reminiscent of an Andrew Wyeth painting of a barn all morphed into Mediterranean villas with turrets and moats and underground parking for forty. But unlike the rest of the residences in her surrounding neighborhood, Halley's

Winnebago had three rooms, not thirty. And they were in a row, with the kitchen in between the other two. The seats in the eating nook folded down into beds, so the dining room became my bedroom. At night, Swentzle and I would curl up there together like a pair of quotation marks. He would quickly fall asleep and begin snoring like a chain saw as I lay beside him, my thoughts ping-ponging wildly back and forth between overwhelming panic and an almost manic glee. To say I was confused about the direction my life should be taking is to understate.

The Halley of that period, with her shimmering magenta hair and small gold eyebrow ring, was focused mainly on her low-paying job as Dr. Richter's receptionist, not because she was interested in the field of reception per se, but because of her unrequited crush on Dr. Richter. He was only thirty then and cute in a young Jewish executive kind of way. Halley's attraction to Dr. Richter made the other hospital employees apprehensive, because to know Halley for any length of time was to know that she had a sociopath tracking device where her heart was supposed to be.

Of course, no one in the Tarnauer family exhibited much in the way of good instincts when it came to people. But it was in the area of romantic attachment that everyone in our family excelled at being terrible. And in Halley's case, her special blend of incorrect insights combined with carefully honed bizarre expectations ensured that the men to whom she gave her love were never anyone you would leave alone in a room with your purse.

To make matters worse, this was back when Halley was still sneaking around with Scott Peterson behind the back of Amber Frey. It had started innocently enough. Halley had only the best of intentions that day she went to Modesto to help search for Scott's missing wife with one of the vet techs from work who'd known Laci Peterson in high school. Halley later told me that from the minute she laid eyes on Scott, she felt compelled to reach out to him. "I was so moved by the strong, silent way he handled his grief," she said. Next thing we knew, he was phoning her, then flying down to spend the weekend.

"I got a weird vibe from him" was my initial comment after meeting him the Saturday he drove down to have Halley dye his hair blond. Instantly, I knew I'd said the wrong thing. But a couple of hours later, when Mom whispered, "I don't get it.

What's up with the orange hair?" Halley turned on us both like a lioness protecting her cub.

"Scott is in a lot of pain. And I'm just glad I can be there for him," she yelled, her face red, her eyes bulging. "You two are as bad as the assholes in the media. And just so you know, working on a new look is a great way to help a man restart his life." After that, no one dared mention Scott Peterson again, even after those audiotapes of his conversations with Amber Frey were all anyone talked about.

Anyway, Halley was right in the midst of coping with this impressive new low in her personal life when Swentzle and I showed up to stay. In a way, our timing was perfect, because Halley had started pet-sitting for Richter's clients and was way overbooked. She was thrilled to be able to foist the overflow onto me. She also directed me toward an opening at the Doggy Depot, a day care facility that Richter had started in the unused stables behind the hospital. I felt very lucky: full-time employment the same day I arrived, paid to hang out with animals, AND I could bring Swentzle to work. Talk about an embarrassment of riches.

Once I moved in, Halley was glad to have

my problems front and center to distract her from her own. It helped keep her mind off of Scott Peterson. Halley had always been proud of her extensive reading in the field of self-improvement. She bought and highlighted with yellow marker every best-selling book with a personal pronoun in the title. I quickly learned that the key to serene cohabitation with my little sister was to smile and nod while she offered endless intrusive suggestions: I needed to take a meditation seminar to balance the negative chi I absorbed from living with Neil. I needed to refresh my look through laser skin resurfacing and something new called ther-mage. I really had to go to the community center and sign up for a watercolor class, because if I could develop a body of work, I could get an exhibit at the Frame-for-All in the shopping center. But most of all, I needed to give some thought to the idea of donor insemination. The responsibility of single motherhood might just offer me a more purpose-driven life.

As her suggestions piled up around me in a philosophical gridlock, so did my symptoms of asthma. But in the end, I was more worried about passing on the genes of the Tarnauer family to some poor fatherless infant than I was about finding the financing to get resurfaced by lasers.

One thing you had to give Halley: She was completely relentless. I had just spent the day fretting about how to tell her to shut the fuck up without hurting her feelings when she came in the door glowing like a Halloween pumpkin.

"Okay. First off, don't judge me," she started, "but I had the most amazing experience talking to Scott on the phone. I know I said I wouldn't take his calls anymore, but he needed help finding positive ways to view his situation. And when we were about to say good-bye, he broke down and started to cry." She paused and looked at me with a bug-eyed openmouthed expression indicating she knew I'd be as stunned at this detail as she was. "He wanted to thank me for everything I'd done," she continued. "And then you know what he said? He said, 'You have a real gift for helping confused people. You should become, like, a Life Coach.' I was blown away, but I've been thinking about it. I've decided I'm going to check it out."

3
THE CELEBRATION
NEVER ENDS

It was in the middle of an acid rain of unsolicited advice from Halley that I met my second husband, Jake.

The only reason we went to that Beck concert in the first place was that my mother got a bunch of free tickets through an old Scientology connection. I never particularly liked Beck. But I desperately needed a distraction from Halley's manic meddling, as well as from the overload of natural beauty that was life in Malibu. As it turns out, there are only so many spectacular sunsets and fabulous ocean vistas a person can experience in a row before her brain needs an infusion of jarring shit. And of course by "a person," I mean me.

The concert itself was more or less what I expected. After a few beers, I started to relax enough to find all that cutesy eclectic stuff listenable. But Beck looked so goddamn young that I felt more like a friend of his mom's than a fan. Maybe that's why my attention turned to the black-and-yellow houndstooth sport coat on the guy standing in front of me. I was thinking it could only have belonged to a hustler or someone with ironic taste in clothes. As it turned out, Jake was right between the two. He was all smoldering Bon Jovi good looks and trendy accessories. There was something about those two leather wristbands on his tanned scrawny wrists that got me hot. And then I had an idea.

"Push me into him," I whispered to Halley, who looked at me like I was crazy. After I repeated myself, she shrugged and gave me a shove. I went stumbling forward, causing Mr. Wristbands to slosh beer on the back of the guy in front of him. When both men turned and glowered at me, I looked into the light blue eyes of the guy in the houndstooth jacket, and an electrical current passed between us. Next thing I knew, Wristbands and I were pantomiming a conversation that seemed like it might have been very compelling had I been able to hear some of it. There was enough definite chemistry going on that by the concert's end, we agreed to meet for drinks the following night.

From the moment I sat down with Jake at

a table in the Basement, a bar that was nearly as loud as the concert, I was enamored. The thing I liked best about him was that he seemed to be nothing at all like Neil. Where Neil was mercurial and spontaneous, Jake was low-key and methodical. He was also much cuter than Neil and exactly my age. Best of all, when I invited him to the Winnebago for dinner, he instantly clicked with Swentzle. Looking back, I think that is the best explanation I have for why we got married three months later. I fell in love with how Jake fell in love with my dog.

We moved into a six-unit apartment building in Oxnard, about forty minutes north of L.A. and right down the street from his business. If only Jake had been smart enough to find us an apartment next to a freeway, where we could have coexisted in a constant state of thunderous ambient noise, we might not have noticed how little we had to say to each other.

Still, my steamy fantasies about being pinned down on the bed by those nasty rocker wristbands remained strong enough to carry me through the complimentary three-month period of nonjudgmental bliss to which every new couple is entitled. Unfortunately, even during this obligatory hallucination-filled interval, sex with Jake was chilly and infrequent.

Once I could see that there was a worrisome pattern setting in, I tried to delicately bridge this unnerving subject via earnest discussion. But Jake got embarrassed, denying that there was any problem. And it's hard to solve a problem that doesn't exist.

As a follow-up, I tried covert attempts at improving things between us by trying to implement some of the "man pleaser" suggestions Halley e-mailed from lists in women's magazines ("Try talking dirty!"). However, nothing (not even memorizing a "Map to the Prostate") managed to prevent the veil from lifting during month number four, when the lack of sex and the silence surrounding it became as obvious to me as a severed thumb in a cup of vanilla pudding.

By now I had frequent thoughts about leaving but found it hard to devise an exit strategy. Being propelled out the door by the force majeure of a heated argument was out. Jake was so easy to get along with, there were never any last straws. Even worse, on paper things still looked good. Jake made a decent income running Bin There, Dump That, a fleet of twelve crusty forest green metal garbage bins that he inherited from his father. Although not exactly challenging work, it did provide a level of dinner conversation that was in a category all its own. "I had to take the truck to Twenty-sixth Street to pick up Celine and Barbra because they were needed at the construction site where Mariah is working," he'd say about his Dumpsters, which were named for famous divas. Many were the evenings in which I sat across from him at dinner, wondering how to make my face look like it cared.

And once again, it was Swentzle to the rescue. His overamped enthusiasm for absolutely everything, coupled with his limitless affection, pushed me gently along my second rut-filled-road-of-marital-difficulties like a carefully herded sheep. It was Swentzle who made me laugh and Swentzle who gave me optimism and the impression I had an affectionate, happy home. Right up until that surreal day when I found Jake's gigantic stack of gay porno magazines stashed under our mattress while I was making the bed. As shocked as I was, I was also relieved to finally have both an explanation and, at last, a good enough reason to leave.

By now I knew better than to confront Jake with anything so personal. So I did the only honorable thing I could think of under the circumstances: I faked an asthma attack. Once I'd worked up a good strong discordant wheeze, I humbly suggested that I needed to "spend some time alone." If Jake realized that this was a euphemism for "I don't want to be married to you anymore," he didn't let on.

Thus it was with his blessing that I took our old Ford Taurus, put Swentzle in the backseat, and drove back to L.A. exactly two years after I'd left. This time I thought I'd try bunking with my mother while I calculated my next move. Joyce had continued to live in Culver City in the pale green stucco single-level three-bedroom duplex with the big banana palm and the partially dead lawn that was her main part of the divorce settlement from Dad three decades earlier. She was, of course, on her cell phone when I showed up at her door. Her still beautiful face lit up with pleasure at the sight of her unhappy daughter, though not sufficient pleasure to actually hang up the phone. She continued talking while gesturing for me to put down my suitcase in the hall.

"That was a serious buyer," she said when she finally ended her call about ten minutes later. "I have my fingers crossed that this guy is going to launch us." I hadn't been to my mother's house in two years and was astonished to see that the whole place had been transformed into a warehouse of sorts as Joyce led me Lewis and Clark style down a couple of small navigable trails that cut through a chin-high canyon of opened and unopened cardboard boxes. These turned out to be tributaries of a larger river that meandered along a floor-to-ceiling card-board box replica of Bryce Canyon. As our safari inched forward, the velocity of my mother's words and excited pitch of her voice triggered an automatic tune-out mechanism that took me back to the many junior high school lectures I'd endured about L. Ron Hubbard.

"You know how no one likes to take down the Christmas tree," Joyce was saying as I rejoined the program already in progress. "That's because everybody loves Christmas! Even the Jews! And that got me thinking . . . the reason we don't decorate the rest of the year is because no one really knows what to do for the smaller holidays!" We arrived at a makeshift workstation. "And then I had this breakthrough," she continued. "Why not a tree that adapts to every holiday year round? A tree so alive and relevant that it's like a member of the family! And then I thought, Well, that can be my slogan: 'Like a member of the family!' And the next thing you know, here we are in rooms full of prototypes!"

With a flick of a wall switch, a dozen small potted pine trees, each differently decorated, lit up. Joyce swept her hand majestically toward them. "America, meet the Every Holiday Tree! Now you can decorate to your heart's content twelve months a year!"

As I looked around me at this multiseasoned wonderland, I felt an unexpected sadness. The Every Holiday Tree had taken over my old bedroom. On the other side of that double-layered barricade of cardboard boxes and potted plants was the corner by the window where I used to curl up with my portable radio in grade school and wait for the deejay to read the dedications I'd called in for myself. And later, in high school, I'd sit in that same spot listening to Nirvana and dreaming about driving up to Seattle to rescue Kurt Cobain from Courtney Love. Kurt would materialize beside me, lock his sad, soulful eyes into mine, and see a reason not to kill himself after all. Now there was a worktable full of carved wax models for future ornaments in various stages of completion. "Happy Presidents' Day," said a wax miniature of Mount Rushmore, detailed with enamel paint so brightly colored that it made all of the presidents look like they were wearing permanent lipstick and eyeliner.

"Every tree comes with a starter kit of two dozen ornaments plus a string of custom lights for each of your big nine classics: Halloween, Thanksgiving, Valentine's Day, Easter, Fourth of July, Mother's Day, Father's Day, Labor Day, Memorial Day. Everything for $89.95! Plus 'a quibble-free guarantee'! Do you like that? I kind of borrowed it from the Miles Kimball catalog." As my mother yammered on, it occurred to me I was looking at what had become of the unspent money her parents had left for our college tuition.

"Anyway, this is just to get the ball rolling. Everyone will need to buy more. And that's where the real cash is. In the extras." Joyce lifted a sketch pad full of drawings off the desktop. "You gotta see our Patriotic Line," she said as she leafed through the pages. "We've got the plans for a special set of two eagle-topped topiary-style cypress trees for 9/11."

"You're doing this by yourself?" I said, as amazed at the scale of this new project as I was by the fact that Joyce had never bothered to say hello or ask me a single question since I'd walked in the door.

"Ng is helping me," said Joyce, turning in

the direction of a rustling sound somewhere down the boxes trail, where a small, middle-aged man of Korean descent dressed in a cowboy shirt and ironed jeans was emerging over the box horizon.

"Hi there," he said, smiling broadly.

"Ng, show her your 9/11!" Joyce urged giddily. Ng held up a wax ornament shaped like the World Trade Center. It was wrapped in an American flag punctuated by a lightning bolt. "Ng is the sculptor who is making our prototypes. I am working on getting the rights to the real names of everyone who died so we can do a gold-and-silver-embossed three-thousand-bead garland."

"If we don't get, we change the spelling of names a little bit. Who gonna know?" said Ng with a big mischievous grin.

"Oh, Ng. Stop," said my mother, pursing her lips and shaking her head. She stroked the branches of one of her trees like it was her cat.

"Mom, don't you think people might still be a little hinky about the whole 9/11 thing?" I said after a heated discussion with myself about whether to bother saying anything.

"I couldn't agree less," said Joyce. "Someone will make that first commercial move. It might as well be us. We're taking the whole kit and kaboodle to trade shows and distributors."

She shut off the lights, and I began to follow her back toward the kitchen. "When did all this start?" I asked, realizing I had been avoiding my mother's calls for months.

"Well, you know how I had been praying for a new calling," she said, speaking with the intensity of someone unwilling to admit to even one idea of normal size in a lifetime of grandiose moments. "And then one night last winter I woke up and this whole thing came to me like it was channeled from a divine source. All my life I have been working for the benefit of others. And now God is rewarding me for having lived selflessly by leaving a pile of destiny where I couldn't fail to step in it."

After that, I hung around only long enough to have an instant coffee before deciding to head back to Halley's. Once again, my timing synced up with another of my sister's career changes. She had pared down her work schedule in order to have the time to follow up on Scott Peterson's advice. She was finally becoming a Life Coach.

"It's just so perfect for me," she said the minute I walked in. "I can work at home! A lot of it's done on the phone! Put your bags down anywhere. Let me read you something." She ran to get her workbook.

"You have a diet anything to drink?" I asked, exhausted.

"Check the fridge," she said, carefully scanning the pages. "Okay, listen: 'Questions to ask yourself if you're thinking of becoming a Life Coach.' " She resumed reading: " 'Are you a good communicator?' Definitely! Everyone knows that! 'Do you sincerely wish the best for everyone?' Totally! 'Would you like to design your own workday?' " She paused and stood, open-mouthed, mimicking the shock she imagined I must be feeling at encountering this photo-realistic portrait of her. " 'Would you like unlimited earnings potential?' Duh! I think I could be talked into that!" She continued, " 'Are you an authentic person, living your values and experiencing success?' These are all so me, it's scary. And guess what? I'm almost certified; I already listed myself on Google! Now it's a matter of trusting the universe to bring me clients."

"Wow!" I said, bewildered. "Sounds promising."

"In the meantime, I'm going to practice on you. Wait till you see how healthy this is going to be for you!"

"Can we wait till tomorrow?" I pleaded,

filling a dish with water for Swentzle. "I am wrecked from driving and moving and leaving my husband. I also might be getting asthma."

"Sure," she continued. "Just listen for one more second: 'Even if you're not absolutely sure what you want in life, a Life Coach can help you create a plan to achieve it.' Isn't that so incredibly perfect for you?"

It only took about twenty-four hours for me to realize that being Life Coached by Halley was not the most difficult part of living with her. Halley was still swirling in the turbulent headwaters of Scott Peterson, now in prison and awaiting trial. Having me in residence gave her an outlet for endlessly dissecting, analyzing, and obsessing on the details of his case. I learned to nod thoughtfully and say nothing as she paced, drank wine, and chain-chewed Red Vines while hurling epithets at a biased media.

"They are so totally out to get him," she would rail. "No one ever prints Scott's side. No one. Ever."

"What is Scott's side?" I asked, only once.

"I can't talk to you about this," she said, and stormed out of the room, furious.

Luckily, I was only at Halley's for three days before I landed a pet-sitting job for Shawn Garcia, a forty-two-year-old sales manager for Dun & Bradstreet who lived up Latigo Canyon in a big rambling house. She needed someone to hang out with Celestine, her shih tzu, for a week while she attended a marketing conference in Denver.

It was difficult getting back into living my life in the midst of someone else's details: going to bed staring at framed photos of unidentifiable loved ones; brushing my teeth surrounded by their bottles of vaguely threatening antiaging preparations; listening to unfamiliar voices who called themselves "me" leave answering machine messages. It was unsettling to know that any place I put something of mine was a place it didn't really belong.

But none of that mattered in light of the one thing that did: Swentzle began to look old. I had noticed a few months before that his back end wasn't cooperating when his front end tried to stand up. If I patted him too hard on his butt, his knees began to buckle. And was it the sun shining on him, or was his face getting awfully white? Still, as long as he continued greeting everyone with enthusiasm bordering on hysteria, I figured he'd bounce through everything okay. I wasn't sure how old he was, and I preferred not knowing. But on the second night of house-sitting, while playing three-man "chase me" with the adorable but mentally challenged Celestine, I noticed that Swentzle couldn't come up the few stairs that led from the backyard into the house. I coaxed him. He wagged his tail. Every noise and facial expression he made indicated desire to come. But he couldn't make his legs carry out the orders.

He had been mainly healthy until now. This came much too quickly. It seemed nightmarishly unfair.

Next day on my lunch break, Dr. Richter agreed to give Swentzle a checkup. "I don't think it's his hips," he announced after X-raying him free of charge. "Looks to me like a ruptured disk. There's corrective surgery that could help, though Swentzle's getting up there agewise. Still, if you'd like to talk to an orthopedic specialist, I have one coming by later this week to consult."

"I have great success with this surgery," the orthopedic surgeon said after examining Swentzle. "I'd say he has a ninety percent chance for increased mobility."

I was elated. "That's incredible," I said to Richter afterward. "You know how much I love Swentzle. But how do I get four thousand dollars?"

"If you can come up with half, maybe we can work something out for the rest," said

Richter, who had become very fond of Swentzle himself. A percentage of the dogs he helped ignored him or bit him and worse. But the greeting Swentzle gave him every single day made him feel like he was a dearly beloved member of the veterinary community.

"Ordinarily I don't recommend surgery for a thirteen-year-old dog," said Richter. "But if he's got a ninety percent chance for greater mobility, we should go for it."

"That's ridiculous. You can't spend that kind of money on an animal who's going to die in a couple of years anyway," said my mother when I tried to borrow a little money.

"I dropped a hint with Maura," said Halley, who, God bless her, was empathetic. Maura was a successful actress and Halley's steadiest pet-sitting client. When Maura was younger, she was known for playing the pouty, spoiled, eventually dumped rich fiancée of the romantic lead. But now that she was in her mid-forties and more likely to be cast as the insufferable, snobbish rich mother of the very same character she'd once played, she was thrilled when she got a lead in a new television series, even though it meant playing the representative from the planet CRSK in a show about the first Intergalactic United Nations. With her impressive new TV salary in tow, Maura was feeling benevolent. She generously agreed to hire me to pet-sit and advanced me the two thousand dollars to help my boy Swentzle recover.

And with that spectacular gesture of compassion, the clouds parted and the sun came back out. My spiraling depression was replaced by gratitude and hope. The gods had smiled. I had been granted the only thing I really wanted: more quality time with Swentzle.

I felt so good about that 90 percent figure that I didn't particularly worry when I brought Swentzle to the hospital the following Monday. I just kissed him on his fuzzy snout and said I'd see him in a few hours.

That was the last time I ever saw him alive. The anesthesia they gave him stopped his heart.

When Richter told me, I was grief-stricken like never before, like I didn't know I could be. I didn't feel like I could face my life without Swentzle. His presence next to me everywhere was something I relied on for joy, for comfort, and for balancing moments I found terrifying. I was filled with a lacerating self-hatred for putting him in jeopardy. He had been in good health. All he had was a back problem. If I had left well enough alone, he'd still be alive. So he couldn't come up the stairs. Big fucking deal. Why didn't I just stay downstairs with him?

"This rarely happens" was what both Richter and the surgeon said as I stood there, sobbing pitifully. "The odds are low for these kinds of complications. He must have had some kind of preexisting condition we didn't spot." But hearing this didn't help at all. Neither did "You did what you thought was right" or "How could you know? The surgeon said ninety percent."

"No one would turn those odds down," Richter reminded me.

"But you said you were worried about surgery on a thirteen-year-old dog. I should have listened to you," I sobbed.

Without Swentzle, the world was a much darker place. I would panic every time I remembered he was gone, then quickly spiral into self-loathing so dense, there was no way to see past it. There was no comfort for me anywhere. Nor did I deserve any. Even talking out loud to Swentzle, repeatedly apologizing for betraying him by putting him in harm's way, only made me feel much worse. No wonder no one could stay married to me. I deserved to be unloved. I killed my own dog.

I was in a very black mood the day Halley presented me with personalized pet-sitter cards she printed for me on her computer. "You're a pet care professional now," she lectured. "Time to kick your business into gear." She'd also made a list of career-related places where I should solicit work: animal hospitals, pet supply stores, shelters, whole-food markets, dog parks. Which is why, about two months later, I found myself walking into the pound.

I had no intention of looking around. I didn't want to think about replacing Swentzle. The shelter itself looked like a covered parking garage that had mated with a small airplane hangar. It was a stark and impersonal building, like a prison but dirtier. Clean enough for dogs, but not clean enough for pedophiles and rapists? I thought with disgust.

The walls were lined with unpleasant-looking regulation animal cages. The ones closest to the door were full of pit bulls making heartbreaking faces that beamed, "Hey. Girl. Come over for just a minute. You'll be amazed at how much chemistry we have." I was still feeling much too vulnerable to look any of them in the eye.

That was before I accidentally (well, was it really an accident?) saw my future son sitting alone in a big dank cement cell. He was all black with a white flame on his chest and ears that stood straight up like Sister Bertrille's wimple on *The Flying Nun.* He looked like an oversize toy some child abandoned when the basement flooded. The sign on his cage said he was eight months old and a mixed breed. Someone had turned him in for digging holes. That didn't seem fair. Holes weren't against the law. Holes and squirrel patrol were what most of these guys did best.

He looked like maybe part Lab, part German shepherd. Or German shorthaired. Something German. Or something else? He was huge for being that young, like a kid with size twelve feet. When I knelt down to say hello, he stumbled over, cautiously wagging his tail way down low, like a flag of surrender. I put my finger into his cage, and he started gnawing on it, looking up at me with unwarranted trust. His cautious expression said, "I don't know what I'm supposed to do. Is this okay?"

And right then, in that single moment, it was all over.

"I give up," I said to him. "Let's you and me go home." I had never fallen for something so quickly that didn't keep me up nights sorting truth from lies or worrying about contagious diseases. Adopting someone from the pound was a bit like picking a mail-order bride from a catalog: an instant lifetime commitment made to a stranger based on superficial first impressions.

All this was whizzing through my head as I signed the paperwork and paid the fees. But it wasn't until I actually picked up the squirming, disoriented young animal to carry him out to my car that I started to feel woozy. At that moment, a Department of Animal Control employee, in an unflattering khaki uniform, walked past, her face expressionless from a long day of shoveling shit, hosing piss, and dealing with potentially tragic dog scenarios. Suddenly she smiled broadly. "Oh, how sweet. I love that little guy," she said, stopping to rub my new dog on the belly. This relaxed me a little. Maybe my instincts had improved. Maybe every decision I made was not the wrong one. "I'm so glad you're adopting him," the worker said, calling to her friend, who was hooking a leash to a bucking beagle, "Hey, Jennifer, she's adopting that little black pit."

"You think he's a pit bull?" I said, feeling a wave of nausea. A dog with a checkered future was not what I had in mind.

"That's what the jerks who tied him to

the front gate in the middle of the night wrote on the note they attached," she said confidentially as I sank further into buyer's remorse. Why in the world had I taken the clean slate of my new life and mucked it up with a black pit? Here I was on the wrong side of a second marriage so ill conceived it hadn't even lasted two years. And now I was proving that apparently I had learned no lesson at all about making bad, spontaneous, emotionally based decisions.

By the time I sat behind the wheel of my car and put the dog on the seat beside me, I was plotting a return trip to bring him back. "I have no business taking responsibility for another life," I said, looking my new charge squarely in the eyes and feeling my heart break when I saw how happy and trusting he acted. It was scary the way dogs — well, all animals and children — could so easily be taken hostage, forced to blithely accompany any idiot who decided to take them home, all the while tragically failing to comprehend what kind of potentially awful hand they were being dealt. And suddenly I was back at New Year's Eve in the eighth grade, listening to Joyce, after too many highballs, announce for no real reason that Halley and I had been accidents. "Honey, I want to apologize for being such a shitty

51

mother. I knew from the moment you were born that I wasn't cut out for it," she said, crunching ice cubes and mixing herself another whiskey sour, confident that this simple act of blunt contrition absolved her of a decade of terrible mothering.

I felt shaky and light-headed as I drove toward Halley's. In order to regain a sense of calm and order, I started to talk out loud to the panting black-and-white puppy perched on the seat next to me, looping my fingers inside his collar to keep him from diving off the front seat. Talking aloud to dogs I sat for always made me feel more in control. Maybe they weren't listening, but then again who ever was?

It didn't take long for me to realize that trying to restrain the puppy and steer at the same time was a serious driving hazard. So I pulled the silly animal into my lap, despite the fact that he was really too big for that. Now, as I continued to drive and talk, I began scratching him behind his silky ears, just the way I used to comfort Swentzle. Either the ear scratching had a calming effect or the puppy found me unbearably dull, because in a couple of minutes he closed his eyes and dropped his head down on my thigh like a velvet pouch full of marbles. He began to make little grunting noises. Having him asleep on me like that made me feel protective. It was tragic the way baby everythings just assumed that your intentions were good. They needed you, but only for all the good reasons: affection, companionship, shelter, food, entertainment. Unlike humans, who more than likely needed you for twisted reasons, secret unpleasant reasons, if they needed you at all. Just thinking about the fragility of life and the brutality of nature made me all teary-eyed. By the time I pulled the car into the long unpaved driveway that led to Halley's Winnebago, I knew I wasn't taking this puppy back.

4
UNLOCKING THE
DOORS TO DESIRE

According to that well-respected Internet novel-writing manual of which I previously spoke, "It is important to aim for one startling image on each page." The manual suggests that we try to equal or surpass this image of a sunrise at sea by Philip Caputo in *The Voyage:* "A golden shimmer appeared where the horizon was supposed to be, then a red sun pushed up, like the head of some fiery infant bulging out of the gray sea's womb water giving birth to its opposite element."

Anyway, it only took me twenty-four hours to relax into my role as the new puppy's mom. In a rare stroke of luck, he was already housebroken. That detail made me feel even more protective. Here the poor thing had cooperated with somebody on bathroom etiquette, presumably to gain their goodwill, and still they threw him away.

Not only did I not bring the puppy back the next day, but by the day after that I couldn't stand to be away from him. I began getting permission from my assorted clients to bring him along on jobs. Everyone who met him said "Fine," then got down on all fours to speak baby talk to him. He even fit in easily at the Doggy Depot because, I was proud to see, he played well with others.

At first I had no idea what to call him. Halley thought I should name him "something sexy. Like Caesar. Or Rashad." When those didn't seem right, I tried a couple of typical college professor dog names: Amsterdam. Gershwin. Faust. Archimedes. And when proper nouns sounded too affected, I consulted an Internet list of the most popular dog names: Max, Jessie, Molly, Jake, Buddy, Bear. But a golden shimmer appeared that pushed up, like the head of some fiery infant bulging out of the womb of names, when I called out, "Chuck," and a drooling brown-eyed puppy looked over at me enthusiastically, no clue that his big pink tongue was hanging out of the side of his head like a dripping wet dish towel.

On The Day Everything Changed, I was working off my debt to Maura by house-sitting for Johnny Depp, her slightly neurotic 110-pound unclipped Bouvier des Flandres.

Halley, who had been Maura's house-sitter for years, was thrilled to pass me the torch so she could finish up her Life Coaching course. Her relationship to Maura had become so maternal, it seemed inevitable that Maura would become Halley's first client.

"This works out super for me," she said, "because I can't be her pet-sitter and command the respect I need."

"You're saying I require less respect than you?" I asked.

"You always have to take everything I say and twist it," she said, incensed. But the truth was that Halley had been carefully cultivating Maura's dependence ever since that first time they met at the Animal Hospital, when Maura brought Johnny Depp in to have a Super Ball removed from his small intestine. As the surgery dragged on, Maura took Halley to Starbucks and bought them each the coffee equivalent of a hot-fudge sundae. To thank her, Halley gave Maura a complimentary tarot reading, something she often did when she was trying to forge a new bond. "You drew the Seven of Cups and the Wheel of Fortune. That shows an opportunity that will develop into something very positive," Halley said. And she said it in a voice that made Maura feel hopeful. Halley had that effect on people because she genuinely believed the homilies she spoke. When she said, "Everything happens for a reason" or "If it's really meant to happen, then it will" or the beloved classic "When one door closes it's because another one is about to open," Halley inspired so much optimism that the sweet but high-strung and overwrought Maura, a recovering alcoholic, was soon afraid to make a decision without first consulting her. Should she say yes to a decent part in a small prestigious but low-budget independent film that wouldn't get wide distribution? Or would she be better off in a big brainless creatively bankrupt comedy that would rake in a lot of money and put her name back in front of the public? How would she know when she'd met her soul mate? Was he by any chance the handsome twenty-five-year-old Eurasian kid who was just hired to play her hybrid human android assistant on the series? And if not, could she go out with him anyway, since he was cute and coming on to her? Would the soul mate be willing to wait? And by the way, did Halley know how old the soul mate was going to turn out to be? Because if he was younger, should she get an ass lift?

The weird part was that Maura's blind

faith in Halley's prophetic wisdom rubbed off on Halley herself, who began to believe she was more keenly intuitive than regular people. This, she figured, might be the key to success in her Life Coaching practice. So she jumped ahead and printed up a trifold brochure with her picture on the front, as the course recommended. Then she began leaving stacks of them in the entrances to acting schools, yoga classes, health food stores, and small theaters. But as it turned out, her first clients all sprang from Maura's parties, where she made the acquaintance of Maura's pantheon of panicky actress pals. At last, Halley's lifelong dream of a charismatic identity was being realized. To help it solidify, she dyed her hair jet black and bought a pair of black-framed glasses with plain-glass lenses like the ones she saw Cameron Diaz wearing in the vitamin aisle at Whole Foods. From that point forward, Halley was ready for action.

"It's important that we identify your self-limiting beliefs" was her opening sentence to me the next time I walked into the Winnebago. "Here are some common examples of what I mean." She read from her workbook: "I am too old. I don't have a university degree. I am too fat."

She stopped and looked worried. "Oh my

God, these are all so me. I must need a Life Coach." For a moment, she seemed to spin out of control. "Do-overs," she said, pausing to take some deep breaths before she continued, "Okay. Repeat after me." She read from the workbook: "I am not too old. I am very educated. I am slim and attractive. I am a great football player or mathematician."

"Halley, I don't think you can become a great football-playing mathematician just by repeating it a lot," I said.

"There you go again with the self-limiting beliefs," she scolded me, shaking her finger. "Can you begin to see just how you hold yourself back?"

For the next few weeks, I never knew what I'd walk into with Halley. She might be chanting a litany of slogans to help her feel invincible. "I am the deliverer of dreams," she would say, changing the emphasis to a different word each time she said it aloud. "I unlock the doors of desire."

Other times she'd insist that I talk to her about my problems so she could practice her listening techniques. These included but were not limited to head nodding accompanied by encouraging noises like "Mmm," "Yes," "Aha," "I see," and "Do go on."

"Be honest with me," she would plead.

"Do I look like I'm into what you're saying? Is it better if I lean forward, tilt my head a little, peer over my glasses, and make a thoughtful half smile? Could you tell I was syncing my breathing up to match yours?"

"You were?" I said. "Don't do that. It's creepy."

"Not if it's for your own good," she said, consulting her workbook. "We are going to be using what is known as the nondirective method, which will allow your unique creative abilities to emerge from the deep high weeds that are choking the plot of land that is your life."

"Halley, be real," I said. "What unique creative abilities?"

"I'm sorry. Do-overs. We were supposed to begin with 'the can do method.'" She scanned back a few pages. "Okay, starting again. 'What do you hope to achieve by having me as your coach? What is it you think I can provide that you don't have already?'" She leaned in and stared intently with a little half smile, her head tilted, arms uncrossed.

"I don't know. This whole thing was your idea." I shrugged. "Stop syncing up with my breathing. I hate it."

"Why must you fight me every step of the way?" she barked. "How can I be a good coach if you don't encourage me?"

"Okay, okay. I'm sorry," I apologized.

"Thank you," she said. "So what do you want to accomplish?"

"Accomplish?" I said, knowing I needed the right answer to move this along. "Well, the only thing I can think of is I've always kind of wanted to write a book."

"And what keeps you from starting?" Halley continued to steamroll. "Fear? Like 'How can I do that? What if I'm not smart enough? What if I'm not a good enough person? What if it turns out I'm just a loser who can never succeed?' "

"Geez," I said, thinking her scenario very harsh, sorry I'd confided my secret fantasy. "Not those. Though they're all kind of true. It's more like I feel so intimidated by the idea of important literary themes, it makes me afraid to start."

"What kinds of themes do you mean?" said Halley, clueless.

"You know," I said. " 'The conflict between the ideal and the real' or 'man's inhumanity to man.' All the big writers like Jonathan Safran Foer and David Foster Wallace and T. Congressman Boyle know the list by heart. I should probably just find some dumb workshop where a teacher would give me assignments."

"Exactly," said Halley, giving me a round of applause. "And when will you commit to taking that step?"

"Today," I said, figuring she'd have no way to find out if I did it or not. After which I was so happy to have her permission to leave that a golden shimmer appeared where the horizon was supposed to be, like the head of some fiery infant bulging out of the gray womb of being trapped by a Life Coach who was also your sister.

"You know what else occurs to me?" Halley said, standing beside my car as I unlocked the doors to let Chuck in. "This Jonathan Safran Foer and this David Congressman Foster have something that sets them apart."

"Talent?" I offered, sliding behind the wheel. "Connections?"

"No, a scary middle name," said Halley. She stared at me as though she'd had a great vision. "Look at the difference between John Jacob Jingleheimer Smith and John Smith. So give that some thought."

Then right before I began to back down the long driveway, she ran up to the window a last time.

"I am so born to this," she said to me, smiling with great delight.

5

PAXTON

Halley hadn't even received her coaching certificate in the mail yet when Maura insisted on becoming her first paying client. "I'm supposed to be helping her to create a strategy to achieve her objectives," said Halley, popping one bite-size individually foil-wrapped dark chocolate Dove bar piece after another into her mouth while she searched for an outfit that offered her a compassionate yet authoritative look. "What objectives isn't she achieving? I know she wants her own fragrance, like Jennifer Lopez." She looked panicky, then corrected herself with deep breathing.

Luckily for Halley, *United League of Galaxies (ULOG)*, Maura's show, had gone into production. Maura was too busy doing press to think about anything else. Her interview in *O* featured a photo of Maura and Halley, in velveteen tracksuits, power-walking, right next to one of Maura feeding Vince Vaughn pudding on a big wooden spoon. By the time she was interviewed in *TV Guide,* Maura's pat answers included one that credited her Life Coach with turning her career around.

And just like that, business was brisk for Halley. The people who were willing to pay four hundred dollars a week to "help pop the cork of potential" figured they might as well work with the woman who helped TV's Maura Kenney be reborn. B- and C-level actresses hoping to hit an eleventh-inning run in their careers now sought Halley's wisdom.

After Maura's series began taping, she began spending nights at her new pied-à-terre in the Hollywood Hills. So I'd find myself living in her house on Mulholland Drive, sitting for Johnny Depp, sometimes for weeks in a row. This would usher in yet another way that the job could be weird: Once I had adjusted to my new setting, I would find myself falling in love with someone else's animals, furnishings, books, appliances, and room design. I'd start to think I recognized those genial old people holding up babies in the engraved silver frames on the mantel.

And then Maura would announce she was coming home for the weekend, and I would be expected to vacate.

I knew it made no sense, but I would feel hurt.

Of course, there were certain aspects of living at Casa Maura that I was glad to leave behind. Chief among them, the small but ardent group of fans camped on the other side of the electric gate at the base of the driveway. The cry of joy they always made that turned to "Oh shit" when they saw it was only me who was driving the car coming toward them was dispiriting, to say the least. Though not to Paxton, the guy I had been seeing for over a year. He seemed to get a thrill out of making Maura's fans wonder if the guy in the aviators was someone they should know.

I'd met Paxton at the Animal Hospital when Dr. Richter hired him to build some "dog vacation apartments." We eyed each other for a couple of days. Then he handed me his card, which read, "Paxton: The Insolent Handyman. What the fuck is your problem?" Paxton could have had a thriving construction business were it not for how much he hated being told what to do. He practically dared his employers to fire him.

"Any moron could do this bullshit," he'd

snort every time I gave him a compliment. It was important to Paxton that he not succeed at being a handyman, the better to maintain his fantasy of alternative media stardom verging on indie cult success. Nothing mattered to Paxton more than his rebel status. *Off the Grid,* the weekly radio show that he did at 3:00 A.M. every Friday night for a college radio station, had been gaining a steady following. "Stalking the Zeitgeist" was the phrase he used for his blurb in the *LA Weekly.* Maybe there was no money in the show yet, but at least one night a week the sound of Paxton's drab insolence really served him well.

Paxton was attractive in a dark, withholding kind of way. He had a tight, lean body and one of those unreasonably deep Johnny Cash/Barry White/Warren Zevon voices that sounded like melting rubber on hot asphalt. Just the pitch alone made casual remarks like "Yessss" and "C'mon now" and "Wait just a minute" sound sexy and strangely profound. At the time, I was so off my game because of my most recent divorce that it took weeks for it to sink in that the big wicked smiles he was flashing me were flirtatious.

One afternoon, after we tried an experimental Starbucks lunch date that seemed like it wanted to keep going, I invited him over to Maura's for dinner. The look on his face when he walked in the front door of her house was ecstatic. Paxton felt like Maura's house was the house he was meant to have. It had one of those enormous bathrooms with a freestanding tub and a big picture window that looked out onto a garden full of drought-friendly indigenous plants. It had a solar-heated pool with a sand beach at one end and a Jacuzzi that was fed by a small waterfall at the other. It had the big *Architectural Digest*–layout kitchen with an island in the center, nestled under an obligatory hanging rack full of glistening copper pots, not a single one of which had ever been used, since Maura didn't know how to cook. But she certainly knew how to shop. Store employees all over the country who worked on commission would stand and applaud when they saw her coming, because if she liked an item, she bought one in every color.

Chuck and I especially liked Maura's bed, a California king big enough to accommodate sprawling dogs and amorous humans at the same time.

I suppose I slept with Paxton too soon, because early on my judgment was impaired by our sexual chemistry. Before Paxton, I had gotten so accustomed to faking orgasms that I worried that I had forgotten what it sounded like when I, not a porn star, got aroused. But sex with Paxton was a window onto a new world. He was not only good at foreplay, he had dozens of kinks that he went at with unabashed lust. From the beginning, I was surprised as he attached himself to parts of my anatomy I never thought had any sexual significance. He was also a very good kisser. I loved how he held my face firmly, tenderly, when things got fierce. And on top of all that, he had a great ear for nasty talk, knowing when to use it and when to knock it off.

It didn't take too many weeks in a row of this kind of stuff for me to conclude that I was in love. "HOT SEX" written in capital letters held up very nicely on the list of pros and cons about Paxton I'd started to make.

The cons involved our limited common interests. Besides his radio show, all he really liked to do was go to clubs in search of undiscovered bands, read rock history, play Halo 2, and download porn. He was very wrapped up in the idea of "living off the grid." Which was fine with me. His grid coordinates were his own business.

But I was sorry that I couldn't get him to

surf or ride bikes or hike or snowboard or ski. He wouldn't even walk on the beach at sunset because he didn't like walking on sand and he didn't like sunlight, even when it was fading.

And then there was the little matter of "I love you." For reasons he wouldn't share, it turned out to be something he refused to say. He once managed "I enjoy our time together," but only after quite of bit of prompting. And it was followed by an exhausted "Happy now?"

Taken on balance, this imperfect relationship with its truly outstanding sex was, in my view, still a huge step up from the liaisons that had preceded it. I was long past seeking perfection. In fact, every problem I had with Paxton was actually a piece of cake except one: Paxton didn't like Chuck. And the feeling was mutual. Ordinarily, Chuck was happy to see anyone who crossed his path. Chuck's version of "hello," though mild compared with Swentzle's, was still overwhelming. Especially when it involved Chuck's special spring-loaded vertical leaping and randomly targeted kissing combination, which was sometimes confused with assault.

From the very first time Paxton came into Maura's living room, Chuck stood five feet away, frozen, head and tail lowered, staring. And when Paxton leaned down and held out his hand to say hello, Chuck wrinkled his upper lip and began to back up. Embarrassed, Paxton did his best to recoup by getting on his knees and trying baby talk. But his "heh-wo, widdew puppee" only caused Chuck to add guttural noises to his hostile body language, humiliating Paxton further. For first-date ambience, this was every bit as bad as a grim-faced father waiting on the front porch holding a Bible.

Still, it seemed inevitable that Chuck and Paxton would begin to like each other in time. I figured we'd all wear down one another.

Toward that end, I dedicated myself to rolling with any and all punches. When Paxton was moody, I rode his emotional landscape like a skateboard: jumping over depressions, making kick turns before tantrums, and last-second changes of plan. I only balked when Paxton insisted that Chuck be banned from the bedroom.

I had been sleeping with Chuck every night since he was a puppy and had come to rely on his hot-water-bottle-like warmth and dead weight against the side of my legs as a sign that things were okay. I didn't even mind the restricted movement. Okay, no one is that crazy about waking up with searing abdominal cramps from being frozen into a sleeping crouch by a sprawling dog. But at 3:00 A.M., when I lay awake filled with anxiety, I could bury my face in Chuck's furry neck and be lulled back to sleep by his jigsawlike snoring noises, which made me smile involuntarily.

I also loved the way his feet smelled like corn chips.

On the other hand, Paxton asleep was a lot like Paxton awake: an island unto himself. He had a way of accumulating the blankets like a big lint roller, leaving me naked and coverless at the far side of that giant bed. Knowing that Chuck was miserable out in the hall because I could hear snorting noises where his nose was wedged under the door made me unbearably sad.

Chuck hated it out in the hall. But Johnny Depp hated it more. That was his bedroom as much as it was Maura's. He had pissed in every corner of it to make sure. He did not understand the concept of being exiled.

Ever the wily student of reverse psychology, I would try to repackage the banishment as a special treat. "Yippee!" I'd sing. "Tonight we're all spending the night in the hall!! No more claustrophobic bedroom! We're free!" And then, as if to prove it, I would set up piles of blankets and pillows and toys and snacks just outside the bedroom door. And if that wasn't working, I'd throw in a few pieces of my dirty laundry for a cozy, comforting smell. But no matter how stinky and convivial I tried to make the hallway nest, I knew that all the tail wagging and unbridled joy coming from Chuck and Johnny Depp would abruptly turn into baleful expressions of misery, shock, and betrayal the minute I said, "Stay," and headed back into the bedroom without them. That's why sometimes in the middle of the night, when Paxton wouldn't know anyway, I would slip out of bed and curl up with the two of them out in the hall. That was where I was sleeping The Night Before Everything Changed.

Earlier in the evening, we had hosted a very nice little off-the-grid dinner party with a group of alternative deejays from Paxton's radio station. Paxton liked to invite friends from the station over to Maura's because he thought the lush, expensive surroundings added to his mystique. So we had barbecued fresh shrimp on Maura's enormous, rarely used propane barbecue grill and sat out on Maura's even more enormous deck, drinking that two-dollar Trader Joe's wine that Paxton transferred to a decanter in an attempt to pass it off as something expensive.

It was a very nice evening. I was feeling so relaxed that I wasn't as intimidated as usual by the many references to obscure bands with names full of supposedly scary nouns and bleak modifiers, like Viral Infection, the Little Cripples, etc. But after the alternative deejays had rewrapped their long scarves around their necks, donned their vintage coats and hats, and taken their leave, Paxton and I got into a fight.

Paxton had this thing where he flipped out if he was interrupted when he talked. Of course, no one likes to be interrupted. But Paxton frequently paused for very long periods of time in the middle of a thought. And when he did, everyone was expected to remain silent, pencils ready, awaiting any additional rejoinders. In my case, having been raised in a home where seamless monologues were the norm, I learned early in life to interrupt if I wanted to learn to speak fluent English. On this evening, as I was loading the dishwasher, Paxton was delivering an oratorio about our departed guests.

"The Kirbys are so pro-Seattle, it's painful," he complained. "Come on! Life didn't begin and end with Kurt." Then he paused. I nodded silently, remembering Kurt fondly, correctly assuming there would be more. "And by the way," he said, "while we're talking about painful, do you know you said 'Rosicrucian Death'? We've discussed this more than once." He paused again. I wanted to apologize but waited. A good minute of silence later, it seemed to me the pause had ended.

"Sorry," I said. "I guess what I don't understand is —"

"If you would JUST LET ME FINISH MY THOUGHT!" he exploded. And he said it with such force that Chuck and Johnny Depp started to slink under the table. "Do you EVER want to hear what I have to say, or is everything about you? If I'm boring you, let me know." He paused again. And again, I held my breath and waited. "I've told you at least three times that there is no band named Rosicrucian Death. The band is Christian Death. The singer is Roz. So it's 'Roz of Christian Death.' Not 'Rosicrucian Death.' Do you understand? The people who were here are cutting edge. They all know me for being off the grid. And it's embarrassing to have you act like some fuddy-duddy Malibu goofball in front of them. It's like when my mom would talk about 'The Race Against the Machine' or 'The Limping Biscuits.' "

And then Paxton shook his head in disgust and stormed out of the room. Slamming the door behind him, he stomped down the stairs to make sure the sounds of his disgust left an audio trail.

The dogs watched his exit from beneath a layer of coat hems, hiding deep in the hall closet. I stood still, appalled with myself for not seeing this coming. I heard him enter the office below me, where Maura kept her computer. Embarrassed, I busied myself with cleaning the kitchen. But I was distracted, haunted by enormous feelings of rejection.

By the time I finished polishing the countertops, I was feeling ashamed. I hated conflict. I hated disappointing Paxton. I decided to go downstairs and negotiate a peace.

6
There's So Much I Wanted to Give You

Standing in Maura's office doorway, wearing an expression of eager hopefulness, I reminded myself of Chuck with his mouth full of tennis balls. Paxton was drinking a thirty-two-ounce Guinness and trying to destroy the Covenant on his Halo 2. When he wouldn't look up at me, I realized I didn't have the courage or confidence to move closer, stare harder, then lean my head on his knee and moan sadly, like Chuck would have. All I could do was float out a girlish "Do you hate me now?" that disgusted me the minute I said it. When he continued to ignore me, I was deeply humiliated. So I backed quietly out the door and padded back up the stairs to the kitchen.

A different well-respected manual on writing a novel cautions us to "make every word count. Never let your character eat an apple, when he/she can be eating fried Cheerios."

Be that as it may, I decided to fry myself a turkey burger because frying Cheerios seemed stupid. They're already crispy.

I also made myself a martini (Maura's favorite drink because they required so many purchases: stemware, a shaker, a tray, an ice bucket, jars of olives and onions, books full of recipes, toothpicks). I guess I was rattled from the fight. Maybe that's why I put too much oil in the pan. For some reason, when I turned on the gas burner there was a small explosion, then a big flame roared up, setting a dish towel and a box of matches on fire. Soon there was a bigger fire on top of the stove than there ever had been in the fireplace. "The kitchen is on fire!" I yelled to Chuck and Johnny Depp, who stared slack-jawed. They both wagged their tails lazily, a courtesy wag, as in "Just saying 'hi' " or "Nice job!" Luckily, I wasn't too drunk to remember that the way to stop a grease fire is to suffocate it. But the largest pot lid I could find only smothered part of the fire. Then I remembered how my mother used to throw salt. Emptying every visible saltshaker, I began heaving fists full of salt at the flaming stove. By then the bottom of a yellow curtain over the sink had begun to burn. So I filled a pot full of water and pitched it at the curtain, dousing the flames, soaking myself, and creating large pools of water on the kitchen floor for Chuck and Johnny Depp to sit in and drink.

I was in shock as I stood back and surveyed the greasy black mess I had made in Maura's pale yellow kitchen. There were big tarry smears across the imported pecan cabinet doors. Between the salt and the pools of water, the room was at low tide. This was the first time in my pet-sitting career that I had damaged a client's home. Worse that it was Maura, to whom I was indebted. I was horrified.

I began to cry those involuntary tears of helplessness, self-pity, and rage that well up inside me every time a cop car pulls me over. I wasn't sure what to do next. I tried calling Halley, then my mother. And when I only got voice mail, I began to feel even sorrier for myself. I wanted some reassurance. And I wanted it from Paxton. So I went back downstairs.

Standing in the doorway again, I hoped that enough time had elapsed since the last time I'd tried this for Paxton to have reconsidered. But he was intently focused on his final winning points. When he finally looked up and could see I'd been crying, he shook his head, then exhaled so hard that the hair in his eyes was lifted. "NOW what?" he said.

"I started a fire in the kitchen and almost got killed," I said, upping the dramatic arc, knowing Paxton responded better to melodrama. Women in tears sometimes brought out the best in Paxton, making him sort of paternal. He held up a finger while he made sure his score had been registered online, then came over and put his arms around me.

"You poor thing," he said, which I took as an apology, though he hadn't acknowledged doing anything wrong.

"Come see what happened," I said, tearfully leading him by the hand up the stairs to the kitchen, where he assessed the damage, nonplussed.

"It's only a mess, baby. No big deal. Nothing tough to fix." He spoke with convincing calmness. "We can match that color paint, easy. Then we just hem that one curtain." And he said it so confidently that I felt a lot better.

"Come to bed," he said, leading me by the hand into the bedroom.

I was so moved by his tenderness and empathy that I ordered the dogs into the hall of my own accord. Then, when he and I were alone, I crawled on top of him and attempted to reenact a highlight reel of every porno film I could recall. If anything, it worked a little too well. Thirty seconds after his orgasm, Paxton was wedged deep in the center of a tightly wrapped blanket burrito, snoring loudly. Alone and very chilly on the coverless part of the bed, I was nowhere near falling asleep. It was still pretty early. So I snuck into the hall to hang out with the banished canines, who, of course, greeted my arrival as though it were the answer to their prayers. Soon the three of us were curled up on Johnny Depp's big stuffed dog pod. That's how we all fell asleep.

The next morning, at sunrise, I awoke stiff and achy because Chuck had shifted so his body was on the bed, but his head and lips were on the floor. Johnny Depp had slept on his back, legs and arms outstretched. I had been shoved off the cushion onto the Spanish tile floor.

I got up to make a pot of coffee, and while it brewed, I started mopping up the many pools of water and salt I created the night before. The gummy grease stains on the cabinets only smeared when I tried to remove them. I was trying to figure out which cleaning solvent wouldn't also remove the wood finish when I heard a shuffling noise behind me.

Turning cautiously, I was surprised to see

Paxton. It was unheard of for him to be up before the dogs. But on this day he came in fully dressed, looking uncomfortable. He stood stiffly, arms at his sides.

"Hi, baby. You sleep okay?" I said, ignoring the obvious.

"Yep. Fine," he said, his eyes expressionless, remote.

"What's your schedule like today?" I asked. "Because I thought maybe later we could meet back here and, you know, you said you'd help me clean up this mess. Maura's due back from Hawaii the end of the week . . ."

Paxton stood quietly, staring into the living room.

"Or we could do it tomorrow, I guess," I said after enough time had passed so I was pretty sure I wasn't interrupting.

"Well, I would love to help. I think you know that. But now is a real bad time," Paxton said, shaking his head. "There's something I've been meaning to talk to you about."

The words sounded ominous. I sat down, awaiting a terrible blow.

"I got a gig in Seattle. Doing overnights at KSUB. The big college alternative station there," he said somberly.

"Congratulations!" I said, relieved and

excited. "I'm so happy for you! That's amazing!"

"It is and it isn't," he said, fidgeting with a silver ring he wore on his middle finger. "It's great for me, obviously. But it probably means we have to redefine our relationship."

"What? Why?" I said, feeling my stomach churn.

"I've been thinking about this, and, Dawn, can I be honest?"

"I don't know," I said, my heartbeat quickening.

"Please," he said, taking a breath, looking at me hard. "This is tough on me, too. But this job is a big break. I'll be under a lot of pressure. I thought it'd be best to put things on hold for the time being. . . ."

I sat very still, examining the soles of my shoes. His radio voice was creeping in: a bad sign. "You know I've always told you that given a choice between career and love, I'd choose career," said Paxton. "You want to get married and have a kid. I don't want those things."

"I haven't given any thought to having a kid with you," I said.

"Oh, come on, Dawn. Your life is all about wanting kids," he said, in a tone that was bordering on condescension. "You've been married twice. You take care of animals. And there's nothing wrong with that. You deserve a relationship geared to what you want."

"But I thought we agreed that things were working great for us the way they are," I said, sickened by the way I felt like a child whose daddy was leaving. "We have fun. We have great sex. I even thought we were in love."

"Whoa. Dawn." Paxton whistled, exhaling dramatically. "I've always been straight with you. I never said I loved you. I don't just throw that word around like some guys do."

I got up and walked to the table where Maura kept alcohol in cut-glass decanters like the ones they have in limousines and I poured myself about an inch of some strong-smelling amber-colored liquor.

"What if we just go back to the way things were in the beginning?" I suggested. "No expectations. I'll just come visit on week-ends. We'll hang out, have fun."

"Oh, right. Like that'll work," Paxton said.

I tilted my head back, swallowing the shot of whiskey all in one gulp the way detectives do in movies to steady their nerves. "It's just that I'm so tired of everybody throwing up their hands every time a relationship hits a rough patch," I said. "I did it in both my marriages, and I swore I wouldn't do it again." Paxton stared at me as I walked over to him and put my arms around his waist. "What if we take a couple months to try and make things right? And then if it all still seems hopeless to you . . ."

"You don't get it, do you?" said Paxton, removing my hands. "It's too late for that now." He started to walk toward the door.

"How can it be too late?" I said, beginning to be angry. "This is the first time you mentioned you weren't happy."

"I'm in love with someone else," he said. "There. Are you happy? You made me say it."

"Oh, that kind of too late," I said, sitting down on the sofa, my body starting to shiver. First I felt like someone had dropped an ice cube down the back of my shirt. Then my insides felt like they were on fire. "Why don't you just get out of here," I said.

Chuck and Johnny Depp both walked over and put their heads in my lap. Except for the light beaming at me from their trusting eyes, I felt surrounded by darkness.

"How about I call you later?" Paxton said in his concerned interviewer voice.

"How about you get out of here NOW!" I shouted. "And stop talking to me like you're introducing a three-song tribute to Elliott Smith."

"It's good you're purging your anger," he said, pulling his baseball cap down by the brim. "There's so much I wanted to give you. But I just couldn't."

"What the fuck does that mean?" I screamed at him as he closed the door behind him. "Is that some kind of bullshit for people without a grid?"

I stood and walked zombielike back into the damaged kitchen. Unsure why I was now in the kitchen, I headed back to the living room, where I poured myself another inch of bad-smelling amber-colored booze. Was it Scotch? What was Cutty Sark again? Alcohol at 7:00 A.M. was unpleasant.

Sitting back down on the couch, I started drowning in a sickening wave of rejection and abandonment. I thought I had finished the part of my life where the rug could be pulled out from under me. How had I fucked up so badly again?

Dropping my head into my hands, I started to sob. As the noises that came out of me grew more alarming, Johnny Depp headed back to the coat closet. But Chuck stayed beside me, his head on my lap, look-ing up at me sweetly as the tears rolled down my cheeks. "You're really all I have," I said to him, taking his head in my hands and kissing him on the snout before wiping my runny nose on my sleeve. "You're the only living creature on this planet who gives a shit about me." I sniffled, choking back an enormous sob. "I am a fucking idiot. I have no idea what I'm doing."

Chuck stared at me, his eyes locked to mine. "Come on! You must have at least *suspected* there was someone else," he said. "Couldn't you smell her on his pants?"

My crying stopped abruptly as I stared down at him. His mouth wasn't moving. So why did I think he had spoken? Was it the early-morning drinking?

Now I sat watching breathlessly as Chuck got up and walked to the other side of the room, picked up a filthy tennis ball in his mouth from the spot on the floor where he'd last dropped it, then trotted back to wordlessly deposit it into my lap.

"Here, throw this," he said. "It'll make you feel better."

I sat still, chilled to my core.

"No, really," he went on. "Once you get into it, it's all you can think about. Look, I know you don't trust my judgment because I eat cat shit. Someday I'll explain that to you. But right now do what I say. Just pick up the ball and throw it."

So I did.

7
THE DAY
EVERYTHING
CHANGED

"The adult novel typically requires twenty plot points in which an action is taken or a discovery made that forces the characters to react." So far we've had one action taken and one discovery made. Two down, eighteen to go. Seventeen if you count my move to Los Angeles as an action.

For a lot of reasons, I hesitated writing this book. My biggest concern was that because of all the recent controversy regarding the fuzzy and mutable truth of memoirs, I might have a hard time being believed.

But like I said in the beginning, I had always talked not just to Chuck, but to all dogs. Maybe they never said anything back, but I believed I understood them, as people who love their animals tend to do. When I offered to take them out for a walk, I could hear them all yelling, "Yippee!" When I made dinner, I knew they were urging me to hurry with a pushy, impatient, "Smells great. Let's get GOING!"

But this time the hair stood up on my arms when I heard that other voice. I sat still, listening to my heart pound.

The voice I heard wasn't the common, slightly baritone version of my own voice in my head that I use to talk to myself. It was a gravelly adolescent voice, squeaking occasionally as it lurched from a high-pitched tenor to a deep bass like that of a thirteen-year-old boy. Maybe it was my conscience or my unconscious, my id or superego; one of those tricky invisible selves with a Freudian name that live only in our brains and reveal themselves as one questionable urge or another. In some other century, I might have thought it was a communication from God. But come on. Would God have bothered to go to the trouble of talking to me just to ask me to throw the ball?

"Did you say something just now?" I asked the voice out loud. Even that much made me feel foolish.

"No," it seemed like the new voice said in my head.

"Okay. Good," I said, feeling calmer. I was looking forward to immersing myself in my routine at the Doggy Depot, comforted knowing that at this very moment, impatient people were lining up to drop their dogs off for the day. That was when I realized I was a half hour late. They were probably swearing at me. I wanted to go back to bed and drink myself into a blackout.

Numb and in too much of a hurry to indulge in more than cursory grooming, I braided my hair, then pulled on the same dog-hair-covered hooded sweatshirt I'd worn the day before. Before I left the house, I tried to distract myself with novel-writing manual tip number seven: "Describe the person you see in the mirror to someone you do not know." To my dismay, the person staring back at me had red beady eyes and pale gray skin, like a homeless person. The person in the mirror made me want to call in sick because she looked as crazy as I felt.

I put Johnny Depp and Chuck in the backseat of the car and headed over to the Animal Hospital, driving as fast as traffic permitted, staring glassy-eyed at the car directly in front of me. I turned the radio to KROQ, seeking the hypnosis of familiar music, but instead of smart songs about triumph over bad love, it was some old Oasis song I'd heard five billion times. I turned the radio off.

"Sit," I said to the wall of fur on Johnny Depp's back, which was all I could see in my rearview mirror. He paid no attention.

But Chuck, who had been standing beside him, moved to the front seat to sit beside me. When we came to a stretch of open road, he stuck his head out the window.

"Chuck! No!" I said, pulling him back into the car by the collar. "You know better than that."

"Well, you know better than to turn on KROQ and you still do it," Chuck said. "They're always playing that same Oasis song. And you always turn it off. I, on the other hand, never fail to encounter a jigsaw puzzle of odors, and actual pieces of matter rushing at me at fifty miles per hour when I put my head out of the car. I know where we are and who is around and what they all had for dinner. Oh, man! I'm still not over that time someone in front of us threw out a partially eaten burger. Next time that happens, I'm catching that thing on the fly. Watch me."

I waited before speaking. "Am I making this up?" I finally said. "Have I found even a scarier way to torture myself? Why do I think you are talking to me?"

"Dude," said a voice a full octave deeper from the backseat, "dead possum on the right. Check it out. Big one."

"Wow," said Chuck, back out the window. "Nice. Can we stop?"

"NO!" I said, finding this all very disturbing. The last thing I needed was for my basic view of the universe to be up for grabs. Within seconds I was so dizzy that I was afraid to drive. I turned right, off the highway, into a small market parking lot and just sat there. Now no one was saying anything. I clung to the quiet like a life raft.

"Why are we stopping?" it sounded like Chuck asked. "Are we gonna go get the possum?"

"No!" I said, to him or to myself, sounding agitated. "I don't like to drive when I'm this upset."

"Upset? About what?" he said.

"Hello? She was dumped this morning," said Johnny Depp.

"Having discussions with myself in three voices seems like a really bad sign," I said.

I looked at Chuck to see his reaction. He was making that same incredibly enthusiastic face that I generally think of as "smiling," even though it might just be panting from heat or from physical exertion.

"Why now, today, do I suddenly think you are talking to me?"

"Well, like that grid guy said, you're not getting any younger," said Chuck. "Sorry. I'm not good at time. I could be totally wrong. Maybe you are getting younger."

"I can assure you I am not getting any younger," I said.

"Whew. Got that part right, anyway," he said, pausing for a minute. "Okay, here's the reason, then. I thought you needed someone to talk to. Someone that you can trust, I mean."

I looked at him, feeling a swell of emotion.

"And until that person comes along, you might as well talk to me," he said. "That was kind of a joke. At least I hope it was. I don't understand jokes too well."

"So I'm just making this up to cover my feelings of desperation?" I said. "Because this does not sound like the conversation I would be having with you."

"I would have expected more from him myself," said the voice from the backseat. "He's deceptively simple-minded."

"You have the nerve to accuse me of being simple-minded?" said Chuck, turning toward Johnny Depp angrily. "You? The fancy Bouvier who stood in the hall yesterday and said 'food' thirty-five times in a row . . . ? And I counted, by the way. This was you yesterday: 'Food! Food! Food! Food! Food! Food.' No variety of phrasing. Always the same inflection. No development of tone. No expansion of theme. 'Food! Food!

Food! Food! Food! Food! Food! Food!' "

"Well, someone had to say something," said Johnny Depp. "I was afraid we'd starve. You know as well as I do that she's arbitrary about mealtimes."

"I'm not arbitrary," I said. "You always eat dinner at five."

"And I'd like to point out that it's five at least twice a day. Maybe more," said Johnny Depp. "Where are we going?"

"To work. To the Doggy Depot. You know that," I said. "We go there every day."

"We do? That festive gathering of dogs we always run into?" he said, awestruck. "You organize that for us?"

"He calls me simple-minded," snorted Chuck as I pulled the car back onto the road. "Fucking Bouvier des Flandres. *Des? I love that. Des!!!* Never trust a dog with a pretentious French name."

I began to focus hard on remaining calm, despite the nagging concern that something was terribly wrong. My reflexes seemed okay. Only when I remembered the incident with Paxton did I feel a surge of unwanted tears. Did he have such a hold on me that he could jar my sanity? If so, that was doubly upsetting. Okay, he was good in bed. At least that explained my attachment. But big deal. Fuck him and the grid he fell off of.

"The 'water down the face,' " said Chuck, "what is that?"

"It's involuntary. It happens when I'm very upset," I said.

"It's like a high-pitched noise, only wetter," said Johnny Depp, starting to cower. "It's not my fault, is it? Are you mad at me? I won't do it again. I swear."

"Of course it's not you!" I said. "I don't know if you can empathize, but it hurts when someone you love dumps you."

"You're joking, right?" said Chuck. "How do you think I wound up in the pound? At least grid boy didn't try to have you gassed. I still don't know what I did to those people. Or why you like that grid asshole so much."

"He's not only an asshole," I said, sorry to have to defend him. "At first he was smart and sexy and fun."

"How was he fun?" said Chuck. "Did he play ball? No. Did he bring meaty snacks? No. And he made such a big fucking deal when I drooled on his pants. How much fun was that?"

"He was a little germ-phobic. But he was fun in bed," I said, wishing I would shut up.

"Depends who you ask," said Chuck. "He threw us out."

"I think she's talking about the humping," said Johnny Depp.

"Oh," said Chuck. "Well, I hope you're not pretending he's the only one you can find to help you continue the species. What's the population of Los Angeles, for God's sake?"

"I think it's about four million," I said.

"At least half of them would do it with you," he said.

"I'm not comfortable talking to you about this," I said cautiously.

As weird as everything had all been so far, now it was getting weirder. "It's different for me than for you. You don't seem to have any standards," I explained. "But as a woman . . . it's my goal to have sex only with guys I love."

"That's just stupid," said Chuck. "Had a look around at the rest of the animal kingdom lately? I'll have sex with anyone who doesn't try to kill me."

"And even then, as long as their butt smells good, I'm in," said Johnny Depp.

"It's more complicated for people," I said. "Well, for girl people. We want to plan a future. We want someone to take care of us."

"In other words, you want someone like you," said Chuck.

"Put yourself up for adoption," said

Johnny Depp.

I pulled the car into the lot at the vet hospital, parking in the shade under the eucalyptus trees. "You guys okay back there for a minute?" I asked, suddenly wondering if I was now supposed to discuss my every move with them. It began to dawn on me how much of my life they had witnessed. How much retrofitted commentary was there going to be?

"We'd rather come inside with you," said Chuck.

"And I'd rather you stay here," I said, thinking it not smart to relinquish my alpha title too quickly. "I'm still not ruling out that I am talking to myself. But if I am, as your alpha, I give you permission to kill me."

As I got out of the car, alone, I thought I could hear Johnny Depp mumble, "See? I told you it wouldn't make a damn bit of difference if you could talk to her. None of them listen."

Inside the hospital, at the reception desk, Halley was training her replacement. The reception area was a big airy room with A-frame lines and big picture windows left over from when the structure was an International House of Pancakes. Though now decorated with many paintings of pets, it still had the bright, antiseptic look of a seventies ski chalet. Halley was at the computer, showing a twenty-something girl with dyed black hair, dark red, almost black lipstick, and matching nail polish how to print out bills. Apparently something was making Halley nervous, because she was chain-chewing Red Vines.

"Dawn, this is Mikayla, Dr. Richter's niece. I'm going to need you to show her the ropes out in day care," she said.

"Nice to meet you," I said to Mikayla, who stared at me like a flounder, not moving a single facial muscle.

"Boy, she looks thrilled," said Dr. Richter as he walked past, on his way into the hospital. "Good morning, team," he said. "Dawn. Halley. Morticia."

"Hey, Uncle Todd," Mikayla said in a monotone, unsmiling.

"Halley, you got a minute?" I said.

"Not really," Halley said, nervously shoving another Red Vine into her mouth. "What's up?"

"Paxton dumped me about an hour ago," I blurted out.

"Oh, honey!" said Halley, looking alarmed. "I'm so sorry. Let me just finish showing Mikayla our billing system and I'll be right out. Are you okay?"

"Well, not really," I said. "You know how it is."

"I was dumped a month ago," Mikayla said, nodding solemnly. "Best thing you can do is embrace it. Like Nietzsche says, 'When you look into the abyss, the abyss looks into you.'"

"Nihilism at eight A.M. Yikes," I said, heading out the door.

"Jesus Christ, did you forget all about us?" said Johnny Depp when I got into the car. "Come on . . . we're dogs. One minute equals one week in here."

Hooking them to their leashes, I led them past where Judy Shwenk was standing with Gilbert, her Pomeranian, next to Greta Cutler and Handsome, her Irish setter. Grant Repka was coming up the driveway with Dinky, his miniature dachshund, as Beau Miller and his pug, Hensel, climbed out of their van. It was a big crowd for this early in the morning.

"Sorry, guys," I said, opening the back gate and forcing Chuck and Johnny Depp inside. I preferred to admit my client dogs one at a time as a precaution against territorial wars, even though lots of these dogs were regulars and knew one another.

Today, it seemed like many of the dogs were almost as sleepy as I was. So I took a seat at the picnic table under the sun umbrella in the center of the corral, the best location for keeping an eye on everyone. The landscape of the place looked a lot like my mood: torn, mauled dog toys full of tooth marks, shredded old couches, soiled dog beds, partially stuffed animals with missing limbs and eyes.

I opened a book I had borrowed from the shelf in Maura's bedroom: *101 Ways to Please a Man.* Maybe this is why Paxton left me, I thought. I bet if I counted up all my man-pleasing ways, I wouldn't get any higher than about thirty. I wondered what the minimum requirement might be. That's when I realized I could hear a lot of muttering around me. At first I thought maybe someone had a radio on in the parking lot. But when I heard intermittent growling, I realized it was closer than that.

"Whoa. Jackpot. Big piece of gum. And I'm not sharing," said a high voice.

"Dude, it's covered in dirt," said a deeper voice.

"My favorite: muddy Nicorette!" said someone else.

"No way. It's strawberry Bubble Yum with a light coating of topsoil," said the high voice, "AND flavor's still there. Back off.

All of you. Now."

It occurred to me that not only was I hearing Dinky talking to Gilbert and Handsome, I could hear all of the other dogs mumbling to one another.

"You new?" said a nasal voice, which turned out to be Kokomo.

"No. You?" said Johnny Depp.

"It's my first time," said Kokomo. "Is there a sign-in?"

"Everyone pees in that corner," said Handsome. "WHOA! Check it out! New squeaky ball over here!"

"Go ahead and take it. I don't go for squeaky," said Kokomo.

"You're kidding. Where did you grow up? The pound?" said Johnny Depp.

"We had squeakies in the pound," said Chuck defensively.

Wow, I thought. If I am losing touch with reality, I have taken a giant leap forward. I stood up and walked closer, knowing that they would all look up.

"Can you guys hear me?" I asked, not speaking out loud.

"Nope. Can't hear a thing," said Dinky, staring right at me. Then she swallowed the gum in her mouth lest I take it away.

8
AND ANOTHER DOOR OPENS

The front gate to the corral flung open, and Dr. Richter poked his upper body in. "Dawn? Can I borrow you for a second?" he called. "Roxy's running late, and I need someone to hold Raja while I shave her stomach."

"Sure," I said, following him as Chuck ran to my side.

"Damn, that bastard gets to go everywhere," I could hear the group behind us grumbling.

"You're leaving us here to starve?" Johnny Depp moaned.

"Thank God we're blowing this dump," said Chuck, trying to force his way out. "These assholes are so on my nerves."

"Stay," I said to him.

"Me? I have to stay?" he said, confused and unhappy.

"Just for a minute," I said. "You're the alpha. You're the pit bull. Keep an eye on things for me."

"Oh. I'm in charge? Well, that's different," he said. "So anyone gets out of line, I can kill them?"

"There will be no killing," I said, looking down from the other side of the fence. "Be good! I'm serious!!"

"Thanks," Richter said to me when I caught up with him. He was carrying a Westie into the surgery room, where he put her on a stainless-steel examining table. "This is Raja," he said. "We need another X-ray of that obstruction on her pyloric valve." When he handed her to me, I could feel Raja tremble.

"It's okay, Raja," I said as Richter plugged in the electric clippers, "he's just going to shave a little hair."

"Tell him I'll bite him if he tries it," Raja said.

"I think she bites," I said to Richter as Raja growled.

"Oh, you know her?" he said. "I'll give her a sedative." He went to the refrigerator for a vial and syringe.

"He touches me, I'll report him to the ASPCA," said Raja.

"Ssh. It's okay," I said, stroking her reassuringly, holding her head and torso tightly.

"Can I ask you a question?" I said to

Richter as he prepared the injection. "You work with dogs all day. You ever feel like they talk to you?"

"Well, sure," he said. "Lay her down on her side."

"Fuck you," said Raja. "Leave me alone or I'll piss on you."

"They give signals with their bodies, with the noises they make. . . ."

"She might need to go out first," I said.

"Good call," he said, turning off the razor. "She's pissing as we speak. After I give her this painkiller, take her out so she can empty her bladder." He tiptoed around behind us with the loaded syringe.

"How stupid does he think I am?" said Raja nervously, rolling her eyes back in her head, trying to follow Richter's movements. "He thinks I don't see him sneaking around back there? Look, tell him I ate one serving of garden hose. And a gym sock. We can skip the X-ray." She jumped as the needle entered. "YEOW. Shit!"

"Now go walk her before the meds take effect," said Richter.

"Okay," I said, lowering the dog to the floor. "One more question. You don't actually hear dogs talk in sentences, do you?" I hooked Raja to her leash. "Telling their opinions and stuff? I'm not saying that I do.

I was just wondering if you did, since you're a vet and all."

"Well, sometimes I think I hear them say, 'Fuck you,' " he said.

"Yeah, they seem to say that a lot," I said.

"If you mean do they confide their troubles like I'm Dr. Dolittle, no."

"Doesn't surprise me," said Raja. "I've been coming to this putz for nine fucking years, and even when I repeat myself he doesn't hear. He . . . Whoa. What's in that shot? I am toasted."

Before we could leave, Roxy, the head tech, appeared in the doorway. She was almost six feet tall, athletic-looking, with short bleached-blond hair. She never deigned to talk to me. Today, as always, she was looking right through me. For some reason I was not important enough to merit her attention.

"Good morning, Roxy," I said, pretending not to notice her coldness. I handed Raja to her, lest she think I was after her job.

"Thanks." She nodded, taking the dog but looking past me.

"This is Roxy's last day of work," said Richter. "She's getting married and moving up north! I don't know what we'll do without her." Roxy gave him a warm, winning smile.

"Congratulations!" I said to the back of Roxy's head as she looked away. "How exciting to be starting a new life!" And when she didn't respond, I headed back outside, thinking, I don't know what I did to make you hate me, lady. But good luck to your new husband. He'll definitely need it.

Halley was waiting for me by the Doggy Depot gate.

"Sweetie! What happened with Paxton?" she asked with grave concern. "I thought things were going so good."

"That's the kiss of death," I said. "The only way to make love last is to want it over."

"You know, I always had kind of a bad feeling about him," she said. "Have you been drinking? Why do I smell booze?"

"I'm a mess," I said. "I might be having a breakdown. I'm not thinking straight. And I feel like Chuck has been talking to me. Do you know anyone who has a good shrink?"

"What do you mean, Chuck talking to you? You mean you see his mouth moving and hear a voice speaking English?" Halley said attentively, her expression distressed.

"I hear a voice in my head," I said.

"That's wonderful!" she said, her face lighting up. "Auditory hallucinations! We studied those in Life Coaching. I know exactly what's going on. It's happened so

105

far with every one of my clients. Your latent creativity has surfaced! It's communicating in a distinct voice so you will pay attention. It's a very good sign, like a nightmare!" She smiled broadly. "All my clients experience something unusual from coaching. Maura started salsa dancing. Skylar is playing the zither."

"I heard of a good shrink," said Pinter, a standard poodle who had come over to have his butt scratched. "I hear my mom say how much she likes her."

"You didn't just hear that poodle recommend a shrink, did you? Because I did, and it's making me very nervous," I said.

"As your Life Coach, I say: Let your right brain come alive," said Halley, "and get to know your true self!"

"Or get the name of the shrink from my mom," said Pinter.

"You're having a creative rebirth!" said Halley. "Just like I predicted! One door closes and . . . ?" She waited for me to finish her favorite sentence. "And . . . ?" she prompted. "Come on!" she said, ignoring how irritated it made me. "And . . . ?"

"Another door opens," I said quietly.

"Ta-da!" she said, holding her hands over her head triumphantly as she did a little victory dance. "Exactly."

"Except I think I'm running out of doors," I said.

"Well, as your Life Coach, my question is this: What advice would *you* give to you if *you* were your Life Coach?"

"Halley, don't Life Coach me right now. I tried calling you last night during an emergency. Where was my Life Coach then?"

"I was with Kirk," she said.

"Who's Kirk?" I said.

"Oh, no one." Her tone turned giddy. "Only the man I'm going to marry. The Knight of Swords. From the tarot reading I gave myself. I Life Coach his cousin Skylar."

"With the zither," I said.

"Correct. He's in real estate. The bus stop at PCH and Coastline Drive, by the red light? That's the man I love, right on that bus bench. You know how some people the minute you meet them it's like you've known them forever?" A look of dreamy ecstasy drifted into her eyes.

"No. But I've known people forever, and it's like I only just met them," I said. "Which reminds me. Do you know where Dad is? I called him and no one picks up. I need him to help repair some fire damage."

"Fire damage?" said Halley, turning frantic. "Oh my God. Not at Maura's? Is it bad?

You've got to get that taken care of before she gets back. She's my most important client. I would have to advise her to fire you."

"Well, I'm trying to take care of it," I told her. "Take it easy. The last thing I need is a hysterical Life Coach."

"I bet Kirk can help you. He's amazing," she said. "I'll bring him by this evening to look at the damage."

"How well do you know this guy?" I said, already worried.

"Well enough that we were in sync instantly," she said. "Something I hope you can experience one day. It's way hot."

"You know that's exactly what you said about Scott Peterson, right?" I said, aware it was the wrong thing to say.

"And I have asked you a number of times to not keep throwing Scott in my face. Everyone makes mistakes," said Halley, becoming livid. "And everyone would make that mistake if they met Scott. And since you brought it up, it just so happens he wrote me a very nice letter to congratulate me about my picture in *People*. He's so good with words." Halley paused indignantly. "When I saw Amber Frey being interviewed, I heard her say 'I seen' and 'supposably,' and I thought about how Scott must cringe every time that woman says 'in-ackrit.' "

"A man convicted of killing his wife and his baby has bigger problems than Amber Frey's command of English," I said.

"You so need to work on empathy," she snapped. "Sometimes I can't even talk to you. I'll bring Kirk about eight."

After Halley left I sat there, feeling cold, leaden, and sad. Chuck sat beside me and laid his head on my feet. When other dogs came over to try and get me to play, he was protective. "Not now, asshole, let her be," he said when Handsome approached with a squeaking hot dog on a bun.

"Work on your timing, moron," he said to Franny when she brought a filthy piece of rope to tug. And the next thing I remember was when Pinter's mommy arrived to take him home. "By the way," I said to her tentatively as I signed them out. "Do you know anyone who knows a good shrink?"

"I have a fabulous shrink," she said. "She's a little humorless, but she's got great insight." Then she wrote the shrink's name on a scrap of paper.

9

ONE OF THE SPECIAL THINGS WE ALL SHARE

In all of my life, my dad had helped me out only two or three times. The last time was when he hooked up an engine to a tiny windmill for the science fair in the fifth grade. So the fact that he would come through for me when I needed him now was deeply touching. Okay — maybe I did have to call the shop three times before he called back. The important thing was that once I found him, he came right over.

"Ball?" said Chuck, approaching with a mouth full of ball.

"Maybe after I get cleaned up," I said to him. His jaw went lax as he dropped the ball to the floor in disgust. "By the way, now that we can talk to each other . . . My dad is coming in a couple of minutes. So don't go crazy at the door when he gets here."

"You talk to me like I'm a complete idiot," said Chuck.

"I'm sorry," I said, embarrassed. "This is

still so new to me. I don't know quite what you do and don't know. Do me a favor and tell Johnny Depp —"

"Got it," said Chuck, exiting as I went into the bathroom. I had just sat on the toilet when the closed door crashed open and Chuck burst in, followed by Johnny Depp.

"What're you guys doing?" I said, startled as they both rushed over to give me a kiss. "Why do you always come in to kiss me while I'm on the toilet?" I asked.

"Makes us feel close to you," Chuck said, surprised I would ask. "Peeing is one of the special things we share."

"No offense, but I'd prefer you to stay outside," I said.

"Oh," said Chuck, tail lowered. "So that's how it is."

"Hey, man. Don't take it so hard," said Johnny Depp.

"She means you, too, dude," said Chuck.

"No way! She does not," said Johnny Depp. "Really? She does?"

"Okay . . ." I sighed, feeling guilty. "You can both stay. I didn't know it was such a big deal." Which was when they both turned their heads, then raced out of the room at top speed, shrieking and hooting loudly.

"Someone's at the door! Someone's at the door!!!" they both yelled.

"I just told you, it's my —" I called, knowing they couldn't hear.

"Hey. Get away from the door, you miserable jack-off," I heard Chuck shout at my
dad. "I'll rip your ass in half."

"Me too! I'll rip your ass in half, too!!"
yelled Johnny Depp. "We hate you. We hate
you. We hate you. We hate you."

"You guys, knock it off," I said, racing to
open the door. "I just told you . . . it's my
— Hi, Daddy," I said, hugging him.

"Come on in! Great to see you again!!"
screamed Chuck.

"Thank God you're finally here!"
screamed Johnny Depp. "We missed you.
Where you been? Welcome back! Who are
you??"

"SSHHHH!!" I said to them both. "That's
enough! QUIET!"

"Shut up," I heard Chuck say to Johnny
Depp, who was still barking. "It's her *dad*.
. . . Idiot Bouvier des Flandres. Des? Give
me a break."

I could see my father's candy-apple red
1957 GMC pickup truck out in the circular
driveway beyond the door. Ted was looking
a little tired but still very spiffy in his vintage
1957 yellow-and-black bowling shirt, ta-
pered black jeans, and two-tone shoes. Add
to that his carefully greased-up hair and he

was a classic photo of his hero Eddie Co-chran come to life. If Eddie had made it to middle age and kept his figure.

"You look great, Dad," I said.

"Check out the gold-toe socks," he said, lifting his pant leg to show me. "Found 'em online. Vintage '57."

"Way to go!" I said, at a loss for what to say.

"Look at this place," he said, surveying the surroundings in awe. "I could get used to this."

"Deena in the car?" I said, seeing no sign of his third wife.

"She's in the car all right. On her way to Tempe to move in with her sister," he said. "Whoa! Jacuzzi with a waterfall! Do you know if they rent this house out for porno films? That Jacuzzi looks awfully familiar."

"Dad, I don't want to talk about that kind of thing," I said, leading him into the kitchen.

"Aw, c'mon, Dawn. Lighten up. You sound like your sister," he said, hoisting himself onto the countertop to get a closer look at the paint damage. "Piece of cake," he said to me, jumping down and bounding toward the front door, signaling for me to follow him.

"So you and Deena are on the rocks?" I

said. "I'm shocked."

"The rocks are a step up from where we are," he said, opening the back of his truck. "Eight months, over and out."

"That was quick," I said.

"Yep," he said as he piled cans of paint and putty and different tools into my arms. "But as you get older, come to find out the best things in life are quick. It took a few decades, but I finally achieved my life's goal of combining marital bliss with a one-night stand."

He locked up the truck.

"So you've already got another girlfriend?" I asked as we hauled cans, brushes, rags, assorted tools, and a ladder back to the house.

"Try three of 'em." He chuckled, wiggling his eyebrows.

"And they're okay with this?" I asked, helping him set up the ladder.

"Sure," he said. "Well, they don't know, exactly. See? After we primer it, we can match the paint color perfectly."

"What does 'don't know, exactly' mean?" I said.

"Well, ya got to throw the word *love* around a little," he said. "But listen . . . I never told a single one of 'em I wasn't seeing other people." He searched for a brush.

"Of course, I also didn't tell 'em I was. That gray area is a thing of beauty. So here's what ya do: First thing in the morning, take that screwed-up curtain to the dry cleaner and get it hemmed. Tile cleaner'll fix the counter stain. How's things going with old whose-its, the artsy-fartsy dude you like? Mr. Goatee."

"He just dumped me," I said quietly.

"Dumped my baby girl?" He stood glaring for a full minute, shaking his head, his lips compressed. I was pleased by his reaction. "That's a damn shame. I'm so sorry to hear that," he said. "But let me ask you something." He paused, looking at me intently. "What did you do to piss him off?"

"Got upset when he said he loved someone else," I said.

"He said that? What a freshman. You're lucky he left," he said. "You never say you're seeing someone else to someone you're seeing. It makes it too hard to come back. You always keep that option open, case something happens, like they win the lottery. So, this color paint? Not yellow enough?"

"A little more yellow," I said.

"A relationship with the opposite sex is like buying a new American car," he said, mixing paint. "It starts out looking great,

115

but it only keeps going for about two and a half years. Then you spend the next two and a half years trying to restore it. Words of wisdom from yer daddy."

"So you're saying it's hopeless?" I said, picking up a small brush to do the corners while he rollered the bigger areas.

"Well, women nowadays don't have the patience to work things through like they did when I was coming up," he said.

"Mom claims she could never get you to work things through," I countered, eager to hear his defense.

"No, ma'am. She couldn't. That's true," said my dad, not looking up from painting. "People didn't do that sort of thing back then. No one heard of it yet. We all thought, You get married and everything is taken care of. Like a vacation package. Run into problems? Have a kid! Problems solved."

We were interrupted by crashing and scrambling as Chuck and Johnny Depp departed at top speed to the backyard, screaming at the tops of their lungs. I wanted to join them.

"I may be full of shit," said Dad, surveying his work with pride, "but damn, I'm good at covering up a big mess."

"Thank you so much, Dad," I said. "This means a lot to me."

"No problem, sweetie," he said, washing his hands. "Listen . . . you haven't got a little scratch you can lend your old man, do you? A couple hundred? Even fifty? I'm headed down to Baja for a week to meet up with Varla after she drops her kids off at her ex's. So, nice guy that I am, I told her I'd take her shoes in to be fixed. Now I find out Kelly wants to come down the following weekend."

We had started to pack up the cans when I found out why the dogs had been barking. Halley let herself in the front door at 8:00 sharp. Right behind her was a guy who looked like one of the tousle-haired "Alive with Pleasure" people from the Newport cigarette billboards. He was tall, square-jawed, ready to put on a pair of Dockers and laugh heartily at the innocent pleasures of a sprinkler in summer with his shirtless buds from Abercrombie & Fitch.

"Dawn, Daddy . . . I'd like you to meet Kirk Farren." Halley grinned, blushing.

"Hey," said Kirk, reaching out to shake my hand. "Halley's told me so much about you, I feel like I know you already." We stood there smiling, shaking hands, a bit longer than was comfortable.

"So you're related to one of Halley's clients?" I said, finally breaking the tense grinning silence.

"My cousin Sky introduced Halley and me on the phone. Then we exchanged e-mails a few times," said Kirk. He seemed a winning combination of forthright and bashful. "But we met in person for the first time last week."

"It's not possible that it could be so few days," said Halley, sliding her arms around his waist.

"You kids enjoy yourselves, best things in life are quick," Dad said, winking. He took a partially smoked cigar and a lighter out of the rolled-up sleeve of his bowling shirt. "New American car," he whispered, elbowing me and smiling. "Listen, either of you happen to have a couple of twenties I can borrow? I'm good for it." He touched the cigar butt to the lighter flame and puffed a few times to get it going.

"Sorry, Dad, I didn't get to the cash machine," said Halley.

"I got it," said Kirk, pulling some bills out of his wallet.

"Good man," said my dad, grinning as he took the money.

"My pleasure," said Kirk, now turning his attention to me. "Halley said you've got something needs fixing?"

"It's all taken care of," said Dad. "Unless

you can sew."

"Actually, I can," said Kirk with a disarming grin.

"I told you he's amazing," said Halley, widening her eyes and dropping her jaw for emphasis. "He's been to cooking school. He knows calligraphy, carpentry, gardening. Cars."

"Just this one curtain?" Kirk asked as I showed it to him. "Sky's got a sewing machine. I'll do it in the morning." Then he began to help Dad pack up the brushes and cans.

"That the original 287 or'd you rebuild?" Kirk asked him, nodding his head toward the pickup in the driveway.

"Original 287!" said my dad. "Hey, this guy's good!" He giggled, giving Halley a thumbs-up as Kirk helped him carry all the stuff he'd brought over back out to the truck.

"I finally hit the jackpot," said Halley when we were alone. "I feel so lucky. Though it's not about luck. I made this happen. I was ready. Like I tell my clients: To find the right person, you must first BE the right person. And if anyone works at being the right person, it's me."

"He seems very nice," I said.

"He's so much more than nice," she

gushed, overwhelmed.

"I feel like I should remind you to slow down," I said. "You've only known him a few days."

"On one level, yes," she said. "But I am learning to respect what I call the 'I' factor. For instinct. Did you know that before the Louisiana flood in 2005 turtles all started laying their eggs on higher ground? Because when you're tuned in to instinct, life makes sense at a more cosmic level. That's why everything is clicking for me now."

"Too bad we weren't born turtles," I said. "Though what you gain in instincts, you might lose dealing with that neck."

"Cool guy," said Kirk, closing the front door behind him as we listened to my dad's truck roar down the street. "I envy you. I never knew my dad."

Kirk headed into the kitchen to get the frayed curtain as Halley looked at me, beaming.

"Halley, listen. I have to thank you. You've been so helpful to me these past few months," I said a few minutes later as we said good night at the door. "Thanks for bringing Kirk by to help save my butt."

Halley gazed at him with the blissful expression of a meditating monk. Then the two of them held hands and floated out the door on a beam of light.

10
"GOOD NIGHT"

After they left, I felt better for a while.

"Do you guys have to go out?" I asked the dogs, thinking I'd get into bed and read. Both of them were following me from room to room while I locked doors and turned out lights. Chuck ran to the back door and stared at me.

"Okay, okay." I sighed. "I'll come outside with you."

"Just for a second. I have to piss where Johnny Depp just pissed," he said as I walked quietly across the wet grass.

"Another couple nights like this and I own the backyard outright," Chuck whispered to me as he and Johnny Depp followed me back into the house.

I locked the doors, closed the windows, and climbed the stairs to Maura's bedroom. Then all three of us crawled into her bed. My plan was to scrutinize Halley's book about "loving the self-absorbed" until I found a psychological syndrome that would reduce getting dumped by Paxton to an easily dismissed cliché. Perhaps something in a secondary narcissistic disorder or a borderline personality?

As Chuck curled up beside me, Johnny Depp began to circle endlessly, as he always did before he lay down.

"I gotta ask you . . . why do you always circle before you lie down?" I said.

"As opposed to what?" Johnny Depp asked, astonished by the question. "You mean not circle? How would I tamp down the leaves and twigs and get comfortable?"

"What leaves and twigs?" I said. "This bed is twig-free."

"Hmm. I see your point," said Johnny Depp, pausing for a second before he resumed circling. "But did it occur to you maybe that's because I circle first?"

"Okay. Fine," I said, pulling the pillow over my head. "That's it for tonight. Good night, you guys."

"Good night, Mom," said Chuck.

A jolt went through me. "What'd you just say?" I asked.

"Well, I don't know what I'm supposed to call you," he said.

"Mom is fine," I finally said. "It just came

as such a shock. Good night, so . . . eh, Chuck."

"Can I ask a question?" said Chuck. "I can still smell Swentzle everywhere. On bushes, on your jackets. At home on the floors. Why are you so hung up on that guy? He took off!"

"Chuck," I said as he looked at me blankly, "Swentzle didn't take off."

"So where is he?" he asked.

"Swentzle died," I said carefully. "Died is when the body . . . uh, wears out and stops living. Swentzle got sick, and I tried to help and . . . Let's leave it at that."

"Just like I said. He abandoned you," said Chuck. "If I got sick, I'd stick around."

"Chuck, there's not a contest between you and Swentzle. No one is replaceable. Swentzle went everywhere with me for eight years. He helped me through a lot of difficult times. He was a good boy. But missing him doesn't mean I don't love you."

"I don't think I'm buying it," he said.

"How about this?" I said, delicately recycling something I'd heard on *Oprah*. "I *found* Swentzle. But I *chose* you."

"You still think I'm a good boy, right?" he said, coming over and sniffing my eyes. "Can I put my head on your legs?"

"Sure," I said, closing my eyes. "Now go to sleep."

"Did he do this, too?" he said, curling up next to me, head on my knees.

"He preferred to sleep on the floor, in the corner," I said.

"Typical," snorted Chuck. "Well, good night, Mom."

"Good night, Chuck. Good night, Johnny Depp."

"He's out cold," said Chuck. "And Mom? You're a good girl."

"Thank you. That's very sweet of you, Chuck," I said.

Though what I was really thinking was: This is too fucking weird.

11
KINDA LIKE MY FAMILY

According to the novel-writing manual, "The structure of your story must involve three disasters plus an ending. Each of the disasters should take about a quarter of the book to develop." By this clock, we're now at approximately the midpoint of Act Two, where we should be encountering "the second and third disasters which are caused by the protagonist's attempts to fix things, thus forcing Act Three."

So it's a happy coincidence that we're almost to the part of the story where Halley throws me out.

The day started out okay. Maura moved back into her house and didn't notice anything wrong with her kitchen. Unfortunately, this forced me to move back into the Winnebago on the morning of Halley's thirty-first birthday.

"Her boyfriend's smell is all over everything," Chuck said as we ran inside for the first time in weeks to drop off my bags. "I better get busy pissing or he's going to take title."

"Don't you dare piss in here," I said, hooking him to his leash.

"Swentzle pissed in here," he said. "In every room."

"Ridiculous. He never pissed inside," I said, irritated.

"No, he totally did," said Chuck. "He pissed by the bed. He pissed in the kitchen. He pissed under the table. Can't you smell it?" And then, despite my protestations, he tried to pee three times on the way to the car.

"How can you have to pee so often?" I said as he jumped in the front seat.

"Well, there's two kinds of peeing," he said. "There's regular peeing, because you have to pee. And then there's auxiliary competitive peeing. For acquiring an empire. I'm all about the real estate."

When we arrived at work, the first thing I saw was Dr. Richter's niece Mikayla sitting on the biggest dog bed at the Doggy Depot, her head on her knees, asleep. When Chuck ran up to her and sniffed her hair, she jumped.

"Good morning," I said.

"That's one way to look at it," she said,

standing in an effort to rouse herself. "Whoa. Rough night. We went to see MCR, and then we were up till four drinking Stoli and Diet Rockstars."

"Ah," I said. "Well, everyone will start showing up in about fifteen minutes, so you have time to mainline some coffee."

"Mind if I sit back down?" she said. "I feel kind of vomity."

By 9:00 A.M., Mikayla was asleep again in the king-size dog bed. Eleven dogs were signed in and looking for entertainment and action. Now that I could hear them talking, I realized that the Doggy Depot was a favorite hangout, like a bar. While some sat around chewing on squeaking latex, gnawing on cow hooves, or destroying stuffed animals, others told stories.

Dinky, the miniature dachshund, liked to dominate with her list of favorite moments when pieces of food dropped on the floor. "Fall of last year — a huge piece of chicken. Kinda tough, but it must have been six inches long, and I'm not exaggerating!! I just started swallowing it whole before anyone could take it away, like I was a cobra," she said, to quite a few chuckles. "Boy, talk about your golden precious memories. Another time a housekeeper dropped an open can of mixed nuts right in front of me and they went rolling every-where. I went racing through that nut field, sucking up cashews like a goddamn ant-eater."

"You lucked out," said Franny, the Dobie mix. "My mother is so anal. If she drops anything, it's gone in a heartbeat."

Of all the conversations I listened to, the dog I was most concerned about was Brandy, a hyperactive seven-month-old golden retriever puppy. I never really liked her owner, Kent, a show business attorney. But until I heard Brandy talking, I didn't understand why, since he paid me on time, smiled, gave me tips. And I was always glad to see big, goofy Brandy, whose frantic puppy energy made her the canine equiva-lent of a meth freak. She'd go springing into the air every time she spotted a fly. She'd roll on her back in the dirt when she needed to stretch, then climb into your lap and force slobbery, muddy kisses on you until you agreed to play rope tug. But because she was bathed and fed, I assumed she was fine. Now I was hearing her say, "When he goes out of town and his girlfriend, Inger, has her Goddess meetings, she locks me in the laundry room. When I have to go potty, she screams and hits me with magazines. Then she ties me to a tree and leaves me there all night."

"That's what's going on at your house?" I asked her.

"Goddesses don't like dogs, I guess," said Brandy. "But know what time it is now? Rope tug!" She came at me with a mouth full of grimy rope, making urgent snarly faces intended to rev up my competitive spirit. The story she'd told really irked me. Should I say something to her dad? What was I going to say? "Your dog told me your girlfriend is mean"? And then what would I do? Go to Animal Control and tell them a dog, with no signs of physical abuse, told me she was being mistreated? What if it turned out I was mentally ill and causing all these people trouble for no real reason?

I was knocked out of my dilemma by Chuck, who was barking at a guy standing behind the gate with a basset hound on a red leash. He was probably in his early forties: wire-rimmed glasses, plaid short-sleeve shirt, long hair that fell to his shoulders. He was staring hard in my direction, trying to get someone's attention. When I approached, he smiled. And when he smiled, his face lit up. "I was just wondering what you guys charge," he said.

"There are different rates," I explained. Then we stood talking for such a long time that we accidentally woke up Mikayla. His name was Collin Kerensky, and he was an assistant curator in ancient history at the L.A. County Museum. Seems nice, was my first thought. I patted myself on the back for listening to my instincts.

"Everyone, this is Margie," I said, leading his basset hound over to meet the others. "This will be one of your jobs," I said to Mikayla, as she did some leg stretches against the picnic table. "You need to make sure that any new dog is introduced to the other dogs without incident."

Chuck was the first to come over and say hello. "That's my boy!" I said proudly. "The welcoming committee!"

"Margie?" said Chuck. "Nice to meet you! Let's fuck!"

"Whatever," said Margie, yawning widely, curling her tongue, looking bored and distracted.

"Chuck!" I said, pulling him off of her by his collar as he tried to mount her. "Take it easy. You just met her."

"Best time to have sex," he said. "Before we find things to fight over." He ran back to Margie's side. "Come on, girlfriend, seize the moment! We may never pass this way again." I pulled him off her a second time. He whined unhappily.

"Your dog reminds me of my ex-boyfriend, Humpy Otis," said Mikayla. "Talk about insensitive and sex-obsessed."

I sat down on the torn upholstered couch at the far end of the corral, pulled Margie onto my lap, and began to rub her long silky ears. She looked up at me with the most beautiful clear brown basset hound eyes.

"Nice to meet you, Margie," I said to her. "Where you from?"

"I don't know. We just moved here," said Margie.

"So, new to the area? No friends or relatives?" I asked.

"We have those," she said, gazing languidly at nothing in particular. "May I ask you something important? Can I have a bowl of stew?"

"Didn't your daddy feed you before you got here?" I asked.

"Yes. But I'm ready to go again," she said. "Think about your answer while I stare at you like this." She fixed me with a big-eyed, moist-lipped stare, a small bit of drool accumulating in the corners of her mouth.

"We don't serve meals here, Margie," I said, not looking.

"Well, let me come at it from another angle," she said. "I might recall more details about my life if I had stew."

At noon, I left work to go to my very first shrink appointment. I also planned to use my lunch break to get Halley a birthday present. As I walked to my car, my cell phone rang.

"Just checking to see if you're okay," said Halley, "and to make sure you know that Mom and Ng are coming at eight. Kirk is making some kind of chicken with morels."

"You need me to do anything?" I asked.

"No, no," she said. "We're fine. Just don't freak if you see, like, suitcases around. Kirk might be staying for a little while." I raised my eyebrows. But before I could officially begin the casting of aspersions, she said, "Oh God, Maura's on my other line. I have to take this." And there was a dial tone.

About 12:30, I pulled into the driveway of the Double Tree Inn–size mansion in Brentwood where Pinter's mommy's shrink saw her clients. White-haired and in her fifties, Jacqueline Willis came to the door of the guesthouse she used for an office and greeted me with a surprisingly warm smile. She was wearing a chic but rumpled beige linen pantsuit, low-heeled pumps, and frilly socks, giving her the appearance of both a silly teenager and a no-nonsense academician. Seated on her gray plaid couch, I gazed into her mostly empty aquarium.

"I like to begin by asking new patients why they're here," she said, studying me as I studied her lonely sea anemone.

"Well, I am concerned that I . . . I don't want to say I'm mentally ill," I said. "I should mention I've had very lively conversations with myself since I was a kid. But now I think I am talking to animals. Well, only to dogs. It wouldn't bother me except that I feel like they're talking back. In different voices, which I can hear in my head but not see. No mouths are moving."

Jacqueline Willis stared at me so intently, I wondered for a second if there was a ball she wanted me to throw for her.

"The whole thing is making me nervous for a bunch of reasons," I said. "One dog told me her owner's girlfriend locks her out of their house, which is right by a busy highway. So I'm worried she — the dog, not the girlfriend — will get hit by a car. That kind of thing."

"These conversations with dogs are anxiety-producing?" the shrink asked. I nodded. "What I am hearing you say is that talking with the dogs provides you with a way to punish yourself. Who else in your life causes feelings of anxiety?"

"Everyone," I said. "My mother. My father. My two ex-husbands. My sister, who says she's my Life Coach. My boyfriend, who just dumped me. Actually the only one who doesn't usually make me anxious is my dog."

"Exactly. I think the dogs for you are safe and so have become a nonthreatening way for you to confront the anxiety of the punishing parent," she said. "In Freudian personality construction, we call it the superego. Your unconscious has given you a device that allows you to punish yourself without real jeopardy."

I think that's what she said. Now it was my turn to stare.

"Well, the dogs do seem like family to me," I said. "Though my real family doesn't listen to me like the dogs do."

"That's a good sign," said Jacqueline. "You're beginning to visualize a more functional, more attentive family. I would like you to keep a detached eye on the way the whole thing is working. We'll examine it in greater detail next time."

Then she spent the last five minutes of my forty-five-minute hour figuring out which double-booked appointment for the following week could be moved in order to fit me in.

12
POSITIVE
IDENTIFICATION

The shrink was right about one thing. From the minute I turned down Halley's long driveway and saw my mother's car, I felt anxiety. I hadn't seen her or her car in two months.

It was good that I was around to witness her arrival with Ng, carrying a very large wrapped package. Otherwise I might not have recognized her. My mother appeared to have had a rather large amount of plastic surgery. If I'd been called down to the morgue right then to identify her body, I would have had to rely on her favorite lime-green woven silk pantsuit and her large silver bangle bracelets to make the identification positive. She looked kind of like an actress who had been hired to play her in the made-for-TV movie of her life. The transformation was dramatic enough that I had to focus on keeping my face from contorting into an Edvard Munchian expression of shock.

"Hello, darling," she said, coming toward me, arms outstretched. It was a relief to hear her familiar raspy voice coming from those much plumper lips. "Remember Ng?"

"Yes, of course!" I said, oddly buoyed by the fact that he still looked the way he had last time I saw him.

"You look different, Mom," I said cautiously.

"Oh," she said, running her hand through her mahogany hair. "People say that whenever I get my hair colored. Like it?"

"It makes you look fifteen years younger," I said, hoping her reaction would reveal something.

"It couldn't have come at a better time," she said. "Now that I'm out repping the Every Holiday Tree, a youthful look is critical."

"Relevant to the young people," said Ng, nodding genially. Ah, I thought. Ng's the new me.

"Mom!" said Halley, stepping out onto the front steps of the Winnebago, eyes widening as she took in the new Mom.

"Happy birthday, sweet girl," my mother called out to her, just as both of their cell phones started to ring.

"I'm sorry. I have to take this," they both

said at the same time. Then they each walked a few feet away and began to talk.

"Hello, Maura," I heard Halley say. "Can I call you right back?" Hanging up, she turned to Ng and me. "Kirk says dinner is ready." Her phone rang again. "I have to take this. I'll meet you all inside." She disappeared into the Winnebago.

"There! All done," said my mother, clicking her phone shut. "Where'd she go off to now?"

"Dinner ready," said Ng, picking up the giant package.

"Not a moment too soon. I'm ravished," said Mom.

"I think you mean famished," I said. "Ravished would mean you've had sex forced on you."

"I guess what I mean is I've been ravished so now I'm famished." She winked at Ng, putting her arm through his.

Inside the Winnebago, Halley and Kirk had really been decorating. There were new brass candlesticks and three different arrangements of flowers. There was a red gingham tablecloth and matching place mats and cloth napkins I didn't recognize. "Those are Kirk's," Halley whispered to me, nodding her head in the direction of two large suitcases outside her bedroom. "Sorry about the phone call. Maura's about to go on Jay Leno. I said she could try out her comedy shtick on me." Her cell phone rang again. "Hang on, Maura," she said into the phone, making the "just a minute" finger at the rest of us. "Why don't you all sit down. I'll be right back!" She sprinted into her bedroom.

"It looks beautiful in here," I said, putting the low-cal, low-carb, low-fat, high-protein cheesecake I'd special-ordered for Halley onto the counter, then taking a seat at the far end of the flower-and-candle-laden table. Chuck curled up under my chair.

"Does everyone want champagne?" said Kirk, stepping out from behind the stove, looking like a cordon bleu chef dressed for casual Fridays in his rumpled red-and-white-striped apron embroidered with "Bon Appétit."

"How lovely to meet you, Kirk," said my mother, smiling broadly, holding up her champagne flute.

"My pleasure!" said Kirk, pouring champagne and grinning like a Cheshire cat. "Halley's told me so many fantastic things about you. How you used to be a model and a political activist and an educator and a restaurant critic."

"Lucky for you, Eddie Haskell was always

my favorite character on *Leave It to Beaver,*" said my mother, winking.

"Mom never really got her due," said Halley, returning from the bedroom, glowing like a radioactive isotope. "She was the first person to review coffee with the language people had mainly used for wine. What phrase was yours, Mom?"

" 'Hearty, complex, and bold,' " said my mother with a degree of humility more appropriate to having discovered the genome. "They only used those words to describe Zinfandel until I made them synonymous with Colombian roast."

"And now I hear you're an inventor, too. What a Renaissance woman!" Kirk went on. I exhaled a little too loudly, because when I looked down, Chuck had placed a tennis ball in my lap and was staring at me.

"Throw this," he said. "You need it."

I picked it up and tossed it. He scrambled after it. He was right. I felt a little better.

"Are we all here now? Paxton isn't joining us?" asked my mother cheerfully.

"Ixnay, Mom," said Halley through closed teeth, like a ventriloquist. "Sore subject."

"Oh! *Finito?* Why am I always the last to know? I'm sorry, Dawn," said my mother, crushed and offering more sympathy than I wanted. "He was adorable. And a looker!"

"A toast," said Halley. Everyone hoisted their glasses. "Thank you for being here to celebrate this very special birthday with —" Her cell phone rang again. "I have to take this," she said, checking the number, then running out the front door. "Sorry. Back in a second."

"So!" said Kirk, picking up the hosting duties where Halley had dropped them. "Did she already mention we're going into business together? Starting a Life Coaching institute?"

"NO!!" gasped my mother. "Woweee!!!"

"Maura! Telling Jay that Johnny Depp took a dump in the house is genius," said Halley, loudly enough that we could all hear. "Congratulations! Now go try to wind down with an inversion."

"Lecithin to settle her nerves!" Kirk called to her.

"And lecithin will calm your nerves," said Halley to Maura.

"Would everyone like some prosciutto and melon?" said Kirk, placing a platter in the center of the table.

"Mmm. My favorite," said Mom. "One of the best pieces I ever wrote when I was at *Lady Gourmet* was about the poetry of prosciutto and melon. I called it 'A Revelation,' a word that had not yet been associated with prosciutto and melon."

"The black-and-red jacket looks stunning," Halley yelled into her phone. "Everyone will tell you. Wait till the show airs."

"Sexy but also classy!" Kirk called out to her.

"Kirk says you looked classy AND sexy," Halley shouted. "I predict a rebirth tonight after people see the show! Job offers! Phone ringing off the hook! Wait and see!!" She clicked the phone shut and came back inside, looking worn out.

"I hear from Maura twenty-five times a day," said Halley, sitting down. "She's exhausting. God help me if she bombed."

"Halley, Kirk just told us about the institute. That is phenomenal!" said my mother with a mouth full of prosciutto, rolling her eyes in ecstasy. "Talk about a revelation, this is ultra yummy!! Kirk, I don't know what it is about you, but you already feel like family to me."

"Halley's a godsend," said Kirk. "She's changed my life."

"A toast to happy couple," said Ng. We held up our glasses.

"And to you," said Kirk. "Joyce and Ng. The way you two combine work and love is absolutely inspiring."

"And to Dawn," Halley added, not wanting me to feel left out. "I'm so proud of how much progress you're making."

"Well, now that this toast has become politically correct, let's not forget Chuck," I said. As we all clinked glasses, I felt a tennis ball drop into my lap. It was a nice reminder that I had at least one real friend here after all.

13

FLYING PIG PEOPLE

"Open your present, honey," said Mom. Ng hoisted the large package over the table and handed it to Halley.

"Goody!" she said, clawing at the paper. "My mother knows how much I love presents. . . . Oh, Mom. How amazing." Halley pulled the box open to reveal a tabletop model of the Every Holiday Tree, already decorated for all nine holidays.

"Awesome!!" Kirk chirped. The two of them gathered around the tree like it was a hearth.

"It's just prototype," said Ng, "so we have to take this one home. But first one off of assembly line we send to you!"

The conversation was quickly hijacked by the Every Holiday Tree, which was apparently doing everything but hosting its own reality show. "We got the American Legends Limited catalog, THE biggest gift distributor," said my mother with at least twice the amount of enthusiasm she ever showed for the rights of animals or the teachings of L. Ron Hubbard.

"That's the catalog with all the darling winged ceramic pigs I showed you the other day!" Halley explained to Kirk.

"Precisely the crowd we want to reach!" said my mother. "Flying Pig people are Every Holiday Tree people."

"There is good chance Wal-Mart will make deal," said Ng. "Now I have to keep your mother from spending money before we get check."

"I feel so confident, I made a down payment on a new BMW." My mother grinned. "Twelve-cylinder . . . with —"

"Sshhh," said Ng. "Bad luck to celebrate too soon."

"The Wal-Mart executives love the way the concept telescopes from niche marketing to year-round," said Mom, pouring herself more champagne. "And when I told them about the plans for the special 9/11 tree, they really flipped."

"Yes," said Ng. "They said, 'You two first to handle correctly.' "

"It all sounds very exciting. Let me know when you're looking for partners." Kirk winked, passing around a serving dish. "Pureed turnips and new potatoes."

"Good. I don't eat old potatoes," said Ng, laughing loudly.

The rest of dinner was devoted to Halley and Kirk reliving the joyous trajectory of their special union in such minute detail that the telling was longer than the relationship itself. On the bright side, Kirk could really cook.

As he was clearing the dinner dishes, I put the low-cal, low-carb, low-fat, etc. birthday cake on the table. "It's got only three net carbs a serving, and it's sugar-free," I said to Halley. "So you can finally eat a piece of birthday cake without having a panic attack."

"Really?" said Kirk, surprised. "I thought you said you never gain weight because you have such a fast metabolism?"

"Yes. That's true. I do!" said Halley in a stage whisper, thinking I couldn't hear. "My sister gets her issues mixed up with mine. We're working on her boundaries."

"You're working on *my* boundaries?" I said, first stunned, then furious. "Right back. Let's go for a walk, Chuck."

I dragged him by the collar out from under the table, hooked him to his leash, and stormed out to the yard.

"Can you believe my sister?" I said, walking rapidly down the rutted driveway in the moonless night. "She's doing it again. She's back to being Mrs. Scott Peterson. Reinventing herself so she can live in a fantasy."

"I'm clear with all my bitches," said Chuck, pulling me toward some bushes. "If I like one, I hump her till she bites me. Then it's adios, bitch, time for BALL."

"You're a model of decorum," I said, letting him pull me into the brush.

"While we're out here . . . there's a place I've always wanted to pee," he said, manically smelling every single thing around him, pulling me farther and farther into the darkness.

"Where you going?" I said. "Hey. Get away from that poo. That's disgusting."

"You're crazy," he said. "It's not only NOT disgusting, it was left here by a very good friend. I haven't seen this guy since, whoa . . . since the pound! I can't believe it! Ricky!!" He stood and sniffed, then started to chuckle. "Listen to what he says: 'I'm feeling great. Got some roast beef string out of the garbage yesterday. I'm all plugged up. Like I give a fuck!' That's Ricky, the garbage freak!"

I started to pull him away, but he wouldn't budge.

"Hold on," Chuck said, "he's expecting

an answer." He planted himself and took a long leak.

"We should go back inside," I said as he finished. He trotted energetically beside me back to the Winnebago.

"You know what, Chuck?" I said. "Despite the fact that you're intermittently vile, you're the only creature on the planet who I love without feeling conflicted."

"Did you used to say that to Swentzle?" he asked.

"Stop that right now. I told you, this is not a contest." I led Chuck up the front steps, waving to Kirk, who stood talking to Mom and Ng out by their car.

Inside, Halley was cleaning the kitchen. "Sorry I didn't get you a better present," I said to her, trying to help by loading dishes into the sink. "But you know the state of my finances right now."

"Of course I do, sweetie," said Halley, beaming so hard that she seemed lit from within like some kind of a Buddha. "So you like Kirk okay?"

"He seems like a lovely guy," I said.

"It took me thirty-one years to finally become smart," she said. "I just wish he had a twin brother for you. No, wait, that would be way creepy." She began to scour a pot.

"He's really wonderful, isn't he?" she began again.

"He definitely seems very nice," I said, "and he's certainly cute. And crazy about you. But . . ."

"But what?" she said, her tone changing from warm to cold in a nanosecond. "What bummer thing do you want to dump on me that will make me feel like shit?"

"Nothing," I said.

"I heard you say 'but,' " she said.

"Let's just drop it," I said.

"No, no! As your Life Coach, I need to point out to you that by refusing to express what you believe, you are perpetuating a pattern that always served you badly."

"Okay," I said, feeling coerced, "I was kind of thinking that . . . um, going into business together after knowing him such a short time . . . Is that a good idea?"

"What an ugly thing for you to say on this happy occasion," said Halley, her face flushed. "I totally resent it."

"See? I knew I shouldn'ta said anything," I said.

"But you had to blurt it out anyway, didn't you?" she roared back.

"Well, only because you made me," I said defensively.

"Placing blame on others is pointless and

counterproductive. You either believe what you're saying or you're trying to make trouble. Which is it?"

"I wasn't trying to make trouble," I said. "But I have found that until you know someone for a few years, you can't —"

"Where do *you* come off giving *me* advice?" she bellowed. "Where's your fabulous track record? What happened to Neil and Jake, Dawn? Where's Paxton? I have to take this." Halley looked down at her ringing cell phone. "Hi, Jen," she said, switching to her cheery voice. "Good girl. No contact at all. Here's what I want you to do: Write your anger down on a piece of masking tape and stick it to the sole of your shoe. Then when you feel crazed, stomp on it! Rub it in the dirt! Try it and call me back. And kudos for not calling him."

Halley clicked the cell phone shut and took a deep breath. "As for you, the problems you had with your loser husbands are NOT the problems that I do NOT even HAVE with Kirk." She shook her head and glared. "After all the support I've given you. It's hard to believe that my own sister would be all bitter and negative about my success like this. . . ."

"Halley, you've got this all wrong," I said.

"It's a good thing you're talking to a shrink," she said.

"Oh! Lucky me! Approval from the big expert!" I said, enraged. "From now on, save the brilliant Life Coaching for D-list actresses who accept advice from a guru who moves in with someone she barely knows."

"Who said he's moving in?" Halley said, her eyes narrowing.

"The three suitcases were kind of a hint," I snorted.

"Okay — what if he is moving in? So what?" she struck back.

"When exactly were you planning to tell me?" I asked.

Kirk came in the door, chuckling to himself. "Your mother is the bomb!" he said. "And Ng is so . . . What's wrong?"

"We were just having a difference of opinion," said Halley.

"I'm moving out," I announced, surprising even myself.

"Not because of me, I hope," said Kirk.

"No, because it's time," said Halley.

"I'm going to bed," I said, feeling the chill in the room. I began collapsing the dining room table to create my bedroom. Kirk and Halley went into her bedroom and closed the door.

"You know, Swentzle pissed in this corner at least twice," Chuck whispered as I made up the bed.

"Not now," I said, trying to calm myself down, aware that the pulse in my neck was throbbing.

A minute later, Halley appeared in the doorway. She cleared her throat in lieu of knocking. "One more thing," she said. "Assuming you ever get around to writing a book, you may *not* write about me."

"Oh. Like you're so interesting," I said.

"We've discussed you taking a writing class," she said. "You claimed you were committed to it. So be advised that my story is my property. You are legally bound by my wishes."

"Now you're threatening to sue me? Well, happy birthday to you!" I said, crawling into bed and turning my back to her as she clip-clopped out. I lay there in the dark, listening to the sounds of the *Tonight* show theme coming from behind the closed bedroom door.

"I pray Maura gets an applause break or we'll never hear the end of it," I heard Halley say to Kirk.

"I know you're under a shitload of stress," said Chuck, putting his head on my neck, "but before you pass out from a life that is too exhausting to bear, can I get a favor?"

"I guess so," I said. He placed a soggy, muddy teddy bear that was missing its face very gently on my chest.

"Throw this," he said. So I did.

14
A CHANGE IN STATUS

I left the house at 5:00 A.M. so I wouldn't have to see either of them, then went right to a newsstand to buy all the local papers. Chuck and I sat on the patio outside McDonald's as I nursed a regular coffee and Chuck swallowed a breakfast burrito in one bite.

"Just the one burrito?" he whined. "Go get me two more."

"Since when do you order me around?" I said, not amused.

"Since today," he said. "There's been a change in pack status. We've done things your way from day one. Now we're homeless. The pack is pissed off. I'm taking charge."

"You and my sister," I said. "You both have all the answers."

"Your sister's head is shoved up her butt. She's all about wishful thinking," said Chuck, staring at me intently. "I'm the one

154

in touch with that little thing called instincts. That's all dogs have. No one ever accused us of being too cerebral or praised our contributions to the arts."

"So, what are you suggesting?" I said.

"Well, my first decision, as the new alpha: two more breakfast burritos. I need them to help me strategize," he said.

"Okay, but slow down," I said. "No swallowing them whole."

"I can clock in at sixty burritos an hour," he said, sitting tall and puffing out his chest. "If I could get you to buy me that many, you'd be blown away by my technique."

Then he swallowed the next two burritos before they were even unwrapped.

After that, we decided to head to the vet hospital to use their phone before they opened for business.

By 8:00 A.M., I had called every reasonable rental listing that was less than an hour away. "I have only two more places circled, then I'm out of places," I said to the incredibly groggy Mikayla, who staggered in to work at 8:15.

"Cars are already pulling up outside," she said. "You want me to go sign people in?"

"That would be great," I said, too tired to move. Then I peeked out the window and saw a Honda Element with an overweight basset hound in the window. "On second thought, let's both go."

"Hi, Franny. Hi, Kokomo. Hi, Sheba," I said, taking the dogs by their leashes from their harried owners. "Why, look who's back today, everyone! It's our friend Margie!" I said, handing all the other leashes off to Mikayla.

"She had such a good time yesterday," said Collin, smiling wryly. "So we're back for more." He looked spiffy in his tweed jacket, even though it was too short in the arms.

"We all love Margie here," I said, trying to X-ray Collin's inscrutable deadpan expression for personal clues. "How's the history business?"

"A conundrum. As usual," he said. "I have to find a way to present the Phoenicians so that the public will embrace them, like they do the Egyptians. But that means I can't use the good stuff, like child sacrifice. For a lot of people that's a turnoff."

"You need a way to let people have a look at the good side," I said.

"That's what I've been trying to tell the director," he said.

"On a totally unrelated subject," I said, "if you hear about anything inexpensive for rent . . . I'm asking everyone."

"You need a place to live?" he asked.

"Yeah," I said. "I just broke up with . . . well, pretty much everyone. My sister. Her fiancé. My boyfriend."

"I'm sorry," he said.

"I've had better days," I said, fearful that too much empathy from anyone would make me weepy.

"I'm getting off work a little early today," Collin said, handing me Margie's leash. "If you have time later, maybe we can go grab a cup of coffee. Or a cup of noodles. Or a cup of soup. Something in a cup. To pick up your spirits. A cup of gin."

"Sounds great," I said as he headed back to his car. "Later, then," I called to him as he waved.

"Hey, take it easy, Handsome," I said, catching the Irish setter by his collar as he leapt out of the car in front of me. Collin turned and looked back. "Sorry," I shouted. "I wasn't being forward. This is Handsome."

"I get more shit from that stupid name," said Handsome. "Why did they do that to me? How would she like it if someone had named her Big Tits?"

"Do you want me to say something to your mom?" I asked, watching Collin's car turn right onto the Pacific Coast Highway.

"Nah. She doesn't listen," Handsome said as we all walked to the corral. "I've given her hints. Like I don't come when she calls me. She just thinks I'm stupid."

"The professor is way into you," sang Mikayla when I met up with her back inside the corral.

"You mean Collin?" I said. "I don't get that at all."

"Didn't he just ask you to do something later? Dude, he wants to hook up," she said.

I let Margie and Handsome loose in the corral. Margie stood beside me, looking around, as Chuck raced up to her side. "Sex today?" he asked, clamping his front paws around her rear, unwilling to wait for an answer.

"Nah," said Margie, looking back, then squirming free. "I'm starving. Maybe if you get me some stew . . ."

With that, she took off at a full gallop for an empty dog bed, collapsing onto her side in it.

"Frigid stew freak. Get her some goddamn stew, for chrissakes," Chuck said to me urgently, lowering his voice. "Do it and I'll pump her for information about whoseits."

"Excuse me, big shot," I said. "What makes you think I want that information?"

"Instincts," he called, following Margie to the big bed.

"Mikayla," I said, "can you handle things alone here for a bit? I have to go talk to real estate agents."

"Sure," she said. "Look . . . I don't know what your take on this will be, but I have an extra room in my condo I'm thinking of renting. Ever since that troglodyte Otis moved out, I've been too angry to even run an ad on Craigslist. But it's a nice pad. My mother's husband, Keifer, bought it for me. He doesn't like humping my mother when I'm on the premises. If you want to try it out, I'd be up for it."

"Really?" I said, my eyes widening. "I'd be very grateful. I'm kind of in a tight spot right now. If it's really okay, I could go pack up my stuff after work."

"Aren't you hooking up with Margie's dad then?" she asked.

"You're right," I said. "I better go now. You think you'll be okay here alone for a bit? Everyone's checked in. Except Brandy, and they're always late."

Chuck and I headed toward the gate together and were immediately shadowed by every other dog in the place. All of them rushed toward us in a mass attempt to escape.

"I'll be right back, you guys," I said, trying to ignore the way they all stood staring at me with the kind of rapt attention I save for the end of a mystery novel.

"Last time you said that, we didn't see you again for a year," said Handsome, despondent.

"The last time I said that was a few minutes ago when I went to the ladies' room," I said.

"I should probably appoint a temporary alpha," said Chuck, thrilled to be the only one leaving. "But do I need the hassle of reestablishing pack order when we get back? No! Where we going?"

"Up to Halley's to get our stuff," I said. "We're moving."

"Whoa. Very nice," he said, jumping into the car. As we drove, he sat watching the road with such grave intensity that I found it unsettling.

"Something on your mind?" I finally asked him.

"Well, yes." He paused before he spoke. "Can I ask you a personal question that's been bothering me?"

"Sure," I said.

"Why do you not strew your garbage around?" he asked.

"Well, the word *garbage* means discarded

waste," I said. "It's meant to be thrown out. It rots, stinks, and gets maggots."

"Exactly. So since we agree there's no downside at all," he said, "why not roll on it first? When I'm flinging a coffee filter full of grounds, sometimes for a second it's thirty million years ago. There I am, ripping up the intestines of some fifteen-hundred-pound *Phoberomys pattersoni.* Now that was a rodent! And I'm so into hurling those guts around, well, I'd do it every day. Except I know it pisses you off."

"Ripping apart a dead thing and flinging the guts around is disgusting," I said. "Not to mention very hard to clean up."

"See — that's the toughest thing about our relationship." Chuck sighed mournfully. "To make you happy, I have to keep the brakes on all the time. Even when it makes no sense."

"We both have to make compromises," I said as I turned right on the long unpaved road to the Winnebago and parked the car. "We see things differently. That's just the way it is. I don't get why you pull the eyes out of stuffed animals."

"Seriously?" he said. "You really don't get it? The eyes are the caviar of the stuffed animal. If I don't grab 'em right away, someone else will."

I parked in front of the Winnebago, then knocked on the front door. When no one appeared, I let myself in and headed for the corner where all my stuff was still stashed. As rapidly as I could, I repacked my still packed suitcases. I didn't have much: a few books, a few receipts. As I was piling the loose stuff into a large plastic bag to haul out to the car, Kirk emerged from the bedroom, humming something unidentifiable. Dressed in a Hawaiian shirt and big shorts, he still looked like a layout for the Gap. He was startled.

"Hi," he said pleasantly. "What a surprise!"

"Sorry, I guess I should have called first," I said.

"I'm the one who's sorry," he said, "about all of this." He gestured to the things I had packed and shook his head.

"Not your fault," I said. "It was a long time coming."

He shrugged, nodding solemnly. "Maybe it's for the best," he said. "Your sister is under a lot of stress right now.

"I'm going to make some chai," he said as he watched me carry my belongings out to the car. "Would you like some?"

"Thanks. But no thanks," I said, climbing

into the driver's seat. I was about to back out when Halley's car pulled up to block my exit.

"Sorry about the short fuse last night," she said, running toward me, hanging in my front window. "You don't have to leave. Please stay."

"I'm sorry, too," I said, holding back a tide of emotion.

"I'll leave you two alone," said Kirk, heading back inside.

Halley lowered her voice. "But if you do stay, you'll have to adjust to having Kirk here. Because he's here for good. He and I are permanent. We have a million things in the works together. An infomercial. The institute. We just booked a seminar at the Learning Annex for next month."

"About what?" I asked her.

"About our journey. And how becoming the person you want to be is a path to the person you want to be with. Kirk thought to call it 'To Be or Not to Be With.' Isn't that hot? We're going to write it up as a book proposal."

She looked at me cautiously. "That's another reason you can't write about me. Though I only want good things for you. I swear."

I nodded. "Thanks," I said. "I gotta get

going. I'm moving in with Mikayla for now."

"Mikayla?" she said, furrowing her brow. "Well, that's kinda dark! If it doesn't work out, come on back, okay?"

"Can we get going?" said Chuck from the backseat. "I need some fresh air. It smells like dogs in this car.

"If I didn't know for a fact that you'd be upset," Chuck said as I pulled the car down the steep driveway, "I would totally have bitten that Kirk guy."

15
THE SECOND THREE MINUTES

"I'm running a couple minutes late," I said to Mikayla, checking in by cell on the way back. "Did Brandy ever show?"

"Nope. But otherwise everything's cool," she said.

I pulled into a nearby Ralph's market to purchase three big cans of stew. Then, since it was on the way, I decided to cruise by Brandy's house to make sure things looked okay.

I was heading down Kanan Road when Chuck said, "There she is. In the bushes. On the left." And there was Brandy, running in and out of the bushes, then in and out of traffic, only a few feet from a major highway. When I stopped the car on the soft shoulder, she came wagging right over and jumped in the backseat.

"Brandy, bad girl," I said, hugging her.

"Hey, mixed messages," she said. "I love that."

"You know better than to run around in traffic," I said.

"I do?" she said. "There's a Goddess meeting and I'm locked outside."

I looked up at the house and could hear the tinkling of synthesizer music. A lot of women in pastel colors were visible on the back patio. Since Brandy was already in the car, I just took her with me.

I expected to find Mikayla at wits' end back at the Doggy Depot but was surprised instead to see her sitting on a dog bed, listening to her iPod, surrounded on all sides by snoring dogs. Margie was asleep in her lap.

"You know what I like about this job?" she said, smiling as she took out her earpiece. "I'm really popular. Finally." She reached into her back pocket and pulled out an electric bill on which she had drawn a map to her condo. "Turn right off PCH at Rambla Pacifica and go up the hill," she said. "If you get lost, here's the phone number. Right next to the monthly charges. And here's my extra key."

"Great," I said, opening up the cans of Dinty Moore I'd just purchased and pouring the first and largest portion onto a paper plate to give to Margie.

"There definitely is a God," said Margie,

consuming stew in such a rapid fashion that she seemed to be inhaling it. Around us, the other interested takers charged like a stampeding herd of starving cattle.

"You know, my dad is a very interesting guy," said Margie, coming up for air, meat fat glistening on her jaw, gravy and peas coating the hair from her upper lip to her nose. "He usually picks girlfriends based on whether or not I like them." She paused and looked at me. "Stew," she ordered.

"So does your dad have any girlfriends right now?" I asked, pouring her a little more stew, only to watch it be consumed so fast that it was as if it never existed.

"You mean women who sleep on the bed?" Margie asked. "Once in a while. But I have no idea what 'a while' is. More stew."

"Want to hear about my owner?" said Handsome, a long elastic drool leaking from his lower lip.

"My owner lets women get on the bed," said Sheba, pushing to the front of the line.

"Sorry, I'm all out of stew," I said to the salivating dogs.

Margie sighed deeply, then trotted over to the dog bed she liked best and collapsed on it.

The rest of the afternoon was uneventful. First I called Brandy's father and left a message. No one called back. Then I threw seemingly endless amounts of balls for Chuck and his posse. Next thing I knew it was 4:00, nearly closing time. So I figured I'd get gussied up a little for my cup of something with Collin. But there was so little available light in the hospital's small unisex bathroom, it was like trying to put on makeup in the catacombs. Unable to see well enough to apply eyeliner or isolate eyelashes, I settled for some generic spraying and fluffing of hair, hoping for the best. My suitcases were in the car, so I changed from my blue work shirt to a pale pink blouse with a ruffle. By the time I walked out, Collin was squatting by the gate, greeting Margie at eye level.

"Mmm. Somebody's been eating cake," Margie said as she licked his face.

"How was my silly girl today?" said Collin, looking at me and waving. I liked how much attention he paid her. Some of the people who picked up my clients treated them as though they were a problem they had to endure, like a sprained ankle.

"She's great," I said. "Though she keeps saying she's hungry."

"Have you been lying to Dawn? If I don't feed you, how'd you get that spare tire?" he said to her. "Now that she knows she's got

168

me hook, line, and sinker, she's stopped trying to keep her figure." He reached into his jacket pocket and pulled out a handful of packaged saltines.

"I sadeese fra runch," he said, talking while ripping open the plastic packages with his teeth. "What is your dog's name, Dawn?"

"Chuck," I said as Collin held out a fistful of saltines for Chuck. He approached cautiously to sniff them, then picked them up in his teeth and trotted off to a spot he liked under a table to eat them. Nice guy, I thought, watching Collin ply Chuck with crackers. Instincts, I thought. I can finally hear them.

"Once again, thanks so much for everything," said Collin. "Looks like Margie had another great day." Then I watched him pick her up and carry her to his dusty Honda Element.

I debated whether to say anything about our appointment, embarrassed I'd bothered to change clothes. Maybe he'd had second thoughts or a change of heart. Maybe he was married. Maybe I looked awful.

"Have a great weekend," he called as he headed his car out to the highway. I just stood and stared as he drove away.

Maybe my instincts work in reverse, I

thought. Maybe when they say "Nice guy," what they mean is "Dick."

Mikayla looked at me expectantly as I walked back into the corral. To the unspoken question on her face, I shrugged. She nodded, rolled her eyes, and repositioned her headset. Sensing I didn't want to talk, she lay down on a dog bed between two clients and closed her eyes.

I sat back down at the picnic table just as Chuck emerged from under it, licking crumbs off his lips.

"See?" he said. "My three-minute rule works perfectly again. I always know everything about someone in under three minutes."

"You don't know shit," I said. "That guy just stood me up. Your 'under three minutes' thing is completely bogus. And your instincts have been compromised by crackers."

"No," he said. "You're wrong. I'm always right about the first three minutes. It's the second three minutes where everything gets tricky."

16
CRADLE OF FILTH

The expensive-looking Spanish hacienda–style building where Mikayla lived was on a beautiful if precipitous hillside facing the Pacific. Her condo itself had a lot of nice features: a cathedral ceiling, a polished bamboo floor, skylights, big picture windows, a big kitchen with all new appliances. For a nineteen-year-old living on her own for the first time, Mikayla was doing okay.

A left turn when you came in the front door led to three bedrooms off a hallway, each with its own bath. That said, it must also be noted that the place looked like a beautifully appointed slum. Apparently uncomfortable with a degree of wealth and luxury that she didn't want or felt she hadn't earned (or maybe out of anger at her mother's boyfriend?), Mikayla had set about putting her personal signature on the condo décor through sheer neglect.

She slept on a mattress on the floor in the

master bedroom surrounded by a nest of all of the clothes, magazines, books, CDs, pizza boxes, and Chinese takeout food containers that had come through the front door since she'd moved in.

And then there were the walls.

"Such is the human race, often it seems a pity that Noah didn't miss the boat. — Mark Twain" was hand-painted in four-inch black block letters above the refrigerator.

"I don't care if people hate my guts; I assume most of them do. The important question is whether they are in a position to do anything about it. — William Burroughs" was painted in dark green and spanned the whole top of one living room wall, turning a corner to complete itself in the dining room.

"Well, that's cheery!" I said, reading the quotes out loud to Chuck and Brandy. "What do you think?" Chuck was running silently from room to room, nose down, tail up, conducting a thorough molecular investigation as Brandy trailed behind him, biting at his back feet, trying to get a game going.

"Knock it off," he said to her. She continued to do it anyway, so he ignored her.

"Well," Chuck said after a few minutes of this, "the place looks like a real shithole. No wonder I love it so much."

"It stinks good," said Brandy, rolling on her back in a waist-high pile of sheets and towels.

"I wonder which room is ours," I said, peering into the two other bedrooms. One was bare except for many posters and photos of pale haunted Goth luminaries: Cradle of Filth, Inkubus Sukkubus, Switchblade Symphony, Fall Out Boy. The far corner had been decorated as a shrine to My Chemical Romance, complete with hundreds of pictures, candles, and a vase full of doll heads on sticks arranged to resemble a bouquet.

The other room had a bicycle, a computer, a Sony PlayStation, a plasma TV, and a boom box with many speakers. In the center of the room was a futon done up like a bed.

"Which should it be? The temple or the arcade?" I said.

"Hi!" said Mikayla, making a sudden entrance. "Are you okay with all this? Some people, like my mom, get kinda freaky about the mess." She took off her sweatshirt and dropped it onto the floor. "You can have either room. But if you take the one with the TV, it comes with a lot of visitors."

I put my suitcases down in the middle of the shrine room, inflated my air mattress, and pushed it against the far wall. When I lay down on it, I found myself looking up at the silver letters on a purple-and-black background of the poster for Cradle of Filth. All around me, the pale spooky faces and dark red lips of the angry alternative rocker boys stared down at me. What, I wondered, did these poor tortured children have to be so upset about? Investment difficulties? Too many love choices? Unreliable room service menus?

I felt displaced, disoriented, like a detached booster rocket left to drift in space, with no destination.

"Don't go to sleep yet," Chuck whined. "Let's go check out the neighborhood."

"We're going out and have a look around," I called to Mikayla, who was now on the floor in the living room, legs up on the wall, talking on her phone. She waved at the three of us as we went out the door.

Our new street had a sidewalk so steep that it was almost vertical. It went winding up the hillside past expensive, enormous architecturally-important-looking single-family dwellings. Chuck wasted no time peeing on everything he could. "There's a lot of real estate to acquire around here," he said, pulling me up the step incline. "Gotta grab it before the bubble bursts."

"Slow down," I said. "Can't you walk

without pulling?"

"I'm not pulling," he said.

"You are, too," I said. "We're almost running."

"We are not," he said, pulling so hard that I almost tripped.

"HEY," I said. "Slow down! I want to know what you think of the neighborhood."

"Well, the street has two overflowing garages. That's a good sign," he said, stopping to sniff. "People with disgusting garages like dogs."

"They do?" I said, impressed by his observation.

"They don't?" he said. "Did I get that one wrong?" He stopped to pee again. Then without warning he began pulling me so rapidly into the street that I fell forward.

"Why are you pulling me into traffic?" I said, angry, trying to restrain him. "You want to get us killed?"

"I'm sorry," he said, upset. "Goddamn asphalt butterflies. The street is infested with 'em. I guess I snapped."

"You do know that those butterflies are in the air?" I said. "What you're chasing on the ground are their shadows."

"That's chilling," he said.

"Dude, that's freaky," said Brandy, grinding our progress to a halt so she could examine the post of a mailbox. "Hey," she said to Chuck, "check this out."

The two of them stood still, sniffing the post and laughing.

"Okay . . . I've had enough of this. Let's go home," I said, wondering what *home* even meant now.

Mikayla was gone when we returned. It was still light outside, but I felt so unsettled, I wanted to hide in bed under the covers. Chuck lay down on my legs as Brandy went trotting from room to room, inspecting things.

When I woke up it was dark outside. Both dogs were sleeping beside me. Mikayla was standing in the doorway, wrapped in a Japanese robe, her hair wet from a shower.

"Would you like a bowl of cereal?" she asked sweetly.

"No, I'm fine," I said. "What time is it?"

"It's about ten o'clock," she said. "You okay?"

"Sure. Great. Except, you know, kind of depressed."

"I prefer depressed people," she said. "It's unnatural to be too up. Like my fucking mother, who's all 'Let's go out and do this. Let's go out and do that.' All day long. And I'm like, 'Who are you to say what I should do? You were a coke freak in the seventies.

Where do you come off telling me that Otis is no good? Just because he does X?' Though in his case she was right. He is no good. But she didn't know that. She just made a lucky guess."

"We'll have to discuss this further at some point," I said. "Unfortunately, right now I'm really wiped out."

"I totally get what you're saying," she said. "If you need any blankets or pillows, check the laundry pile in the hall. One last thing. The guy you broke up with? Paxton?"

"Yes," I said warily.

"I kind of know him. I was a huge fan of his show. I had a crush on him until I found out he's, like, forty."

"He is an old coot, isn't he," I said.

"He doesn't look all that bad considering," she said, consoling me. "And now I'm your roommate. So how cool is that?"

"Maybe not so cool if you know he dumped me," I said.

"You're kidding! I heard you dumped him. Because he got that show in Seattle," said Mikayla, suddenly full of dangerous information. "I mean, that's a lucky break. A chance to go to a real station because Roxy's father was program director. My stepfather, Keifer, works at Sony. I tried to make him hire Paxton so he wouldn't have to leave. But Keifer wouldn't do shit. Even though he's got tons of ideas for bands to sign from Paxton's show."

"Roxy who?" I said, not wanting these answers at all.

"You know. Roxy from work," she said.

"Dr. Richter's Roxy?" I said, recalling her hostility. "You mean, she and Paxton . . . ? Were they . . . ?"

"No. It's not like that. I don't think. It was just a really great opportunity. Or that's what he told me."

"You talked to him about all this?" I said, stunned. "He told you I dumped him?"

"Kind of," she said. "I was around and he was around and I didn't want him to leave. I offered him your room. Before I offered it to you, I mean."

"So if Paxton and Roxy weren't . . . why is she moving to Seattle?" I said.

"All's I know," she said, "is that her father needed a host."

"Whoa," I said. "I had no idea of any of this."

"Really?" Mikayla looked surprised and a little proud. "How weird is it that I know more about your life than you do? That is so freaky. I hope you're cool with it." Her cell phone rang. "I have to take this. Sorry," she said, leaving me alone in my bed feeling like I'd been run over by a truck.

"Chuck?" I said, nudging him where he lay asleep on the floor. "Come up here next to me?" He climbed up onto the mattress and curled himself into an apostrophe by my right side. I buried my face in the fur on the back of his neck.

"You're such a good boy," I said. "I feel really awful. I want to disappear."

"Please don't disappear," he said, picking his head up, his voice full of anxiety.

"I can't really disappear. Even if I want to," I said.

"Whew. Close call," Chuck said as I rubbed his giant doe-like ears.

17
GODDAMN
GODDESSES

At about 5:00 A.M. I found myself staring at more of Mikayla's hand-painted words on the ceiling above my bed: "Ah, *mon cher,* for anyone who is alone without God and without a master, the weight of days is dreadful. — Albert Camus." Still dizzy from the details of what I had just learned about Paxton, I wasn't ready to be called *mon cher* before I'd even had coffee.

"Yeehaw," Chuck said, waking up ecstatically happy as always. "What a nice surprise! A stinky new place to live!!"

He bounded out of bed, ran across the room, and returned with a mouth full of squeaking vinyl lambchop for me to throw. To entice me further, he placed it on my stomach.

"Ball?" he said. And when I didn't pick it up, he added, "I realize it's not an actual ball per se. I'm speaking euphemistically." Then he picked it up in his mouth again, raised himself on his arms to my eye level, and stared at me before dropping the chop on my chest. "What's wrong? Not that grid jerk again?"

"No. Of course not," I said. "There's a lot of stuff wrong: Famine. Genocide in Africa. The war in Iraq. The idea that I was not only dumped, I was also betrayed."

"What war in Iraq?" Chuck said, suddenly worried.

"It's been going on a couple years," I said.

"Yeah, but they started it," said Chuck defensively.

"No, we made a preemptive strike," I explained. "That's when you think that someone is going to do something to you, so you do it to them first."

"Wow. You can do that?" he said. "So if, like, we're on a walk and I see a dog that I think might kick my ass, I can jump him and hurt him before it even occurs to him to come after me? That is so me from now on."

"Don't you dare do that," I said, sitting up at last. "They kill pit bulls for a lot less than that."

Checking my messages, I saw that Brandy's owner had called from Honolulu. "I spoke to my fiancée, Inger, who's house-sitting," he said, "and she says to just drop

Brandy off late afternoon. She has a Goddess meeting until four. But after that she's clear."

I called him back right away. "Not unless I get some assurance that this Inger person is not going to leave Brandy out, running loose, again" was the message I left.

"Inger promised me she will not make that mistake a second time. She really loves Brandy and misses her like crazy. So please bring her home at your earliest convenience" was his reply.

Usually work provided me with a kind of safe haven where I could count on being lavished with indiscriminate affection from my clients. Now the things Mikayla had said were piling up into a paralyzing gridlock. I felt attacked, exposed, and preoccupied by what the people around me were thinking but not saying. Which of them had wondered what I knew, then decided it was none of their business? Which of them looked at me with pity? Or felt I had gotten what was coming? Did Richter know about the whole thing? Did Halley? I felt trapped in some Samuel Beckett play where everyone who pretended to like me had a secret agenda. Or was it a play by Sam Shepard? It was some angsty, paranoid Sam.

We didn't have too many clients that day,

so on my lunch break I reluctantly drove Brandy back to her home. Since no one answered the door when I rang the bell, I went around to three different doors, knocking and calling out, "Hello?" Finally, I sat in my car and called the house from my cell phone. A very groggy woman's voice answered. Apparently even Goddesses needed their sleep.

"Hi, it's Dawn from Doggy Depot calling about Brandy," I said.

"She's downstairs," said Inger. "Are you picking her up?"

"No. She's not," I said. "She got out yesterday and spent the night with me. I have her here in my car."

"Sweet feathery lemon-scented Christ," said Inger. "Look, I'm not dressed. I haven't had my coffee. Do you think you —"

I hung up on her. Then I took Brandy and walked back to the front door, where I stood ringing the bell until she came downstairs.

"Okay, okay," she said, opening the door. She was a thin blonde, wrapped in a man's robe, her hair pulled up on top of her head in a barrette. She was too asleep to look at me as Brandy bounded inside. "Thanks," she said, cupping a cigarette to light it as she closed the door with her foot.

By the time I got back to work, I was feeling really off balance. I decided to leave Mikayla in charge for a while and retreat back to her condo. It was the first time I had ever jumped ship when I was on the clock. But the combination of the new Paxton info and the Brandy situation had me so distressed, I couldn't focus on even something as simple as entertaining dogs.

What I wanted to do was get in bed and escape into my book. I felt like pouring myself into an alternate reality. But now I had Halley's new edicts in my way.

"How am I supposed to 'write what I know' and not mention Halley?" I said.

"There's plenty of other stuff to write about," said Chuck.

"Like what?" I said.

"Watch me work," Chuck said. "Just start writing it down."

Chapter 1
Being and Somethingness
By Chuck

My memory is burdened by chaos and cacophony; details, impulses, and desires from this morning and ten million years ago. Flashes from some ancient collective past in Eastern Europe, sometimes only seconds long. I remember roaming with a pack and everything making sense. When the moon was full, we'd all go stalk aurochs. Sometimes when we'd catch one, we'd rip it apart and feast. Back then no one screamed about mud on the carpet. No one said a single word about getting blood on the furniture. No one ever cared if we puked, then ate it and puked again. Why would they? Everyone did it. No one batted an eye. Sometimes I remember everything, and sometimes I don't know what I remember; the creodonts begat the miacis begat the cynodictus, then tomarctus. Or was it the cynodictus after the creodonts, then miacis? Sometimes it seems like yesterday, I can almost smell them all. And then the wind shifts and I hear a yelp, a shriek, some kind of cry. Is it a wild boar? A hyena in its death throes? Or is it that rubbery undercooked lambchop that squeaks when I bite on it? Why does it squeak? Is it still alive? Did I stalk and kill a squeaky latex animal? Why is it so red, yet there is no blood? Is it grotesquely undercooked? I have so many questions for which there are no answers. Like why, when I see the garbage can on the kitchen counter, do I flash for a moment to the African veldt and feel a raw metaphysical urge to leap upon it? Why do I want to tackle that can, to kill that can and rip it open, then throw back my head in a joyous cry of bloody communion?

18
THE THREE-MINUTE TEST

Fuck Halley and her legal threats. I'm legally entitled to write my story. And if she doesn't like the part she's in, she can sue me. If she wins, I can always change her name. Besides, I don't have any money. Good luck when she tries to collect.

So anyway, the next day at work, two disturbing things happened. First Patricia Foster, mother of a very nervous Tibetan apso named Skittles, showed up, red-faced and furious, to inform me that a dog communicator she had put on retainer said that the reason Skittles was refusing to eat was that he was being treated abusively at Doggy Depot.

"That's just not true," I said, knowing that nothing ever happened to Skittles under my watch. He slept from the moment he arrived until the moment he left.

"I don't feel like eating because she and her damn husband scream at each other all night," Skittles mumbled to me while his mother stood there yelling. "Tell her to keep her voice down. She's giving me colitis!"

It didn't seem wise to pass along this information.

"Sometimes if there is a lot of emotional turmoil in the home, a dog will stop eating," I ventured. Patricia Foster glared, then demanded I give the animal communicator a call. When I said I was too busy, she likened this to a criminal unwilling to take a lie detector test. That was upsetting. But not nearly as bad as what happened next.

Kip, who drives the ambulance, pulled up so quickly that he hit the curb. He jumped out and lifted a large yellow dog onto a gurney, then pushed it rapidly toward the back entrance to the hospital. When he saw me watching him, he called out, "Brandy. Hit by a car."

I felt the blood freeze in my veins and my heart stop in my chest. "Is she okay?" I said.

"She's alive," he said, closing the door behind him. In seconds, I went from sad to angry. This was my fault. I should never have let that Goddess get anywhere near Brandy. I had felt that sickening ping in my guts when I'd dropped Brandy off. Talk about ignoring my instincts.

I went over to the gurney just as Claire,

the new head tech, was injecting Brandy with anesthesia. "He's going right into surgery with her," she said.

"Sweet feathery Christ was right," I said, kicking myself for turning Brandy over to that wretched Goddess. It was so upsetting that later, when I saw Collin's car pull up to drop off Margie, I didn't have the strength to deal with whatever excuse he was planning to offer. I ran into the back and hid in the kennel.

But he came looking for me.

"I'm so sorry," he said. "As soon as I got in my car this morning, I remembered us getting a drink. I was almost too embarrassed to show up today. I'm really sorry. I feel terrible."

"It's okay," I said. "I wasn't in the mood to drink anyhow."

"I try not to do this," he went on, "but I'm afraid I'm famous for it. At work they say I operate better in the first century than in this one. I have a fog bank for a memory. Pathetic. I just want you to know how bad I feel."

"It's fine," I said.

"No, it's not fine," he said. "I feel ridiculous. Hey! Chuck! Look what Uncle Collin brought you! I expect you to put in a good word for me with your old lady." And then he opened a paper sack he was holding and handed Chuck a Big Mac. Chuck looked at me cautiously, clamped his jaws over it, and ran under a table before I could reconsider.

"I'd like to make it up to you," he said. "Can we please pick another time? This afternoon? Tomorrow? Next week?"

"Well, let me check my schedule," I said, pretending to rifle through papers on my clipboard as he went into the hospital to pay his bill. While he was gone, I consulted my instincts. They reminded me that since they had betrayed me so often before, it would be dumb to give them another chance.

"What a great guy," said Chuck, emerging from under the table, licking condiments from his lips. "What'd I tell you? Those first three minutes say it all."

"Like I still trust your judgment," I said to Chuck. "You are so easily bought.

"I'm too busy right now to make plans," I said to Collin when he came back. "I'm sorry. Maybe somewhere down the line." I watched the lower half of his smiling face deflate like a punctured beach ball.

"Great! Well, keep me posted," he said, trying to preserve a friendly demeanor as he drifted back to businesslike. He leaned down, kissed Margie good-bye, waved, and left.

"You are so wrong," Chuck said as Collin drove off. "I pegged the guy in one minute flat. I'm always right. And I can prove it. If you will but give me a chance to demonstrate." That was how it came to pass that Chuck and I went to the dog park in the canyon after work.

"Check it out," Chuck said as I hooked him up to a Flexi leash so he could have a little more leeway. "Whenever we see someone who passes the three-minute test, I'll bark."

He put his head down and lurched forward, dragging me in a zigzag so fast, I almost fell on my face.

"What are you doing?" I yelled to him. "Slow down."

"Asphalt butterflies," he said. "Why am I the only one who seems worried about them? Okay. Let's start again. Ahead and to my left . . ." He stopped and began to bark, causing a five-year-old boy to get so frightened that he ran crying to his mother.

"Don't bark like that," I said. "You're scaring children."

"Where's he going? He's the one I'm talking about," Chuck said with great urgency. "Follow him and ask him to dinner."

"But he's only about five years old," I said.

"You didn't say age was an issue," he said. "I myself have dated one-year-olds."

"Sorry," I said. "Doesn't work with people. Non-negotiable."

"Your loss," he said as we walked in silence. He put his nose to the ground and began to sniff the feet of all who passed. I could hear him muttering under his breath as he moved among them, "Asshole . . . Moron . . . Creep . . ." Then his ears moved forward. "Here we go," he said, head lowered, sniffing. He stopped. "Guy on my right. Go get him."

"Chuck, he's wearing a wedding ring," I said. "He's with his wife and kids. And even his parents — or maybe they're hers. Take a look!"

"How many more excuses are you planning to invent to make this completely impossible?" he said, staring at me. Then, dropping his head, he again began moving forward, pursuing certain smells. "Moron . . . Creep . . . Creep . . ." I heard him mutter, "Yikes. That one's a mess." He froze.

"Okay, I'd like to see you find something wrong with the guy ahead on my left," he said. "Quick. Get his phone number."

"At the risk of pissing you off," I said, "he's at least eighty."

"No one is ever good enough for you, are they?" said Chuck. "Next time you're wondering why you have so much trouble, take a look at how you behave." And then he began to race headlong toward the water fountains, pulling me straight into a cocker spaniel. "Hey, Curly! Got time for sex?!" he yelled.

"Your territory or mine?" she yelled back.

"Mine," he said, peeing. "I own this whole park." Grabbing her by the back legs, he turned to me. "See how easy it is? Go ask out her owner."

"Excuse me," said a very large man with salt-and-pepper hair, dressed in a tan poplin jacket and matching stay-pressed slacks, who upon closer inspection turned out to be a woman. She was not amused by Chuck's indelicate attempt at intimacy with her dog. Glaring at me, she pulled the spaniel away by her collar.

"Would you mind controlling your dog?" she said, annoyed.

"Sorry," I said, grabbing the angry Chuck.

"It's only slightly obvious why you've had a lifetime of troubled relationships," Chuck growled as I dragged him toward the car. "You haven't tried one of my suggestions. Not one."

"Because," I said, "they're inappropriate

and crazy."

"So?" he argued. "I think almost everything you want me to do is crazy. The only reason I do half of what I do every day is that it matters to you. Nearly all of it goes against my instincts." I unlocked the car, and he jumped in. "Do you have any idea how much I like to disembowel small animals?" he continued as I started the engine and headed back toward Mikayla's. "But do I? No. Because you don't want me to. If it was up to me, I'd poo and piss everywhere. I'd shred your pillows and your furniture and throw the stuffing around. I'd eat that pair of shoes you have on right now. In fact, you probably don't want to hear this, but my instincts tell me to eat my own vomit, because millions of years ago when a mother fed her pups she —"

"That's enough," I stopped him.

"No, check it out," he said. "It's really interesting. The mother would vomit the —"

"ENOUGH!" I finally shouted. But that was not the end of it. Chuck was insistent that I give his instincts a fair shake. So the next day, after work, I agreed to go with him to Santa Monica, about twenty minutes south, for a final test of the three-minute rule.

As we walked the tree-lined sidewalks outside the pricey shops of Montana Avenue, I could hear Chuck once again muttering, "Asshole . . . Asshole . . . Asshole . . ." He kept repeating it like a mantra as we strolled by a window display so bare and spooky it could only have meant expensive designer stuff. "Asshole . . . Asshole," he said outside a jeweler, an herbologist, an overpriced Brazilian café, a Banana Republic. And then he froze a few feet from a guy in a white uniform jacket pulling down the iron grating in front of a gourmet market.

"*That* guy," said Chuck. "Guaranteed. Go talk to him."

"I can't just talk to him for no reason," I said.

"Wrong," said Chuck, "but okay, then push me into him."

"What?" I said. "No, I can't do that." And the next thing I knew, Chuck charged the guy, bumping him in the back, goosing him in the butt, causing him to lurch and then stumble.

"YEOW. Jesus H. Christ!!" the guy yelled as he pivoted on his heel, ready to fight. I found myself looking into the face of a ruddy, sandy-haired middle-aged man with large bags under his eyes. He was attractive in a hard-drinking Irish kind of way, like a pudgier Russell Crowe.

"I am so sorry," I began to apologize as he looked at me. And then, to my great relief, he started to laugh. By now, the insanely friendly Chuck was throwing himself at this guy. They looked like family members reunited after a war.

"This isn't like him," I continued.

"Oh, I'm beloved by dogs," the guy said, nodding toward the awning of his store. "I work the meat counter. That makes me the canine equivalent of a *Penthouse* centerfold." He leaned down to rub Chuck's belly. "How you doin', fella?" said Riley Campbell, which was the name embroidered on his pocket. "Why don't ya come around back? I've got a nice big bone I was saving for someone like you. If it's okay with Mama." I smiled as Chuck continued breakdancing with joy.

We walked to the edge of the block and turned the corner into a small parking lot, where Riley unlocked a back door behind a Dumpster. Inside, he opened a giant freezer and pulled out a prime-rib bone the size of a miniature dachshund. "How 'bout I wrap this up for you?" he said, heading to the back of the deli case as an incredibly wired spring-loaded Chuck bounced along beside him. As Riley was pulling down a piece of waxed paper, I looked him over. He was in good shape. He had broad shoulders, strong arms, and a nice twinkle in his eye. Best of all, apparently he'd passed the three-minute test.

"That is so nice of you," I said. "I'm Dawn. He's Chuck."

"Good meeting you both," he said. "I don't recall seeing you around here."

"I live up in Malibu," I said. "I work at the Doggy Depot. It's a dog day care in back of the Animal Hospital."

"Dog day care!" he said. "Great idea. I'd love a place to leave my dog during the day. Can't bring her round here. She's a little too interested in my line of work, if you know what I mean."

"Here's our address," I said, writing the specifics on the back of a receipt I found in my pocket. "We open at eight. Come by anytime. I'll show you around."

"I might just do that," he said, grinning appealingly.

"Good job. I'm proud of you," said Chuck as we headed back to the car.

"You're sure about this?" I said, putting my key in the ignition. "The guy doesn't seem like my type."

"My instincts say you're going to be pleasantly surprised," Chuck said.

19
A Celestial Visitation

When we got back, the first thing I did was run to check on Brandy. "She's got a broken leg and a fractured hip," said Richter. "She's in a cast. She had thirty-four stitches. But she'll be okay." I started to cry.

"Brandy made it," I said to Mikayla, who was lying on the big dog bed, eyes closed, making occasional loud, blurty noises as she sang to her iPod. When she opened her eyes, she looked like she'd had a celestial visitation while I was gone.

"Awesome," she said. "Okay. Don't freak, but guess who was here looking for you."

"That asshole Goddess girlfriend of Brandy's dad?" I said.

"Paxton," she said.

"Paxton?" I said, feeling my circulatory system stall, then start, and then stall again like a car engine after a snowstorm. "Why? What's he want?"

"Ask him yourself," she said, and I turned

to see him getting out of his Mustang and walking down the driveway toward us. He was looking annoyingly magnetic in a pale night-crawlerish way, dressed in black jeans and a black cowboy shirt with white pearl snaps. His hair was dyed black, and he'd grown one of those goatees with a soul patch that went from his lower lip to under his chin. Like Chris Cornell when he was in Soundgarden.

"Hi," he began as Chuck disappeared under the table. "You got a minute?"

"Not really," I said, rifling through my imaginary work again.

"I don't blame you if you don't want to talk," he said, "but I owe you an apology. Can you give me fifteen minutes?"

"Go," said Mikayla. "I'm fine here without you."

"Mikayla, I don't need a social secretary," I said.

"Oh, come on, all I need's a couple minutes," said Paxton with a self-effacing grin.

"So how are things in Seattle?" I said as I followed him down the driveway.

"Great. Good time slot. Number one indie rock station in the country. And I was miserable." We sat in his car. "You know how I always said that given the choice, I would choose career over love? Well, I'm back here because I missed you." I just sat staring at him. "I even missed Chuck," he said. "When I was with you, I had a sense of belonging to a little family. But I was too fucked up to let anything that good stay in my life."

I was breathing rapidly, feeling light-headed.

"Don't think I haven't been haunted by my own stupidity every minute since I left. Is there a chance we can take a walk later and talk?"

I just sat quietly, aware I was choking back tears. "Please?" he said. "Just let me talk to you, and then you can tell me to go fuck myself. Would that be okay?"

"I guess so." I nodded.

"I'm glad Mikayla gave you her extra room," he said. "Underneath the spook show, she's a good soul. I hear dogs howling. That probably means you should go."

"It probably means Mikayla is doing tai chi," I whispered. "It makes the dogs nuts. They hate it."

"Thanks for seeing me," he said. "So is seven-thirty too late?"

"No, it's fine," I said, getting out of the car, stunned.

"I really do love you, you know," he said.

I just looked at him hard, unable to think of a single thing to say.

As I entered the corral, Mikayla was watching for me, riveted by my every movement. Chuck, on the other hand, blocked my path, making odd grumbling noises.

"You bring that guy back, I'll bite you," he said.

"You're threatening to bite me?" I said.

"Well, no. I don't really bite. But I will throw up on your shoes. And that stink never comes out of leather," he said.

20
"THEMES"

Things that happen in a story sometimes have two meanings: "a literal meaning," where something that happens is just what it appears to be — for example, someone thinking their dogs can talk; and "a figurative meaning," where that same something is "an example of an idea," such as trying to define what is meant by being crazy and what is meant by being sane. "When several different things that happen in a story share the same figurative meaning, we often say that the author is exploring a theme." What my theme might be:

Would it still be considered mental illness if you call the conversations you think you are having with your dog "ruminations with the ego ideal"? How about if you called them "a dialogue with my conscience"?

And also: In the world in which we live, where pretty much nothing is part of a natural process, how do you know when you have connected with your instincts? Can the conversations you think you are having with your dog be a way for your instincts to make themselves known to you?

That evening, Paxton actually showed up on time for our appointment. Equally startling, he squatted down and scratched Chuck's back so hard that it made Chuck's back leg thump. Despite all the nasty things Chuck had to say about Paxton, he seemed to have no problem accepting a large rawhide chew as a gift, like some corrupt senator.

At sunset, we all went down to the beach and walked along the shore, through large truckloads of newly delivered fog so dense that it made the berms of sand look like a cemetery in a low-budget horror movie.

"Soon as I got settled in Seattle, I realized how much I missed you," Paxton said, staring off at the gray horizon. "Without you, none of it meant anything."

"Hmmm," I said, examining my broken fingernails as though they contained a code I needed to crack.

"You think I'm full of shit, don't you?" he said. "Well, maybe you're right. That's what my father always said. Last couple weeks I've been doing a lot of thinking. About why I run away from people whenever we get close. I talked to a shrink. I know I always pooh-pooh therapy, but I found a lot of what she said interesting. Helpful."

A cold, wet wind began to gain some momentum. I zipped up my hooded sweatshirt and put my hands in my pockets.

"Shrink thought avoiding intimacy was an unconscious desire to please my parents by proving I wasn't lovable," Paxton said. "They didn't think I deserved anything. So I didn't, either. I wouldn't even let myself walk on the beach at sunset."

I looked over at him, surprised to see that his eyes were wet. "I'm sorry about the emotional thing," he said, wiping the tears on his sleeve. "This stuff is pretty humiliating." He stood directly in front of me, taking my hands in his. "Thing is: I love you. I always have. I never used to tell you because I was too much of a mess. And while I know it's probably pointless to ask you to give me another chance, I promise if you do, you won't regret it. I see things so differently now." He took one of my hands in both of his and held it tightly, almost like a little kid. "You deserve to have a man in your life who loves you," he said, leaning in to kiss me gently on the cheek. "I always said you deserved someone better. Now I want to be him."

When he said that, I flinched at first, because it rang kind of false. But the more I thought about it, the more I realized that the only reason a calculating guy like Paxton would say something so corny and over the top was that he was finally saying something real.

That was when I realized how many feelings for him I'd been trying to block. The pain of wanting to be with someone — with him if he would let me — came flooding over me. When we hugged, I was choked with emotion.

Still, I broke from our embrace after a peck on the cheek. The enormity of my feelings for the warmer, bigger Paxton was simply too terrifying. The wound was still much too raw.

"Look, all I'm asking is that you let me hang out with you. Play it by ear. See how it goes," he said. I couldn't tell if I was being smart or stupid when I said yes.

After he went home, I lay down on my bed, leaned back on my pillow, and stared up at the ceiling. The nicest moments from the evening swirled around me. That was when I noticed that Mikayla had done some fresh graffiti: "Almost all of our sorrows spring out of our relations with other people. — Arthur Schopenhauer," it said in red block letters right under the Cradle of Filth poster. And then in parentheses beneath it, "Good luck anyway. Love, M."

The tiny ray of sunshine that was pushing through the blackout curtain I had drawn around myself made me smile.

"See, that's the cool thing about life," I said to Chuck, who was curled beside me. "You think you're looking down a long empty road of never-ending darkness. Then something happens and you realize it's not that long or dark or never-ending. There's a Thai restaurant, a good coffeehouse, and a decent bookstore in that little mini-mall just ahead."

"I don't know what you're talking about," said Chuck.

"It's a way of saying that what happened yesterday isn't necessarily the same as what's happening tomorrow," I said.

"That's why we need instincts," said Chuck. "Without them we're lost. All is chaos."

"Well, I'm trying to learn that from you," I said. "But right now I feel like my instincts are telling me things will be okay. I have a new place to live, a job I like. I have you. And maybe even love. At the very least, my odds of meeting the right person are better now that I'm finally BEING the right person. Right?"

"Your instincts have been co-opted by your goofy sister," said Chuck.

I hugged him. And felt really peaceful and happy as we drifted off to sleep, like I was wrapped in one of those perfect golden pink clouds that look too much like Disney cartoons to be real, even though they are.

21
Do You Like Horses?

The next morning when I came to work, I found out we had been fired.

"Patty Foster is filing some kind of a nuisance suit against Doggy Depot," said Richter. "I know you guys are doing a great job. I think she's out of her friggin' mind. But the insurance company dropped our policy. Until I find another company to carry us, we have to shut down. By the way, do you know how to get hold of Brandy's people? No one answers their phone, and I need his permission to do another procedure."

I tried calling Team Brandy immediately. But the silence after the beep when I called and left messages for Kent and the Goddess was the only one I heard that day. From then on, my world was filled with the whining of stressed and inconvenienced dog owners coming to grips with the reality that the burden of caring for their animals was being handed back to them.

More explicit were the dogs themselves. "You're fucking kidding me," said Handsome.

"This is such bullshit," said Margie.

"Do you make house calls?" asked Collin. "Margie likes a walk every day, but my schedule is . . . well, I get so distracted I forget to walk her. Next thing I know it's dark out, and poor Margie's still sitting there staring, pressuring me, hoping beyond hope. . . ."

"I can do that," I said, although till then it hadn't occurred to me. When Handsome's owner overheard, he wanted to hire me, too. The promise of income, however small, made things a little less frightening. But as the day wore on, it began to hit me that I had lost my real job.

I tried calling Brandy's owner periodically. In the middle of my fourth unsuccessful attempt, I was interrupted by a call from my Life Coach.

"I heard about the center closing," she said, her voice full of anxiety. "We need to create a new strategy right now!"

"I'm working on it," I lied, resentful that I was expected to accept her unsolicited advice but not allowed to offer any.

"What would it take for you to act instead

of just thinking?" she said. "What can you hope to accomplish in life unless you . . . One second. I have to take this call."

"Halley, I don't want to talk now," I started.

"Okay, sorry about that," she said a few seconds later. "I've got a new client. The wife of a famous serial killer, if you can believe that. I'm trying to get her to deal with her anger issues by doing an exercise where you physicalize the baggage of rage by hauling around an actual bag full of rocks representing —"

"Halley, I'm in the middle of . . . I have to go," I said.

"Okay, I just want to add that it all boils down to you being mainly a green, which means prone to peacemaking, and underrating your own talents. What you need to do is —"

"Halley, I'll figure it out," I said.

"Good," she said. "Now you're talking more yellow. . . . One second. I have to take this call. Hello? . . . Hello? . . . I guess she got disconnected. One last thing. What I said the other night, I said as Halley. But as your Life Coach, I see you needing a more purposeful life path. So I think you should definitely be writing your book. Any way you want to."

"Thank you," I said, cutting her off before she recanted, thrilled that now *I* had another call. "I have to go."

"Hi, sweetheart," Dad said. "That kitchen repair holding up?"

"Great, Dad . . . she didn't notice a thing," I said.

"Glad to be of service," he said. "Everything else good?"

"Actually, no. I just lost my job," I said weakly.

"Honey, I have lost a job once or twice in this life," he said. "You know what they say? 'Take This Job and Shove It'? Anyway, listen, I'm in kind of a tight spot. Would you mind me giving your cell phone number to a little girl I met Saturday when the Cheaterslicks played a chili cook-off in Chatsworth? She doesn't know I'm in Cabo."

"You're in Cabo?" I said. "Right now?"

"Pumpkin," he said, "you gotta come sometime. It's paradise."

"So you want me to lie to this girl for you?" I said.

"No! It's not like that!" he said defensively. "I need you to help me protect her feelings. You know how women get. If she calls, take a message, like you're my assistant."

The next call was from Mikayla, speaking

in a voice so drained of energy, it sounded like an audio sinkhole.

"How come nobody warned me that this fucking job could end before I resigned from the receptionist job?" she said. "Right now all I want to do is hurt someone."

"Are you okay?" I said, kind of alarmed at how upset she sounded.

"No," she said, then, "I gotta go."

I was heading for my car when I saw Riley Campbell coming across the lot toward me, wearing a big smile.

"Came to check the place out. Now a good time?" he asked pleasantly. He had a great smile, kind of impish, very warm.

"Good is not the word," I said. By the time I finished explaining the whole thing to him, he was so overcome with empathy, he invited me to a party he was having.

"It's a monthly gathering of my closest friends in the food biz," he said. "Everyone cooks something. It's a hoot."

A reasonably attractive stranger inviting me to a party buoyed my spirits. It gave me confidence, made the world seem to hold greater possibilities. I liked the idea that there was more on deck than just Paxton.

"Don't you dare say no," said Chuck. I had already said yes.

When I got home that night, scrawled on

the living room wall, on top of a coating of primer, was "I loathe people who keep dogs. They are cowards who haven't got the guts to bite people themselves. — August Strindberg."

There was also a note on my pillow, written on torn notebook paper in big block letters with a red Sharpie.

"I can't take it anymore. Everything I touch turns to shit," it said. "I'm a screwup, a demon seed, the poisonous ruiner of everything. By the time you read this, I will be gone. M."

"Whoa," I said to Chuck, feeling my heart start to race. "Should I call 911?" Then I looked up and saw that Mikayla was standing in the doorway. "You okay?" I said. "You know the place closing isn't your fault, don't you?"

"Yeah, I know," she said sheepishly. "Sorry about the note. I was hoping to steal it back before you got home. Since I wrote it, I decided getting fired is the best thing that ever happened to me."

"So you're not leaving town?" I asked her.

"No, I still am," she said. "Otis is taking a cross-country trip to photograph naïve installations. Like a house that some old lady in Yreka built out of milk of magnesia bottles? So I thought I'd go. Except I'm afraid if I do my stepdad will sell this place. He's always talking about cashing in before the housing bubble bursts. So I was wondering if you'd stay here and give me, like, four hundred dollars a month, which I can use for travel expenses. It's still cheaper than rent."

"I guess so," I said, feeling a bit like Porky Pig looks after being hit on the head by a frying pan. My eyes seemed to be spinning in different directions as I tried to comprehend my finances and my life. "But . . . don't you hate Otis?"

"Not HATE hate," she said. "I won't get involved with him ever again. I'll blow him occasionally. But no more sex. No way."

"Blowing him isn't sex?" I said.

"Get real!" she said, laughing. "A dick in your face? Anyway, if I could get the four hundred tonight, we're leaving in the morning." And then her phone rang and she left the room. The discussion was over.

I stopped by the cash machine on my way to Riley's, since he had asked me to be there at 7:00. I felt so out of practice for socializing with new people that I changed clothes six times, finally deciding on jeans and a fitted jacket over a black tank top: friendly, with a degree of polite restraint. A little bit pretty, a little bit scary, like Condoleezza Rice.

Riley lived in a small Craftsman-type house in Venice, a few blocks from the ocean. It was full of office waiting room furniture and decorated with driftwood sculpture and tiki heads. It had a nice seventies surfer feel.

There were about forty people there, mostly couples. And a huge steam table along one wall. Everyone brought something: Riley made a corned beef; his friend Kevin, who owned a Greek restaurant, made roast lamb and moussaka; his friend Kegger, who ran a sausage company, brought sausages. There were vegetables and salad, brownies, and a peach pie.

"We meet once a month, and everyone makes what they're into," Riley explained. "We call ourselves the Meat Men. If you come next month, our new shirts and hats will be ready." He laughed, grabbing us each a Dos Equis, then took my hand and began to introduce me to his friends. It was a noisy room, but Riley was very attentive. He had the kind of smile that made everyone smile back.

I was very taken by the amount these people liked him, and one another. Although there was quite a bit of drinking, Riley and company were happy genial drinkers who frequently broke into choruses of jaunty old Irish folk songs where they referred to themselves in the third person. In general, there was more toasting, backslapping, singing, laughing, hugging, and discussion of irradiated meat than at any party I'd ever attended. Soon Riley had his arm around my shoulders, a sexy, muscular arm that set off surprisingly swoony submissive urges in me. I wanted to lie back and let him take over. It all felt really comfortable.

"This is Larry, acting president of the Meat Men," Riley said as I shook hands with a smiling, pear-shaped man, his shiny round face decorated by a fringe of reddish hair and an expensive pair of titanium-rimmed glasses. Both he and his wife, Lorraine, a short, heavyset woman in a tight black T-shirt that said "Grandmas Rock," appeared to be in their late fifties.

"Larry and I have been best buds for twenty years," said Riley.

"Riley's the man," said Larry. "There's no one better."

"Great to meet you both," I said, amused to be encountering a group of people I would otherwise never have met: a little older, a little more conventional, more on the grid than off. They were the kind of people I would see waiting on line at Costco. And they all seemed really nice.

This is turning out to be a lot of fun, I thought as Riley grabbed another beer, then took my hand and led me out to the patio. Is it possible that Chuck actually made a good match for me? I wondered as I stood among the Christmas lights, Japanese lanterns, and tiki torches from Cost Plus that Riley had used to dress up his yard.

"Hey! Do you like horses?" Riley asked, and when I nodded he took me by the hand and led me to the far side of a surprisingly deep grassy area. Behind a stand of pepper trees on the other side of an ivy-covered fence, I could see a couple of friendly-looking horses staring in our direction. One minute we were cooing at them, trying to inspire them to come toward us by pretending to have food, and the next Riley was giving me a deep emotional kiss that was so electrically charged it knocked me off balance. When, a moment later, he began running his hands up my shirt, I didn't resist. I knew we were moving too fast, but I figured that slowing things down wouldn't be a problem. Then, out of nowhere, Lorraine and Larry appeared and, to my great surprise, put their arms around us. Lorraine leaned in to kiss Riley as he was kissing me.

That was it for me.

I stepped backward, holding up my hands like a traffic cop. "Whoa," I said, my only immediate thought being to buy time. "I . . . uh . . . have to go to the ladies' room. Be right back," I stammered, racing toward the house, Riley at my heels.

"You okay?" he was shouting. "Everything cool?"

"Yeah. Emergency. Bathroom. Gotta go," I said. Once inside the bathroom, I locked the door and turned on the water. I flushed the toilet and waited a few minutes, peering into Riley's empty medicine cabinet. After what was hopefully "a while," I opened the door a sliver. Riley was talking and laughing only a few feet away. Luckily his back was to me. I slipped out behind him, walking as rapidly as I could. Now, as I passed through the room, I realized that many strange tableaux were beginning to take place. Over by the CD player, I could see what looked like a flash frame from a fifties stag film: a close-up of someone's pale, hairy flesh, black socks, and wristwatch. There was a quick cut to someone removing his pants, then a pan across the room to the front of the buffet, where two fleshy women, both in their forties and nude from the waist up, were wrapping themselves around Kevin, one of the Meat Men. When I realized that all he was wearing was a barbecue apron and a chef's hat, I was startled enough to go into a skid on a glossy patch of waxed floor, causing me to ice-skate toward the front door.

"Goddamn high heels," I muttered, nearly crashing into a foursome of revelers, then regaining my balance and pushing ahead, not waiting to hear the jokes being made about me.

The minute I hit the cool night air, I took off my shoes and, holding one in each hand, began to sprint barefoot down the block to my car. As I put my key in the ignition, I saw Riley step out into the front yard to look around for me. A right turn at the corner, and I was out of his line of vision. I was never more glad to see the Pacific Coast Highway.

When I got home, Chuck was lying patiently on the floor by the door. Mikayla was out. "So?" said Chuck. "How'd it go?"

I shook my head and hurried into the bedroom, aware that my complaints would sound insane from Chuck's perspective.

"Did you pick this guy out because of his access to meat?" I finally asked him.

"Not only that," he said. "He seemed humpy. He seemed happy. He smelled like liver and blood. Seemed like a win-win situation."

"Oh, he was humpy all right," I said. There didn't seem to be any point in discussing the evening further.

I was just about to turn the lights out when Mikayla returned from a long evening of saying good-bye and closing up shop. In a great mood, she pulled up her shirt to show me her new tattoo. "The more we look forward to anything the less we enjoy it when it comes. — Arthur Schopenhauer" was now on her abdomen between both hips in red three-inch Old English lettering with black highlights.

"You know what? I'm going to miss her," said Chuck after she took the pile of twenties I gave her and went into the next room to pack.

22
MEN WHO
DIG FOR WATER

First thing in the morning, someone finally picked up the phone at Brandy's house. I interrupted the Goddess in the middle of a belly-dancing lesson. "You know, Brandy is going to need another surgical procedure before she can come home," I said.

"That's fine. I'm, we're, not ready for her here yet," Inger said in a flat voice. "We're still having the floors refinished."

"Could you have Kent call Dr. —"

"I'll tell him. I gotta fly," she said, hanging up abruptly.

Immediately my mother called, her voice so infused with manic delight that I had to hold the phone away from my ear.

"We've been picked up by SAV-ON!" she shouted. "We're an industry! Do you know anyone reliable who will work cheap? Hint hint. Halley tells me the Doggy Depot is closing."

A sharp ping in my stomach indicated that

my instincts advised against it. But logically, I figured that for a short time it couldn't be worse than working at TGI Friday's.

I wasn't thinking clearly.

Before I went over to Collin's to walk Margie, I stopped by the hospital to visit Brandy. She was groggy from being on a morphine drip, not too able to communicate anything. Claire, the new head tech, let me sit in Brandy's cage so I could stroke her drooling head. "You got any of that filthy rope on you?" she managed to say before passing out.

Locating Collin's house that first time was a little tricky. He lived in Park La Brea, a strange gated housing development in Hollywood full of identical condo units that looked a bit like a Communist vision of utopia from the fifties. When I stopped to pick up Margie, I found a note tacked to the front door that said, "Key on ledge." Collin was also considerate enough to leave the front door unlocked, for the convenience of any burglars who couldn't read. Apparently, he had great faith in the crime-fighting ability of the overweight woman in the guard booth who waved me in, not even checking for my name on her drive-on list.

I found Margie seated on the couch, staring out the front window. "He really wanted to stay and say hi to you, but he had to go to wherever it is that he goes," she said.

"Yeah, right," I said. "He's just dying to see me."

"He also told me to tell you to give me all of whatever is in that very large dish on the second shelf from the bottom in the refrigerator," she said.

"Funny how he forgot to mention that in his note," I said. I looked around while hooking her to a leash as Chuck ran through the smallish condo, examining everything. The living room was dominated by a cluttered desk on which were many piles of carefully tidied papers. The rest of the room was overwhelmed by waist-high piles of books, creating a literary cityscape against a backdrop of crowded floor-to-ceiling bookshelves that formed the horizon.

"Organized, but not very clean," said Chuck, sniffing everything. "No wonder he continues to get my highest rating."

It turned out that Margie's idea of a walk was to stand in one place and sniff, moving as little as possible. "I can't believe how long she takes on each bush," Chuck whined. "It's like walking with a sack of onions."

By the time we all got back, Collin was sitting on the couch in the front room, a cardboard carrier containing four small cups of Starbucks in his lap. "I hope you appreciate the ordeal this purchase was for me," he said, handing me two of them. "As a language purist, I can't bring myself to say 'grande latte,' knowing that the rest of my sentence is going to be in English. So I sidestep it by buying two small cups because the people of the Starbucks nation still understand 'small.' If you don't like stale scones, please eat one anyway. Otherwise they'll go to Margie, and she is starting to look like a duffel bag."

I followed him into the kitchen, where he pulled out a chair for me in front of a small table. "So! Living with Mikayla! She looks like a kind of a heteromorphic character. How's that going?" He sat down across from me, offering his complete attention. I was so pleased I didn't want to wreck things by asking him what heteromorphic meant.

"Well . . . it's kind of like slum living with brand-new appliances," I said.

"Interesting combo," he said. "If you guys are ever buried under lava, in a few thousand years archaeologists will probably hypothesize a violent overthrow of one civilization by another."

"They wouldn't be far off," I said.

The rest of our conversation was about a paper he was writing that examined the highly developed irrigation systems of the Nabateans in the Jordanian desert around the time Christ was born. "The word *Nabatean* was from the verb *nabata*, which means 'men who dig for water,' " he said. "Stop me if you've heard this one already."

"He was hard to understand in an entirely new way," Chuck said when we got back into my car. I had to agree.

23
CONGRATULATIONS

From the minute I walked into my mother's house, she was going a million miles an hour. "We have so much to do," she said. "I have to train people to assemble the kits. I've got to go pick up the labels. So here's what I need from you." She handed me a list. "Go to Trader Joe's and get me a pound and a half of the fine-ground Colombian coffee. Dark roast. A case of large bottles of Orangina. A big bag of dry-roasted pistachios with salt. The unsalted ones taste like sealing wax. In the freezer section they have spanakopita. Four — no, six — boxes. Bring your cell so I can add stuff."

"You want me to go shopping for you?" I said.

"We're out of food around here!" she said sternly. "I also need you to take the BMW to the car wash and drop this pile of stuff at the dry cleaner."

"So I'm running errands for you?" I said.

"Today, yes," she said. "And stop at Target and pick up a carton of Marlboro Lights for Ng. And call your sister. She says you're not returning her calls. Shame on you!"

"I guess it's no worse than any other temp job," I said to Chuck as we headed to Trader Joe's in my mother's car, "although a temp job wouldn't hammer me about calling Halley."

"Where are you right now?" said my mother, finding me via cell in the beverage aisle at Trader Joe's. "I just remembered that Ng likes their body wash. And get the big vanilla-scented candles when you're at Target. About ten."

"Now where are you?" she said, calling a few minutes later as I waited at the car wash. "I need you to move a little faster. I'd like you back here by two to vacuum the front room and help me straighten up. I have a big meeting of possible investors at seven."

"Mom, I am doing the best I can," I said in a tone of voice that made me feel like I was back in junior high. "She's turning me back into a teenage jackass," I said to Chuck.

"Do what I do," he said, sticking his head out the window. "Pretend you can't hear. Ahh. Smell that backed-up sewer!"

There were two messages waiting on my machine when I got home that evening. One was from Paxton, wanting to go for another walk. The other was from Riley Campbell.

"Call him right away," said Chuck, first thrilled, then furious after he realized the call I was returning was to Paxton. When I said we'd love to go for a walk, Chuck slid under Mikayla's cape on the kitchen floor.

"I've got good news and bad news," said Paxton after a long emotional hug at the door. "What d'ya want first?"

"Bad news first," I said. "Then the good news will cheer me up. Though, seems like bad luck to hear bad news first."

"I got my job back at the radio station," he said, grinning wildly. "*Off the Grid* is back on at a better time! Fridays at ten P.M. Only one shift a week to start, but they're already talking about using me for vacation fill-in!"

He handed me a bouquet of flowers. I recognized them as part of the $5.95 garden assortment from Ralph's, but I was nonetheless moved. They were the only flowers he'd ever given me. "That's wonderful," I said, heading to the kitchen to put them in water.

"The bad news is I think I told you I was supposed to move in with Muppet from the station? But he just informed me he's moving to his fiancée's condo in the Westwood corridor. Can you believe it? Fucking leaving me stranded with a ton of work to do." He bit his lip and looked at the ceiling. "So I was wondering, and stop me if this upsets you in any way, is there a chance I could stay here awhile? Mikayla told me she's leaving. I don't know if you know what you're doing yet. . . ."

"Not really," I said.

"If there's any way you could let me stay here for the launch of the show . . . I just don't want to fuck up. It's a real break, and I'm so anxious to get my life going again." He took both of my hands in his, then looked at the floor. "Believe me, I'd rather sleep in my car than wreck everything between us by putting too much strain on our relationship too soon. So if you think this is going to screw everything up, please just say so and I —"

"No, no," I said, feeling off balance. "You can stay here."

Part of me was thinking there was plenty of room. The rest of me was wondering what I really wanted from him.

"For how long were you thinking?" I asked.

"A couple days, a week at most. After that it's completely up to you," he said. "Totally your call. At least I can help share expenses."

As I stood quietly, he wrapped his arms around me and leaned his head against mine. "I know this is a lot right away. I apologize. But Muppet just completely pulled the rug out. If this is in any way a problem for you . . ."

My brain was watching a kaleidoscoping montage of partial thoughts as I stood hugging him back: "I love you." "I never said I loved you." "Rosicrucian Death."

But when he began to kiss me gently on the neck, then lightly on the lips, my thoughts went to Riley and his Meat Men. I thought of fleshy naked ladies and that guy without his pants. I thought about all the creepy scary people in the world I was glad I didn't know.

"Okay," I said. "Let's give it another try."

My guts were pinging. But as we kissed, I also felt something happy unfolding inside — like time-lapse footage of a daffodil blooming in spring. I would have been even happier had I not been so aware of the sound of Chuck's angry growling.

24
MOTEL 6 TAKES DOGS

Paxton and I spent the night together. Sex with Paxton was always good, but this time there were astonishing new layers of raw emotion. Maybe it was all happening kind of quick, but like Dad always said: The best things in life are quick.

One thing I certainly noticed: how it really felt right. Instincts, I thought. Listen to what they're telling you. By the time I got up the next morning to make coffee, Mikayla was packed and gone. Her posters and piles of stuff remained, along with fresh living room graffiti.

"The man of knowledge must be able not only to love his enemies but also to hate his friends. — Friedrich Nietzsche" was painted on top of the coat of primer she'd used to obliterate Mark Twain. "He who despairs over an event is a coward, but he who holds hope for the human condition is a fool" began in the dining room and ended in the kitchen, where it was attributed across the freezer to Camus.

Another personal note to me was attached by gargoyle-shaped magnets to the refrigerator door: "I don't know when I am coming back," it said in block letters on notebook paper. "Keifer, my mother's boyfriend, will probably contact you. Feel free to give him shit. He deserves it. He's a big fucking asshole and most of the reason I'm leaving. M."

I had just delivered a bedside cup of coffee to Paxton when the oft-mentioned Keifer showed up in person. He turned out to be a short, stocky man in his early fifties wearing a lime-green Lacoste shirt with a matching cotton sweater tied around his neck, tan Dockers, and cordovan moccasins without socks. His sunglasses were pushed up to the top of his tan brow. He had one of those "I'm still a young guy" spikey mussed-up hairdos.

"Holy shit," he said when he saw the inside of the condo. "What did you girls do to this place?" Ignoring me as he walked around, he began shaking his head angrily. Then he encountered Mikayla's note hanging on the fridge. His eyes bulged, and his face got red. From that point on, he regarded me with real contempt.

"It wasn't me," I said. "I just moved in a few days ago."

"I don't know who you are, but you're out of here," he said. "Today. Now. There are no dogs allowed in this building."

"I just gave Mikayla four hundred bucks for rent," I said.

"Take it up with Mikayla," he said. "I don't have your name on any agreement. Clear out." Then he turned his back and stood out on the front porch, making calls.

I'd never felt quite so much like a squashed bug before. "We've just been evicted by Mikayla's stepdad," I said to Paxton, my face flushed as I pulled out my suitcase.

"Keifer Berlini?" said Paxton, sitting up. "From Argonaut? She always tells me he digs my show. Let me handle him." He pulled on his pants and left the room.

"We're homeless!" said Chuck, leaping up and down. "We can finally sleep on the beach and eat garbage!"

Paxton was back in a minute. "Well, he was happy to hear my show's on earlier. Said he'd be sure to catch it." He added, "We've got to be out by noon. The painters are coming."

"That's how you handled him?" I asked.

"Come on! Don't be so negative. He's a

great connection for me," said Paxton. "Uh-oh — it's eleven o'clock. I have to go to the record library before it closes. Will you call me on my cell phone when you know what's happening with all this?" Then he pulled on his sweater, kissed me passionately, and ran out the door.

"Maybe tomorrow," said Mom when I called to inquire about spending the night. "Tonight is another buyers' showcase. Every room is in use. Sav-On has selected the Every Holiday Tree for a featured winter gift item." And then she paused to leave room for my congratulations. "As soon as you get a minute, I need you to rent me a rug shampooer."

"There just isn't any space since Kirk moved in," moaned Halley when I checked with her. "And we're so deep into his abandonment issues, it's critical that I'm there for him one hundred percent."

"The place was just tented for termites," said Maura. "Then I'm redoing the kitchen: I'm moving the whole thing outdoors!"

"Well, I'm all out of people," I said to Paxton on his voice mail. "I don't know what to do." Then I dialed Collin and Handsome's mom to tell them I might be late tomorrow, depending on where I was spending the night.

"You know Motel Six takes dogs," said Dr. Richter when I called to check on Brandy. And that's how we ended up in a place that really should change its name to Motel 55.

25
MOTEL 55

Chuck stood and sniffed the seat of a threadbare turquoise-and-brown upholstered chair as I heaved my suitcase onto a small desk that stood beneath a long black painting of the Arc de Triomphe. "You won't believe what they did in this chair," he said, sniffing the seat again, ending with a loud snort.

"Please don't tell me. I'd rather not know," I said.

This was the first time in my life that I'd stayed in this kind of room alone. I pulled the curtains shut, then worried when they didn't make a perfect seal, imagining twisted drooling lurkers waiting outside the window.

As Chuck and I curled up together on the bed and I leaned against the heavily starched pillows, I envisioned terrible things: drug-addled people kicking in the door, Chuck and I both murdered, our body parts strewn around, my photo on the front page of the

Metropolitan section of the *Times,* accompanied by a story reflecting on a life cut short.

"I'm so glad you're here with me," I said to Chuck.

"We're not really moving in with grid boy?" he asked.

"We might," I said. "I'm thinking of it."

"Instincts say no," he argued.

"The same instincts that gave thumbs-up to Riley?" I sniped.

"Well, maybe I got mixed up," he said defensively. "I knew there was something in it for one of us."

"Same thing with Paxton," I said. "There's something in it for me despite the fact he doesn't make a living with meat."

"But how can it be in your best interests to be with a guy who hates me?" Chuck said. "I've been down this road before. At some point it ends with me in a cage at the pound."

"I would never let that happen to you!" I said, shocked.

"Yep, heard that before, too," Chuck harrumphed.

"But Paxton is learning to love you," I said. "Here." And I handed him a rawhide chew to shut him up.

"Why don't you ever have one of these?"

he asked, gnawing on the twisted leathery stick. It rotated in his mouth like a hard, wet cigarette.

"They're just one of those defining differences between us," I said. "You don't drink vodka. I don't chew rawhide sticks. They don't appeal to me."

"It helps if you think of them as the tiny well-developed calf muscles of a chipmunk," he said, chomping merrily.

I cringed and picked up my phone to make a few calls.

"Motel Six?" said Paxton, picking up on the very last ring. "You poor thing. I wish I were there with you. But listen, Muppet from the station says I can stay in his guest room tonight. I said yes because it's walking distance from the record library. If there wasn't so much riding on this . . ."

"No, no, that's fine," I said. "I just thought I'd check in, tell you where we are." As soon as I said it, I started feeling lonely and sad for myself. "I'm going to look at rentals tomorrow," I said. "What time is good for you?"

"Babe, I'm really crazed," he said. "I trust you. You have good taste. You'll find us something great."

"Well, do you have any idea how much you can kick in?" I asked gingerly. "If I knew, I could maybe get a better place."

"That's kind of up in the air right now," he said. "Rent something you can afford on your own. And depending on what happens with my job, we'll upgrade. I love you."

"I love you, too," I said, shocked to hear him say it. It still made me get teary.

After I hung up, the room seemed dingier, stuffier, smaller, lonelier. I really wanted to talk to someone besides Chuck. My mother and Halley didn't pick up. Claire from the vet hospital didn't, either. Out of options, I took out my novel-writing tips. Tip number nine was "Learn to think like a writer. Writers are different from ordinary mortals." I read out loud to Chuck as he lay in bed beside me, gnawing loudly on his rawhide cigar: "According to this, 'They flit through life with antennae tuned to the moods and marvels of the planet. Like a detective, always asking why and seeking the truth.' This sounds more like you than me. You're much better at flitting than I am."

"I'd flit even more if I didn't think you'd get pissed at me," he said.

By now, my anxiety from sitting alone in this room made it tough to focus. I picked up the remote and scanned the available television. All of it seemed jarring: war, tornadoes, child abductions, explosions of all kinds. What about Karbom for my literary middle name? I thought. Sounds like *car bomb,* yet also strangely ethnic in a way you can't quite place, like Coraghessan or Safran . . . Which was when the phone on the bedside table rang. I jumped. Who knew I was here? Was someone in the motel stalking me?

"Hi. It's Collin," said the voice at the other end. "Richter told me you were looking for somewhere to stay. Motel Six sounds dismal. Do they still have those vibrating coin-operated beds?"

"No," I said. "It's not that bad. Chuck and I are sitting, reading and chewing rawhide, depending on who you ask."

"I thought I'd offer you my couch if you need it," he said.

"That is so sweet of you," I said.

"I know. But it wasn't my idea," he said. "It was Margie's. She thinks you'll bring food."

26
A STUDIO PLUS

I woke up every half hour on the hour all night long. As soon as it was daylight, I started calling all the possible listings in the local paper. I didn't exclude much. I even went to meet three Pepperdine students who were seeking a roommate. "I'm too old for that much good-natured giddiness," I said to Chuck.

"Thank God," he said. "There was nothing in that refrigerator except beer and salad dressing."

At the end of the day, with Collin's couch my only real option, I felt compelled to say yes to the one affordable apartment that I could move into immediately. It was about the size of a hotel suite, on the fifth floor of a big old deteriorating apartment house, corner of Western and Third, across the street from one of those enormous Korean grocery stores full of nearly familiar food in unfamiliar packaging with poorly translated names like "Fried Radish" or "Squid Crackers." The building itself reminded me of an aging, mentally unstable actress too broke to afford plastic surgery. The paint was so faded, the floors so scratched and rutted, the carpet so threadbare, that the interior looked like a yellowing newspaper crime scene photo from the thirties. But the fact that the apartment was ready for immediate occupancy sealed the deal. And small pets were permitted. I hoped that if I put a big coat on Chuck, he might strike the landlord as "small."

"We call it a studio plus," said the building manager, forcing a broad but uncomfortable smile full of yellowish teeth as he showed us around.

"Plus what?" said Chuck.

In addition to the tiny kitchen and a tiny bathroom that were adjacent to a medium-size living room, there was a small bedroom featuring a Murphy bed from the twenties, stored behind two doors that almost closed. "We got a brand-new mattress a couple years ago," said the landlord. I was afraid to look. Or to ask him his definition of "a couple years."

After he left carrying the check I'd written for pretty much everything in my account, I sat on the floor of that empty room and leaned against a wall. The steady roar of traffic outside was so loud, it sounded like a fast-moving river. Mariachi music boomed from radios on two different floors. I tried pretending I was in Baja. The reality that this was where I now lived was so depressing, I was surprised to find myself aching for Swentzle. His extreme relaxation and instant adjustment to every new situation always made me feel like everything had turned out just the way he'd hoped. Swentzle seemed at home everywhere and therefore made every place feel like home.

"You're hung up again on that hairy black-and-white idiot you used to live with," said Chuck. "I can sense it. You miss him."

"He had a way of making me feel safe," I said.

"He was so great at safety, he took off," Chuck said, "and was never seen again."

"I told you I'm not talking to you about this," I said. But I did want to talk. The hollow cold feeling of having just moved made me desperate for conversation.

Everyone was at lunch at the Animal Hospital except Claire, who was busy. Nevertheless she let me into the back room to say hi to Brandy. I was glad the medication still had her knocked out. Nothing like trying to explain to a puppy that she needs to relax and lie still.

"If you hear of any jobs, let me know," I said to Claire on my way out.

"How do you feel about bathing dogs?" she said. "They need someone a few days a week."

"What should I know about bathing dogs?" I asked Chuck as we were driving over to walk Margie, after I said yes to the job.

"Whenever possible, don't and say you did," said Chuck. "Brush the dog, add some perfume, leave him the hell alone."

I was sad to see Margie sitting by herself on the couch, staring out the window, when I got to Collin's condo.

"Where's your leash?" I said, not seeing it in its usual spot. As I looked around, I took advantage of the situation to peek inside the only closed door in the place I'd never opened. It led to a second bedroom, which was mostly unfurnished except for a small couch against one wall, a boom box, an oboe, and a music stand in the center of the room. Of course, there was also a wall of floor-to-ceiling bookshelves full of books and cardboard files. The bottom three shelves were crammed with individually labeled boxes that had "Female Classical Composers" scrawled on them in pen.

"Before 1500," said one. "1600–1750," said another. "Female composers 1930–1960" was the third. Peeking into that one, I saw sheet music, reprints of letters, biographical materials, and photos. There were also copies of taped radio broadcasts and live recordings.

Margie's leash was draped over the music stand. Margie herself sat at my feet, perched on her hind legs, pawing at my calves, making noises that sounded like a garage door hinge that needed oil. Apparently she was ready to go. As I was hooking her up, I noticed that something was in the tape player. Curious about this unseen side of Collin, I couldn't resist pressing PLAY. A very odd piece of strangely haunting piano and oboe music filled the room. It was like something written for an Eastern European funeral in another century.

"Come on," said Margie, "let's get going. I hear this all the time."

I turned it off, hoping that Collin wouldn't notice that the tape had advanced.

27
A Beautiful Shade
of Sea Foam

As I was pulling out of Collin's driveway, my mother called and asked me to work "for a while." Today that meant envelope stuffing.

Sitting alone in one of her cardboard box canyons, deprived of all natural light, I found it impossible not to fixate on the way she repeated herself word for word while making sales calls in the next room.

"Not many people know that I was the first one to use the words *fruity, complex,* and *hearty* to describe coffee," she said to virtually everyone. "Don't forget, back then coffee was either *hot* or *cold.* Period. Until I had a vision. And I think you'll see I'm predicting the future again with the Every Holiday Tree."

"I hate to be a pest," I finally said to her when I couldn't take it anymore, "but I just rented a new apartment and I need some money to cover expenses. Do you have any idea when you might be able to pay me?"

"We're good for it, if that's what you're saying," she said, staring coldly. "No one has gotten paid yet. Keep a record and submit it at the end of the month."

Envelope stuffing made me long for running errands.

By the time I got back to the new apartment, I was feeling so devalued that I started phoning everyone I knew, even friends from childhood, hoping for some kind of meaningful bond. Paxton didn't pick up. Or Halley. The only one who picked up was Collin.

"I made a huge mistake," I said, thrilled to have a sympathetic ear. "I hate this apartment. I don't think I can stay here."

"I've felt like that every time I've moved," he said. A half an hour later he showed up at my door with four small cups of Starbucks.

"I love this place," he said, walking slowly from room to room, examining the details as though it were an ancient ruin. "This building was probably fantastic when it was built in the twenties. That's why it held up so well."

"It hasn't held up so well," I said. "The ceiling's coming down in the bathroom and in the kitchen."

"Yeah, but look at the detailing in the baseboards. Look at the wainscoting," he said. "Look at the built-ins. Look at that light fixture. Okay. Don't look too closely. It's filthy. But a Murphy bed! How cool is that?"

"You're not bullshitting to make me feel better?" I said.

"Let's go buy paint," he said. "You can pay me back later."

As we stood over the paint chip display at Home Depot, scrutinizing color cards, he put on his reading glasses. "Morning Moss. Sea Foam. Ocean Mist," he said. "That must have been a hell of a committee meeting the day they decided they needed new 'fun' ways to say 'gray green.'"

"What color appeals to you?" he asked me.

"I guess something bright, cheery," I said, "to counter my extremely black mood. Maybe yellow?"

"Well, in ancient Egypt, yellow was the color of mourning. In tenth-century France, they used to paint the doors of convicted criminals yellow." He picked out a few paint chips with different shades of red and held them toward the light in order to see the colors more clearly.

"That's kind of what I was going for: a

feeling of grief, combined with the ambience of a prison," I said, examining blues.

"A lot of people find blue healing. Tranquil. In ancient Egypt, blue was used for protection against evil," he said.

"So if you were me, would you paint my room blue?" I asked.

"If I were you, I think I'd paint it red. I've always wanted to live in a red room," he said. "But if I were me, I'd paint it eggshell white. I've painted everything eggshell white for the past twelve years. It's embarrassing how easily I submit to boredom. I figured you for someone more daring."

"I can be talked into red," I said, not liking the idea at all but now wanting to prove that he wasn't wrong about my daring nature.

"In China, red symbolizes good luck," he said as we took a gallon of Chinese-lantern red up to the cash register.

"I'm excited about this," I said.

"Me too," he said, grinning and wiggling his eyebrows. I noticed for the first time that he had beautiful greenish gray eyes with really long lashes.

"I didn't realize your eyes were a lovely shade of Sea Foam," I said.

"I've always thought they were closer to Morning Mist," he said, blushing, but pleased to be getting a compliment. He had one of those faces that somehow blinked in and out of attractive based on something unidentifiable: attractive, not attractive, very attractive, kinda geeky. Like broken neon. Or a quantum particle. Now you see it. Now it's gone.

When he took my arm in his as we walked out of the store, I started worrying he'd misinterpreted my intentions. That was when I got the bright idea for a preemptive strike: Fix him up with Claire.

"Are you seeing anyone?" I asked him as we found the car.

"Not really," he said. "By which I mean not at all. You?"

"Yes, actually I am," I said. "He's about to move in."

"Ah," he said as he loaded our haul into the trunk.

"There's someone I'd love you to meet," I said. "Do you know Claire at the Animal Hospital? The new tech who works the front desk? Light brown hair, bangs, pretty. Just got a divorce. I think you two might like each other."

"I don't know." He shrugged. "I've probably seen her."

When we got back to my place, he took a roller, dipped it in a pan of red paint, and handed it to me. I hesitated, then made a big streak across the living room wall.

"What do you think?" I said, instantly panicky. "Is this a mistake?"

"No reason to admit that yet," he said, beginning to seal off the wood trim with tape. After that, it went pretty fast. We finished painting by 10:00. Two people, two rollers, one smallish but very red room.

"I think it looks great," I said. I meant it. I was dazzled.

The phone rang. "I'm taking a break from my playlist," said Paxton, "so I thought I'd come see the new place."

"Talk about timing!" I said.

"Why? What's going on? You sound weird," he said.

"I'm just in the middle of a surprise," I said, suddenly in a better mood knowing Paxton was on his way over. Though when the call ended, I noticed that Collin's once ebullient expression had deflated like a pan of ruined Jiffy Pop.

So, I took a chance and called the Animal Hospital. As I had hoped, Claire answered. I handed the phone to Collin, forcing an awkward introduction. "She says to tell you that Brandy is ready to go home," he said when the call was over. "Apparently no one can get ahold of the owners."

"I'll see what I can do," I promised, unable to tell if he resented what I'd done.

As Chuck and I walked Collin to his car, I said, "I can't thank you enough for all this."

"Not true. You definitely can," he said. "I find thank-yous grating after about four." He didn't even try to hug me good night as he got behind the wheel. "So tomorrow night you want to paint the kitchen?" he asked.

"That would be wonderful," I said, now wanting a hug, relieved he wasn't angry about the Claire thing.

My first reaction upon reencountering the red room again was to feel cheered, energized, pleased with myself for discovering my daring nature, even if the apartment did kind of look like a crack house at Mardi Gras. Still, I was pleased to have made my mark. This was really my first solo apartment, full of my own personal lack of furnishings. It made me feel like someone specific.

"You weren't kidding. It really is small," said Paxton as soon as he walked in. "Did you ask if they'd pay for paint to repaint it?"

"I did repaint it," I said.

"YOU painted it red?" he said. "When?

Just now? And I don't even get a say in the color?"

"I'm sorry," I said, wondering what I ever liked about the apartment or the idea of a red room. "I guess I didn't think that you would care." I watched as he stood looking, silently. "What do you think we should do?" I said, feeling a Pandora's box full of demons taunting me about being left alone flooding through my bloodstream.

Paxton came over and sat with me on my air mattress in the corner. "The molding is pretty," he said, looking around. "What's the Murphy bed like?"

"I don't know," I said. "I've been afraid to look."

I followed him into the bedroom, and he opened the partly closed doors. "Not too bad," he said, sniffing it carefully, then pulling it down from its nesting place. "It doesn't even stink. I don't think whoever lived here last ever used it. Come here." He sat on it and patted the space beside him, bouncing a little until I joined him. "Want to take it for a trial run?" he said, pushing me back down on the bed, then climbing on top of me, smiling. When he kissed me, I was instantly reminded of how much I liked sex with him. It was like being teleported to a wicked planet where being raunchy and hot were not only required, they were also rewarded.

28
CONGRATULATIONS

Paxton borrowed someone's truck and brought his stuff over the next day. He had quite a few things: a desk and chair, an upholstered chair, six boxes of books, three suitcases, and ten big boxes of CDs. The small apartment began to teeter dangerously toward one of my mother's cardboard canyons.

I had just returned from picking up Brandy at the hospital. "That big dog is staying here?" Paxton said.

"Well, for now," I said. "I can't leave her with that Goddess, and her dad is still out of town." In fact, Richter had called the Goddess repeatedly, and when she never came, he finally called me. I called Kent and left him a message at his suite in Honolulu.

"So it's temporary," Paxton said, relaxing as I settled Brandy into an extra-large dog bed I'd brought from the hospital. It was now the largest thing in the apartment.

"She's on tranquilizers," I said. "I don't think she'll be in your way."

Paxton sat down at his desk, shrugging in weak agreement.

"We have to start looking for another apartment," he sighed, opening his laptop and beginning to work.

By now, I had picked up a few more dog care assignments. I walked Johnny Depp daily and bathed him once a week. And Maura and Collin both recommended me to others.

"How did your beau like our paint job?" Collin asked when I arrived to pick up Margie the next morning. He looked like a kid on his way to Sunday School in a shirt and a pair of corduroy slacks that were both so new they had their original packaging creases. I didn't see our usual Starbucks haul.

"He, uh . . . hard to say," I said.

"That bad, huh?" he said. "Probably takes a little getting used to. I had breakfast this morning with your friend Claire. She's great."

"Wow," I said. "You work fast."

"Not usually. In fact, the opposite. But I had to take Margie in for her shots, and I recognized Claire from your description. So we started talking about you, and . . . I don't want to jinx everything by being too optimistic. But we walked over to that coffee shop around the corner. I think it went pretty well."

"No kidding!" I said. "That's so nice!"

"Here," said Collin, offering the always begging Margie a freeze-dried chicken strip. "Claire just loves Margie."

"Claire's great with animals," I said, surprised by the peevishness creeping upon me. I had liked being Collin's most promising bet.

"We might go to a movie tomorrow night," he said. "I'd have tried for tonight, but I didn't want to seem too eager."

"Good plan," I said, feeling a little jealous. "Paxton moved his furniture in today," I countered.

"Congratulations!" Collin said with a warm, genuine smile.

"Well, come on, Margie . . . you ready for your walk?" I said, calling to her in a high, peppy voice. "Chuck! We're going! . . . Chuck?" I called as I hooked Margie to her leash. "Chuck. Come on, Chuck! We're going!" I said again.

That was when I learned that Chuck was gone.

29
ONE MORE USELESS DOG

No tension-filled moment has ever hit me with more terrifying impact than realizing I didn't know where Chuck was. Being dumped by Paxton, assorted automobile wrecks, even being held up at gunpoint once now all seemed lighthearted by comparison.

"Check the backyard under the bougain-villea," Collin suggested. "He's obviously right around here. . . ." He began to me-thodically inspect the condo. "Chuck?" he called into the bathroom, the space under the sink, under the bed, into the closets. "Chuck, come here, boy," he said into the crawl space under the house and the little attic area that Chuck could never have entered without being reincarnated as a bird. "The front door was open a little, I suppose he could've run out. He's got to be right around here somewhere," he said. "I'll drive. You look."

By the time Collin found his car keys, I

had examined the front, back, and side yards of the houses on both sides of his.

Collin moved a thick wedge of files off the passenger seat of his Honda so I could get in.

Although we didn't know precisely when Chuck had taken off, it didn't seem like he could be far. So we drove up the block, yelling "Chuck!" out the window, then drove back the other way doing the same thing while I examined the side of the street less scrutinized.

"I think we might be better off on foot," I said to Collin, "in case he's hiding. Or chased a cat and got trapped in someone's yard." We started walking in opposite directions.

Chuck would tell me to listen to my instincts, I thought. And they say . . . that he is following *his* instincts. There were only a few places I could think of that he had been frequently enough to make them a destination.

"I'm going to check Maura's," I said to Collin via cell.

"I'll keep looking around here," he said, projecting convincing calm. "Don't worry. We'll find him."

But as I drove toward Maura's, I could

feel the panic rising. "Oh, shit! Brandy!" I remembered, calling Paxton and getting his voice mail. "I am going to be a little late. Chuck escaped somehow, and we're looking for him. If you get this, please take Brandy out for a minute before you go."

He phoned back a short while later.

"I would be there helping if I didn't have the show tonight. You know that, right?" He sounded concerned. "If you still haven't found him by eight o'clock, I'll mention it on the air."

"Thanks," I said, rolling down the window and then yelling, "Chuck!"

"I'm just wondering: Does he chase other dogs?" asked Collin, checking in by cell. "I could try those houses first."

"Yes. And asphalt butterflies," I said. "But that's not what happened. He's pissed that Paxton moved in. He hates Paxton because Paxton thinks dogs should sleep in the hall."

"Margie pissed on my ex's leather coat after being thrown out of bed," said Collin. "It didn't help her case much. I'll be in touch."

By the time I got to Maura's it was 4:30. The group of fans at the base of her driveway was up to five. None of them had seen Chuck. I gave them my cell phone number, wondering if that was very smart. What they all wanted was to see a photo. It was clear my next move had to be to print up a poster — an upsetting thought. A montage of all the "Lost" dog and cat posters on display everywhere flashed by. Did any of those animals get found?

With the relentless advance of darkness came an ever-growing terror from knowing that Chuck would become increasingly invisible to traffic.

A sense of having betrayed him overtook me. I had reneged on the promise I'd made to take care of him and protect him. What if Chuck made a wrong turn and wandered into a place where he was viewed as a marauding predatory pit bull? He might get shot, and no one would give any thought to the entire thing again. Even a very smart dog, all alone, in the wrong place at the wrong time, was just one more useless dog to be put into the pound and eliminated.

What if Chuck stumbled into twisted, sinister, animal-torturing children destined to become serial killers? Or angry medieval people who would force him to fight with other animals for sport? What if he accidentally met up with one of those perverted freaks who have sex with dogs? Or a primitive starving asshole who sees them as dinner? What if coyotes got him? What if he was hit by a car? What if he was lying in a road somewhere, injured, bleeding, and in pain? What if he felt threatened and attacked someone?

By now I was driving up and down every street I saw, yelling his name. My eyes were glued to any stray movement. But it was getting harder to see. For each thing I tried to focus on, there were dozens of things I missed.

By sunset, I still hadn't spotted Chuck, but I had seen Kirk's picture on two bus benches. He was dressed in a blue work shirt and holding up an enormous oversize giant wrench, right above large red letters that said, "Kirk Farren. Fix your buying and selling problems. Now."

At 8:00 I turned on Paxton's show. I wanted to focus all my attention on finding Chuck but knew that if I didn't hear any of Paxton's show, he would be insulted. The cell phone rang.

"I'm going to check the local shelters and emergency rooms," said Collin.

"Thanks," I said, only half listening to Paxton contemplate the renewal of garage rock in a post-9/11 world. I turned it off during a three-record set of the Ramones. If there was a "lost dog" bulletin, I missed it.

I was still just driving around yelling

"Chuck!" at 9:00 when the cell phone rang again. It was Mom.

"You need to get over here," she said, her voice so full of hysteria that I feared she'd had a heart attack.

"We just got an e-mail from one of Ng's relatives in Korea. There's a competitor ripping off the Every Holiday Tree. They're about to sign a contract with Wal-Mart where they plan to undercut our price by ten dollars. I already called Halley and Kirk. I need everyone to rally round. So come right over. And bring cheese and crackers. And mixed nuts."

"Mom, I can't. Chuck is missing. I've got to find him."

"Oh, he'll turn up. Animal Control will grab him," she said.

"Right now I have to go put up some 'Lost Dog' posters," I said.

"And this strikes you as more important than helping your mother through a crisis?" she said. "My business, which employs you, is facing ruin. Step back and get some perspective."

"Mom, you have Ng and Kirk and Halley. You're in good hands," I said. "As soon as I find Chuck, I'll come help."

"Wonderful," she said in a withering tone. "And while you're driving around pointlessly, give a little thought to how incredibly selfish you are." Then she hung up.

Ordinarily, I would have gone into a frenzy of calling back and apologizing. But with Chuck missing, none of that seemed to matter. I was deep into a kind of hysteria, replaying a million conversations I'd had with Chuck these past months alongside a never-ending slide show of pitifully touching moments: the way that he always regarded my change of location with such buoyant enthusiasm, the rapt attention on his face every time he put a tennis ball in my lap. No yogic meditator or Buddhist monk had ever been able to live in the present with more commitment than Chuck. And then there was all that time I'd spent pining for Swentzle. What if Chuck didn't know how much I loved him?

30
UNHINGED

When I got back to the Red Room, I found Brandy tied to the foot of the bed, lying in a puddle of piss.

"Dude," she said, "I'm sorry. I really didn't mean to piss the floor. Guess I'm still pretty toasted." She looked around, put her head down, and fell back to sleep again. I woke her, cleaned her, and led her outside for a bathroom break before giving her another pain pill. Then I got out my photo albums to find a clear shot of Chuck for the poster.

There was one of him peering out of the bathtub that broke my heart. Well, they all did. But I chose the one where he was sitting in the driver's seat of my car. When I wrote "Lost Dog" across the top of a large piece of paper, I felt like I was going to be sick. Now it was too real.

"Missed terribly. Needs medicine. Reward," I wrote, hoping the lie about the medicine would make someone try harder.

I was heading out the door to find an all-night copier when Paxton arrived. "Catch the show?" was what he said.

"Yeah, great," I said.

"Does that mean you thought it wasn't very good?" he said.

"No, it was terrific," I said. "I'm just crazy with worry about Chuck."

"Look, he'll be fine. I promise." Paxton came over and put his arms around me. "So what part of the show did you like best?" He went into the kitchen and grabbed a can of beer.

"Everything," I said. "It was all totally great. Do you know where there is an all-night copy place?"

"Kinko's on Vine," he said. "Did you really hear the show?"

"Sure I did," I said. "But I'm not thinking straight. Will you come help me tack up these posters?"

"Tomorrow, yes. Right now I'm beat up," he said. "I guarantee you nothing will happen between now and morning."

"How can you say that?" I asked. "A dog running around loose in traffic at night? What's gonna keep him from getting hit by a car? No calls about the 'lost dog' announcement, huh?"

"Sorry. I didn't get to it. We had to run a ton of public service announcements. And I had to do a lot of office politicking. First day back, don't forget."

"Well, I'm going to Kinko's," I said. "Can I get you to drive me over?"

"Babe," he said, "I wore myself out today. I can't move. I will definitely help you tomorrow. I promise."

"If you drop a bunch of posters by, I'll go out tonight and paper my neighborhood with them," said Collin, who picked up his phone on the first ring. So at 1:00 A.M. I printed about two hundred copies of a poster so upsetting to me I almost couldn't look at it. Then I drove over to Collin's house to get him. While he was finding his jacket, I chatted with Margie.

"Where would you go if you got loose?" I asked her.

"Right to the first person who offered me snacks," she said, "and I would love them deeply as long as they kept it up."

Collin and I stayed out most of the night sticking posters everywhere — on telephone poles, on the fronts of stores, on concrete road dividers where people get stuck waiting to make left turns, on Dumpsters and garbage cans, under windshield wipers. Neither of us talked, but I was grateful for his presence. I had started feeling frighteningly unhinged. A piece of paper flying past made me jump. A car pulling up to a corner too slowly looked suspicious. Every time a homeless man walked by yelling, I imagined he had sold Chuck to a testing lab for a dollar.

By the time Collin and I knocked off at 4:00 in the morning, parts of Hollywood had so many pictures of Chuck, you might think he was playing a concert at the Wiltern.

31
A Very Good Omen

When the phone rang at 8:00 A.M., I raced around the apartment searching for it, finally finding it hidden under Paxton's black jeans.

"Hello?" I said, hopeful and frightened at the same time.

"Thank God you picked up," said my mother. "Have you heard what's going on? Has Halley updated you?"

"No," I said, noting the rising hysteria in her voice.

"Where did I leave off with you?" she asked. "I told you about the Koreans who signed with Wal-Mart to do a cheapy tree, right? Well, turns out the company is owned by Ng's brother-in-law. Can you believe that? We're in complete crisis mode. Ng is with the lawyer figuring out a plan."

"Geez, Mom, that's bizarre," I said. "Ng didn't know anything about this?"

"Only that he told his brother-in-law

about our idea, the way you do family. We don't know what to do now, except wait for the lawyer to file something. And it's international, so it's way complicated. You don't sound very interested."

"I was up all night putting up posters," I said.

"Oh. I see. Your family going bankrupt doesn't concern you?"

"Chuck is my family, too," I said.

"That's out of line," she said. "How dare you compare the two? Chuck is a dog."

"Gee, Mom. Remember when animal rights were so important you couldn't attend my eighth-grade graduation?" I said quietly.

"Eighth-grade graduation isn't a real graduation. It's a way for schools to kill time till summer vacation," she said.

"I'm sorry, Mom, but I have to get off the phone now. I have to leave the line open," I said.

"Well, I'll remember that the next time you need me to do something for you," she sniped.

While we talked, the only person who called was Collin. He'd left a message saying he was stopping at a copy shop to make more posters on his way to work. When I heard he was already up and about, I got dressed and headed out, too. It didn't seem fair to wake Paxton, so I put the groggy Brandy in my car, figuring she'd sleep while I did what I needed to do.

"Where we going?" she said, trying to muster a little enthusiasm as I moved her to the backseat.

"We're going looking for Chuck," I said.

"Awesome," she said. Then her eyes closed and she was out.

I had a list of every pound and vet's office in the area. My plan was to make sure Chuck's picture was everywhere you looked. Whenever my cell phone rang, my heart began to pound. This time it was Halley.

"Mom just told me about Chuck," she said. "Can you hold?"

"Halley, no, I can't hold right now . . . I need the —"

"Sorry about that," she said, disappearing and then returning. "Everyone's got emergencies today. Maura thinks her series is canceled, and you know how crazed she gets when things are fine!! So tell me what happened."

"I was at a client's house, walking his d—"

"Just a second. I have to take this," she said again. I hung up and made it to the Agoura pound before she called back.

"I am so sorry," she said. "That was Mrs. BTK. She is all, 'How do I cope with the guilt?' So I told her, for the tenth time, 'Look, holding on to this stuff won't bring those people back. You've got to let it go.' But I mean, you know . . . Yikes! Right? So I told her to write a list of all the awful things her husband did, then burn the paper over a white candle and release the negative energy. Maybe cleanse the room with a sage wand. That's all I could come up with so far. What's happening with the dog?"

"Halley, I can't talk right now. I'm at an animal shelter. . . . If you could just handle Mom, that is the best thing you could do for me," I said.

"You heard about Ng and — one second, can you hold?" she said.

And I hung up on my sister for the second time in one day.

For the next few hours, Collin and I checked in with each other periodically. I got home to the Red Room around 2:00.

When I walked into the apartment, Paxton was going a million miles an hour. The station really liked his show and had offered him vacation fill-in. He was working every night this week. "Do you understand what a break this is?" he said. "Vacation fill-in is halfway to staff."

"That's fantastic," I said.

"You don't seem very excited," he said.

"I am excited, but I'm crazy with worry about Chuck," I said.

"I will definitely read the announcement about him on the show tonight," he said. "I'm sorry I screwed up yesterday. I'll put your poster up at the station." He gave me a very sweet hug. "Don't worry," he said. "This job is a very good omen. I wish I could help you look, but everyone at the station made me promise I'd nail the influence of seventies pub rock on present-day punk. I have to get to the record library. . . . I hope you don't mind."

"No, it's fine. Congratulations," I said as he packed his briefcase.

"The important thing is we have each other," he said, giving me a kiss on the cheek as he ran out the door. "Maybe you can't see it now, but things are definitely looking up."

After he left, I lay down on the bed. It had been thirty-six hours since I'd slept. I guess I dozed off for a moment. But when the phone rang, I woke up fast. There was a message from Dr. Richter, a number for me to call.

"Hello," said a sweet female voice. So far so good. Sweet. Female. "I think I hit your dog," she said next. Her voice began to tremble. "I was driving north on Wilshire, and he ran in front of my car. I couldn't see him." Now she began to cry. "Coming home, I saw your poster. And I'm so sorry. I'm so sorry. . . . I rushed him to my vet."

"Where is he?" I said.

"The Mid-Wilshire Animal Hospital," she said. "I'll pay for everything."

32
No

"You're the owner of the pit bull?" the vet tech who answered the phone at the Mid-Wilshire Animal Hospital asked me when I phoned a few seconds later.

"Yes, I think so," I said. "Where is he? Can I see him?"

"You're welcome to come whenever it's convenient. I think you should know he didn't survive the surgery," she said.

It was like I didn't hear it right. It was like I wanted to look around to see who she was talking to. And then somebody inside me screamed out, "Noooo!"

33
THE EVOLUTION OF "LA BAMBA"

I had never cried that hard before. It was so forceful and exaggerated, it felt fake. When Swentzle died, I had cried and cried, and the crying lasted for days. But at least, at the bottom of it, I knew Swentzle had been old. This was the most gut-wrenching physical agony and hopelessness, a feeling that I had no reason to live anymore. "Nooo!" someone who sounded like me kept wailing.

"Do you know what you'd like us to do with the body?" the tech asked. "We have a cremation service that we —"

"Can I call you back?" I said, hanging up because I couldn't stop the spasms of sobbing and shaking. A strange detached part of me watching from somewhere else was thinking, *This is the saddest I've ever been.*

"I'll be there in the next twenty-four hours," I said when I called back an hour later. By pretending to sound definitive, I hoped I could still make a difference.

The next thing I did was call Collin; I was relieved that he wasn't there. I didn't want to hear myself explain to him what had happened. Still, I needed to be with someone who at least pretended to care. No one else came to mind.

It isn't my nature to show up unannounced on someone's doorstep, but I just walked up to Collin's front door and knocked. My eyes were red and runny, my cheeks were gray and black from mascara, my hair was matted and straggly. I hadn't showered in two days, just kept pulling on a sweatshirt on top of the sweat-stained and stinky clothes I'd worn the night before.

When Collin came to the door, I fell forward and collapsed on him. Only after I'd soiled his clothes did I realize he was dressed up. He had on a sport coat and slacks with a crease down the front. Sitting in the room behind him was Claire from Dr. Richter's office. They were having dinner.

"Oh my God. I'm so sorry," I said. "I never just show up like this."

"Something happened to Chuck?" he asked quietly. When I nodded, he put his arms around me and stood there, unmoving, while I heaved and sobbed.

"Oh, honey, I'm sorry," said Claire, hugging me from behind. "I'll leave you two alone. I was about to go home anyway."

"Let me walk you out," Collin said, getting his jacket, then putting his arm around my shoulders. We both walked Claire to her car. Once she was gone, we got into his car and he drove me to the Mid-Wilshire Animal Hospital in silence. I couldn't think of anything worth saying, except for the involuntary gasp at the first four-way light when I looked to my right and saw a bench full of Kirk.

"That's my future brother-in-law," I said.

"That rap star sitting on a tank?" Collin asked.

"No, the real estate goon holding the screwdriver," I said.

"I don't know which of them is scarier," said Collin.

I thought of turning on the radio to hear a bit of Paxton's show. But I was in no mood to track the influence of "La Bamba."

It's weird how the total indifference of strangers doing their jobs can feel cruel and terrifying when your brain is in emotional chaos. "Hi, I spoke to someone on the phone," I snuffled to a distracted woman at the reception desk. "I'm here to see my dog. He was hit by a car?"

"The pit bull? Right. You want to come with me?" she said. Collin put his arm around me again as we followed her to a back room, where a dog lay on a gurney, swathed in towels. I started to cry the moment I saw how mangled his legs were.

"I can't look," I said as Collin walked over to him.

"Come here," he said.

"I can't," I said, turning away.

"You gotta come here," he said, pulling me over.

I forced myself to look down. I decided right then that no matter what his condition, I would still kiss him good-bye on the bridge of his furry nose. And it's a good thing I did decide to look down. Because the dog wasn't Chuck.

34
A RANCH IN
VERMONT

Collin and I stared at each other. "I don't believe it," I said.

"Me either," he said.

The drive home from the hospital seemed unreal. The good news and the bad news were both that I still didn't know what had happened to Chuck. This allowed all the vivid grotesque imagery I'd been accumulating to fuel my imagination. And now I felt bad for a whole other reason. Whose good boy was that back there at the hospital? Would they ever find out what happened to him? Should they?

"I can't stand to think of animals being hurt," I said as we drove down Wilshire Boulevard. "I stop watching a movie if they introduce an animal too early in the plot. It almost always means they're going to kill it. Like the rabbit in *Fatal Attraction* or the little dog in *There's Something About Mary.* Why couldn't it have been Ben Stiller falling out that window?"

"I couldn't agree more," said Collin. "I always hated those classic kid movies like *Old Yeller* and *The Yearling* where the beloved pet dies. What would be so wrong with having those damn kids learn their lessons about mortality from watching Grandpa kick? Then at least they'd have the dog around to comfort them."

"Exactly," I said. "If they'd only had the mother committed to a mental hospital in *The Yearling,* the deer could have moved into the house. Then the kid and the deer would've lived happily ever after."

"What do you say we stop and get a bottle of champagne. To celebrate something that almost never happens: unfulfilled tragedy," Collin said.

"Are you sure that's not fiddling while Rome burns?" I worried.

"Well," said Collin, "it's that or stand here, sweating, worrying about smoke inhalation, wondering if some fiddle music might at least lighten things up." So we pulled into the local Ralph's market. While Collin was inside, I reluctantly checked my messages. No new info on Chuck, but of course, a panic-stricken call from my mom, at Halley's.

"Hello, you poor thing, are you remembering to keep a sacred space around you filled
with white light?" said my Life Coach when
I finally returned her call. I pushed back
into the seat, anticipating a drama. "Did
Mom tell you the latest development? About
Ng flying to Korea to confront his brother-
in-law? With papers Mom's lawyer gave him
to have the family sign? So Ng takes off . . .
Just a second. I'm so sorry, but I have to
take this. Maura's started drinking."

"Halley, I'm in a car and . . ." I was saying
as she disappeared.

"I'm trying to get her to do some holotro-
pic breathing," she said when she emerged
from the black hole of cell phone purgatory.
"I'm going to have to go over there in a
minute. Anyway, Ng catches a flight to
Korea, and then Mom's lawyer calls to say
Ng and his brother-in-law are now in ca-
hoots. The brother-in-law offered Ng a bigger piece of the profits. Never mind that Ng
still owns half of Mom's company. Now he
won't take her calls. The lawyer is looking
into her legal options. Meanwhile, Ng's
knockoff is hitting the stores a week before
Mom's. She's berserk. Can you hold?"

"No, I can't," I said, hanging up as Collin
came back to the car. "My family is so . . ."
I said to him as the phone rang again. "I'm

not picking up," I said as it kept ringing.

"I guess I better take this," I said, picking it up.

"I am so sorry I have to keep taking calls," said Halley. "That's the one bad thing about being a Life Coach. Life is so about phones. Anyway, Mom's beside herself. She's here, in my bed. You should really come over."

"Halley, I can't right now," I said as we pulled out of the parking lot and headed back to Collin's. "It sounds like you and Kirk have it covered. What would I add?"

"You know Mom. She starts going on about having the whole family rallying around," said Halley. "Look, I know your dog is missing, honey. But every other obligation in life does not come to a halt because of a missing dog. There are only about fifty billion perfectly lovely dogs who still need a home. Tomorrow you and I and Kirk will go down to the shelter and pick out another fantastic dog whose life you will save. He'll be thrilled, you'll fall in love like you did with Swentzle, and that will be that."

"It's not that simple for me," I said.

"Well, as your Life Coach I want to encourage you to make it that simple. Because it is. You can grieve and begin to love a new dog at the same time. And life goes on. If I give you twenty-four hours, will you come here tomorrow?"

"I know you must be exhausted from handling Mom alone," I said, relieved to have bought some time.

"Thank you for acknowledging," she said, sounding tired. "I couldn't do it without Kirk's love and support. I know this is my chosen profession, but when you add in Mom and Maura, and Mrs. BTK, well, holy shit, you know? Who, by the way, is a Blue, which means she thinks there is a 'right' way to live. I tried having her chant 'I am not my husband,' but her sense of 'I' is so weak that I'm now thinking a cleansing fast might be a more powerful metaphor."

"Well, I'll try to come by tomorrow," I said.

"I don't accept 'try' from my clients," she said.

"Sorry," I said to Collin as I hung up. "I hate when people make calls in front of me. I must seem like a catastrophe to you. My family is out of control, I'm out of control . . ."

"Not really," said Collin. "I never met my father, and my mother is in a mental institution. Luckily for me they don't let her use the phone much."

"Does anybody have a family that functions like a family?" I mumbled, surprised by what I hadn't known about Collin.

"I think so," he said, parking in his driveway. "But my theory is that the 'good family people' hang out with other 'good family people.' Those of us born into the nutcase class seek representatives of our caste to make us feel normal."

For the next hour we sat in his living room, sipping champagne and eating the rest of the stuffed mushrooms he had made for Claire. Brandy woke only when I brought her in from the car. "We're visiting your friend Margie," I said.

"Dude!" she said. And fell back to sleep.

"Guess I'll phone shelters again tomorrow," I said after a while.

"We could also try running an ad in the local paper," Collin said.

"I keep thinking about that poor mangled dog we saw at the hospital," I said. "I hope his owners never find out what happened. That way they can make up a nice lie to believe, like 'A family found him and took him to their ranch in Montana.' "

"Try not to make up any more frightening scenarios," he said.

"You sound like my sister," I said.

"I'm sorry this is happening," he said, shaking his head.

"I should go home now," I said, not really wanting to go.

"Why don't you leave Brandy here for the night?" he asked. "She looks comfortable. Seems a shame to wake her."

He walked me to my car. "We'll find Chuck," he said.

"Thank you so much," I said, sitting behind the wheel, "for everything."

35
THE PRODIGAL SON

It was weird coming home to the Red Room with no dogs in tow and none waiting. Paxton had just gotten home and was lying on the floor, drinking a Guinness and listening to a CD of his show.

"Boy, you look like shit. Rough night, huh?" was the first thing he said as I walked in the door. "D'ja hear any of the show? Come listen" was the second. Grinning, he patted the floor next to him. "I think it went pretty well. Or so the folks around the station were all saying."

"That's wonderful," I said, a deep hole of black quicksand beginning to swallow me. "I apologize for missing the show again. I had an emergency."

"Yeah?" he said, getting up to adjust the speakers.

"Brandy is spending the night at Collin's. He was helping me look for Chuck." That got his attention.

"So the first time I have a real job, you run out the door with another guy?" he snapped. "You sure hate for me to be the center of attention."

"No," I said, too tired to give it much energy. "Someone called to say Chuck was at the Mid-Wilshire Animal Hosp—"

"So that jack-off goes with you to hold your hand? Unless he's gay, he just wants to fuck you. No straight guy acts like that without a motive."

"Come on. He's seeing Richter's tech Claire. I interrupted them in the middle of a romantic dinner," I said.

"Okay," he said, considering this. "I don't mean to be an asshole. But a guy wants to show off for his girl. It's in the DNA. So while we're waiting for your prodigal son to return, can we at least enjoy a few moments of serenity in our clean, dog-free apartment? Even you must have noticed how peaceful it is around here."

He sat back on the bed and turned on the CD player with the remote. "Come. Sit down. Please? Let me play you my show." And when he said it, he looked like a kid who was desperate for praise and attention. It made my heart melt, so I sat next to him. He took my hand and held it while he played me a segment in which he traced the influence of "La Bamba."

"Amazing!" I said, more taken by the way he was beaming than by the show itself. Then the phone rang.

"It's me," said Collin. "You gotta come over right now."

"What happened? Why?" I said, panicky.

"Chuck's on my front porch," he said.

36
Q AND A

Of course we raced right over. This time, Paxton insisted on coming along.

I ran into Collin's house, and there was Chuck lying on the rug, tongue hanging out the side of his mouth. He wagged his tail lazily, as in "Hey. How ya doin'?"

I burst into tears. "Stupid fucking dog, lying there wagging your tail like nothing happened," I said as Chuck offered me the same level of enthusiastic greeting I generally expect when I come home from the store. "Where were you?" I yelled at him as I hugged him. "Talk to me."

"Not while he's here," he said very softly with no inflection, ignoring Paxton, who was behind him in a squat calling to him, trying to say hello.

"Collin, this is Paxton," I said, standing up after Paxton did.

"Nice to meet you," said Collin. "What can I get you both? Coffee? A cocktail?

Apple juice? Ovaltine?"

"No, we're fine," said Paxton. "We really should go. It's late. I'm working tomorrow. But thank you so much for all your help."

"Maybe you want to leave Brandy here tonight?" said Collin. "Give you time to check out Chuck and make sure he's okay. I'm working at home for a few days. It's no problem." And he said it in such a kind way that all I could think of was, I hope Claire loves him. And why don't I? What is wrong with me?

"Great idea," said Paxton. "Thanks."

We got in the car and drove home in silence. I was exhausted, but so euphoric to be back with my boy Chuck that I didn't want to ruin the mood by speaking.

Once we got home, I promised I would listen to the rest of the genesis of "La Bamba" right after I took Chuck out for a walk. As soon as we got outside, he and I sat in my car. This is what I found out.

Chuck's Moderate-Size Adventure

Q. Where the fuck were you?

A. Well, once your little friend moved in, I knew I had to leave. So while you got Margie ready for a walk, I ran down the block. I figured I'd get laid or have a snack, then come back later. After I'd scared the shit out of you.

Q. Oh. That was lovely.

A. I figured I'd be safe as long as I followed my instincts. But the problem with instincts is they only really work in the absence of opportunity. At the end of the next street was this whippet. I don't usually go for them. Too snitty. But this one was way into me. And she was hot. Literally. She was in heat. We were going at it, when the mother or whoever shows up and starts chasing me, down the block, around the corner, down that block. I finally lost her by going under a fence. Then I was stuck in someone's yard. So I'm digging a hole when some old lady runs out, opens her gate, then runs back in the house, screaming, "Go! Just go! Get out of here!" So, I took her advice and kept on running. Only stopped once by a bunch of gardeners to grab a bag lunch. Sandwich. Chips. Cookies. Nice. At that point I wasn't sure where I was exactly. The buildings were closer together. So I thought, Wherever I am, I don't get here much. Let's have a look around. Talk about instincts! Led me right to a pyramid of fish in a parking lot. But it was crawling with too many hissing cats. I reversed course and started back the other way. And now there's nothing familiar around. I go in an open door behind a parking lot full of motorcycles, and I walk into a place where there's loud music. And naked women. That was fun. One of them gave me a salami sandwich. Well, actually, I took it off her plate after she passed out in the back room. Ended up I took a nap with her, and she liked me so much she invited me back to her place. This time I slept in bed. Not with her, but with the one who smelled like birthday cake. Talk about a great cologne. Oh. And by the way, they tried to call you. A couple times. They took the number off my tag. They kept reading the other side out loud. They liked the part where it says, "If I'm alone, I'm lost." No one answered the phone.

Q. Oh, Jesus. I didn't get you a new tag since we moved! I am such an idiot.

A. Good. Hold that thought. I like you sharing the blame. Anyway, the upshot was that they put me back on the street. In pretty much the same spot where they found me. The cake lady said, "Go home." I thought, Good idea. Because at that point I figured you'd be so glad to see me. This would guarantee me the leverage I was after. I checked in with my instincts. Everything seemed to be working. Soon the streets started to look familiar. And then it hit me: I had gone home all right. But I had accidentally gone home to the people who put me in the pound.

Q. Holy shit. That's really weird.

A. For a moment, I was kind of glad to see them. The place looked the same. It hasn't been that long. I could smell that the kids were home. So I walked into the house through the garage. I was headed for Ryan's room when I heard someone yelling. And it was HER. And when she screamed, HE ran in. He looked awful. He was even fatter than before. "It can't be," he said. "I took him to the pound. I got a goddamn receipt. You want to see the receipt?" "I don't care about the receipt," she said, "just hurry and get rid of the damn thing before the kids go nuts again. They think he lives on a farm in Vermont." So fat boy starts acting all sweet. "Come here, Tiger. You want a cookie?" Like I am so stupid that I would fall for that a second time.

Q. This is a very upsetting story. Was that your name? Tiger?

A. I don't want to talk about that. Anyway, now she starts in, too. They each have a cookie, so I figure, fuck it . . . a cookie's a cookie. I grab one out of his hand and am about to grab hers, too, when he catches me by the collar. I growl at him. He screams, "Don't you growl at me!" Then he hits me on the snout with a rolled-up magazine. So I growl at him again. And he hits me again. She's screaming, "Get rid of him right now. And this time I mean it. Get him out of here!" And he goes, "Okay, okay," and he drags me outside and throws me into the car and says, "You shut the fuck up." He's backing the car down the driveway just as the kids run out of the house. So I get up to the window, I gotta at least say hello. And he turns around and swats at me with a rolled-up magazine and screams, "Get down, goddamn it!" And then he drives away really fast.

Q. I hate this story. He took you back to the pound where I got you?

A. But this time when he goes to pull me out of the backseat, I run to the other side of the car. And he comes around to the other door but doesn't close the first door, so I jump out. And run like hell across the parking lot. I'm making good time. I'm almost to the road. And blam! I feel a huge dead weight. And he tackles me. Falls right on top of me. Like a sack of wet leaves.

Q. How terrifying.

A. So I bit him. Hard enough to taste his meat. And by the way, I do not recommend him if he's on a menu. He's tough and fatty. So he's yowling on the ground . . . and while he's recovering I take off and don't stop.

Q. I am so glad.

A. Now I know where I am. My instincts are working again. I remember this from the first ride I ever took with you.

Q. You were just a puppy. How can you remember that?

A. Okay, I also stopped to ask a couple of homeless guys for directions.

Q. You talked to them?

A. I do it every now and again. Only when it's someone no one ever believes. These guys were dead drunk. Or maybe on crack. They pointed me toward Wilshire and Fairfax. I could smell Margie. And that whippet. I figured I'd stop for a quickie, but she started to follow me. I had to do the crinkly nose toothy snarl to get her to go home. I hate to do that right after sex. It ruins the afterglow.

Q. We may be getting into that area known as "too much information."

A. Anyway, when I first got to Margie's I could hear you inside going on about me. I sat out front and enjoyed it.

Q. You were there and didn't come in?

A. Yeah. I saw you leave.

Q. And you let me leave knowing I was in

agony?

A. Well, I figured the longer I stayed away, the more leverage I had.

Q. You little fuckhead.

A. Also, it looked like you and Collin were bonding.

Q. What is this, *The Parent Trap*?

A. I don't get that joke. So let's run a test: Can we throw Paxton out?

Q. You seem to forget that you and Paxton are finally getting along.

A. It's superficial. He hates me.

Q. Ever since we got back together, he has been really nice to you. How dare you manipulate me like that? I am the alpha. I decide what is good for us. Not you.

A. My instincts say that every decision you make is wrong. Everyone takes advantage of you.

Q. Your instincts are wrong at least half of the time.

A. No. The instincts themselves aren't wrong. It's the world that is flaky. All animals know certain things. How do you think we got out before the tsunami hit Sri Lanka?

Q. This is the final proof that I am just talking to myself. How could you know about the tsunami?

A. Well, besides my millions of years of

collective memories? I heard it from a crow, who said the sparrows everywhere were going on about it. Not that I trust sparrows. But in this case they heard it from a tern who split from Thailand.

Q. At least none of them are giving out personal advice.

A. Because they're very self-absorbed. Here are my final words on the topic. Watch when Paxton sees I'm back. Just watch.

Q. Well, you'll have to try to cope and work something out.

A. If I'm around that long.

Q. Are you threatening me?

A. No. I'm just saying . . . It's him or me. Want to play ball?

37
THE RESURRECTION
OF MELKART

Of course he was right. Paxton seemed annoyed at having Chuck back. It was visible in little sidelong glances. The obvious tension was not improved by the fact that because of Chuck's threat, I refused to let him off the leash.

"You're on the leash until I see that you and Paxton are buddies," I said, to which he made a loud snort and collapsed onto his side.

The next day, rent was due. I had barely enough. It seemed logical to approach Paxton about contributing. He was all wrapped up in creating a playlist designed to show the history of the second batch of guys in Mott the Hoople. Knowing it was dangerous to interrupt him, I first went to the store and bought chocolate-filled croissants.

"These are great," he said, his lower lip glistening from chocolate. "Why are you staring at me? What's up?"

"Rent is due," I said sweetly.

"Can you cover me right now?" he said. "I know this is going to become a paying gig. My instincts say very soon. . . . Why is that funny? So now you're going to ride my ass about money? You want me out there looking for busted screens to fix and leaky pipes to replace while the station gives my show to someone else? I was there one week and they promoted me to vacation fill-in. Isn't that fast enough for you?"

"Paxton, I didn't mean to make you feel pushed," I said, "but, you know, I wash dogs two days a week —"

"But that's what you do," he said. "You're different from me. I'm living off the grid. I need time and your support."

"I am supportive," I said. "I'm just worried about money."

"Fine. You win," he said. "You're forcing me to tell you the real reason I haven't got any money. Halley and I have been organizing a birthday surprise for you tomorrow night. You happy now? You can't even let the people who love you do something nice for you?"

I hadn't been thinking about my birthday. Maybe because getting Chuck back had been an answered prayer. But also because of nerves. Turning thirty-seven felt like the end of the cute portion of my thirties.

The next night, the party proceeded as scheduled, even though it was no longer a surprise. The guest list was small — mainly family, but I added Collin and Claire. Halley and Kirk had decorated the Winnebago to look like the world's smallest Mardi Gras. There were balloons and masks and candles and lights. There was a Cajun music playlist picked out by Paxton and a long table in the garden inside the former foundation of the house. Outlined with lights, the ruins looked spooky and beautiful.

Dad was the first to arrive, and surprisingly, he came alone. "Two of 'em found out about each other," he said by way of explanation. "The shit put the fan out of commission. All that's left is Sara Ramos because she's already married. Though I did meet a very cute girl yesterday when the Cheaterslicks played a swap meet in Thousand Oaks. You know, the girlies still come flirting after the show," he said, raising an eyebrow. "Of course, we've expanded the definition of 'girlies' to anyone under sixty. Gotta make hay while I still got the hormones for it. You know as well as I do, before long I'll be trapped in another bad marriage." He handed me a big box of cellophane-wrapped vanilla-scented pine-tree-shaped car air fresheners, then nodded his head toward the driveway. "Looks like your accountant is here."

"He's not an accountant. He's a curator of ancient art. Dad, this is Collin," I said as he and Margie strolled up to us.

"Claire had to work. She sends her best wishes," Collin said to me as he held his hand out to my dad.

"My pleasure," said Dad, grabbing Collin's thin white fingers with his big tan veiny prime rib of a hand.

"Great bowling shirt!" Collin said with unexpected excitement. "Just a guess . . . '57?"

"The man knows his ancient art," my dad said, winking at me.

"Happy birthday, Dawn," Collin said, handing me a large heavy box. "The present was Margie's idea."

"A box of stew?" I said.

"Mr. Artsy-Fartsy's in the house," whispered Dad as Paxton drove up the driveway. "You two back together?"

"Dad, I told you I live with him now," I said.

"Well, you know the Tarnauer definition of living," he winked again. "The best things in life are quick."

"Paxton, you know my dad," I said as they

shook hands.

The thing I never anticipated was that Paxton the music archivist had less to say to my dad than did Collin, who surprised me by connecting the relationship of chariot racing to hot rods. That, of course, didn't stop my father from launching into a monologue on the trouble with women that segued seamlessly into his thoughts on the war in Iraq. That was my cue to go in and help with dinner.

Inside the Winnebago, Halley was cutting ciabatta bread into tiny chunks for dipping into some kind of olive tapenade Kirk had made. Seated at the table, Mom was in her glory playing the grande dame grand drama card. With no word from Ng or the lawyer, she had gone from mogul to mental in twenty-four hours.

"Nothing will make me feel better than to see that little Korean dog eater strung up by his balls," my mother said as Chuck slinked under the table.

"Did Halley already ask you what steps you're willing to take to make that happen?" I said as Halley glared at me.

"The Every Holiday Tree was the best idea I ever had," she said as everyone sat down to eat. "How dare he do this to me?"

"Mom, don't be a rapport ruiner," said Halley.

"I'll ruin more than rapport for that weasel," she said.

"If you don't mind my asking, what is the competition selling, exactly?" Collin asked her.

"Same damn thing," said my mom. "The tree plus the big nine. Easter, Thanksgiving, etc., etc. Presidents' Day."

"What if you tried different holidays from other cultures?" Collin suggested. "Bastille Day. Cinco de Mayo. Or other periods of history? The Phoenicians celebrated the Resurrection of Melkart."

"Oh, that'll be a moneymaker," said Paxton.

"You'd have no competitors. Guaranteed," said Dad.

"He's got the right idea," I said. "You could open it up to other reasons for celebrating. Like the start of football season. The World Series. The Super Bowl. The Academy Awards. Tax refunds."

"Hmmm!" said my mother, some life returning to her face.

"Coq au vin, everybody!" said Halley, tapping on a glass to draw everyone's attention to Kirk's platter of food.

"Beautiful!" said my dad. "You know how

much I love cocoa." My mother rolled her eyes. "Oh, come on, Joyce. You loved that joke back when."

"I loved a lot of strange things back when," said my mother.

"That looks amazing, Kirk," I said. "Thank you, guys, for doing this. What a lovely birthday."

Halley leaned over to give Kirk a kiss on the cheek.

"Those two remind me of you and me back in the beginning, Joycie," said my father, pouring her a third glass of champagne. My mother swatted him with her napkin.

"Where'd you learn to cook like this, Kirk?" I asked him as he served us roasted-chayote-and-red-pepper salad.

"I took a year of cooking classes," he said.

"He's taken woodworking, gardening, calligraphy," said Halley.

"That represents a lotta free time. Bad marriage?" guessed my father.

"That's the only mistake I avoided," Kirk said, blushing. "I just like to be productive."

"It's one of the reasons he's such a fantastic Life Coach," said Halley. "You should work with him, Daddy. He could get all your circuits lit. He really knows focus dynamics. I'm sorry. I have to take this."

She ran to pick up her cell phone.

"I've got so many circuits lit, I'm having rolling blackouts," said Dad, winking as Mom swatted him again.

"Halley wanted me to mention that we got a green light for our new couples seminar," Kirk said, beaming, "based on the one we did at the Learning Annex. 'The Garden of Love: Seeding, Keeping, Weeding, Reaping.' "

"No wonder I got problems," said Dad. "I hate gardening."

"Congratulations," I said to Kirk, suddenly appreciating how he maintained such calm while living with my rattled, hypervigilant, compulsive sister.

After dinner, I opened presents. Halley gave me a gift certificate for more Life Coaching. My mother gave me an IOU for a makeover at Burke-Williams Day Spa, redeemable as soon as she got her Sav-On check. She also gave me two big garbage bags full of clothes. "They were Ng's. He was just about your size," she said to me. "He had quite a few nice pieces. Take 'em, hide 'em, don't wear 'em around me."

Paxton gave me scented soaps, bath salts, and matching powder in a little wooden box.

And then I picked up the long heavy package from Collin. Inside was an oboe, in two pieces. Had he given me his oboe? For a moment, I stood quietly. "I can't take this," I said.

"Hang on. Let me explain," he said, taking the oboe from me and assembling it. "I wanted to give you a really nice present. After what you've just been through and all. You've been a good friend to me and Margie. But I don't really know you well enough to get you something expensive. So . . . uh . . . I can't remember if I told you about how I collect the work of obscure female classical composers? I'm not sure how it all started, but I've got sheet music, live recordings, old radio broadcasts."

"No, you never did," I said, not owning up to my snooping.

"Well, I came upon a piece recently by one of my favorites from the early 1900s . . . Germaine Tailleferre. Rondo for Oboe and Piano," he explained. "I just really like it. The liner notes sum it up pretty well. I went ahead and memorized them in honor of the occasion: 'This good-natured and sunny piece features a rondo theme of long, winding phrases that essentially end where they begin, creating a circular and rather comic effect.' "

The polite announcer-like manner with which he delivered the liner notes made me smile, but I still didn't get what he was doing until he said, "So, if it's okay with everyone, I thought I'd play it for you. Happy birthday."

Then he took a deep breath and began to play the oboe. Long trills and ribbons of notes began to wrap themselves around the room, bouncing off the table in front of him, dancing up the walls to the ceiling, and then spiraling back down. He was a good player. And it was an endearing performance. I was so moved by his trust and good intentions that I was afraid to look down the table to see how the rest of the revelers were reacting. To my great relief, everyone sat quietly for the first few minutes. Although Paxton was staring, expressionless, Halley and Kirk were smiling and holding hands. But about halfway in, my mother's cell phone rang and she stepped outside to take it. The extremely passionate conversation she began to have with her lawyer was so loud, she might as well have stayed put. "Listen, Henry, you tell that Korean son of a bitch that he had no right to . . . No, I know you are handling it, but isn't there some way we can extradite that miserable mugger and prosecute him criminally? I absolutely trust you, and . . . Okay, call me back.

"The lawyer," she stage-whispered when

she finally came back in and sat down. Collin was still playing. If he found it distracting, he didn't let it show.

"They served Ng the papers," my mother whispered too loudly to everyone. "Chased that bastard all over Seoul."

"Mom, shh!" I said, putting my finger to my lips.

"For chrissake, how much longer is he . . . ?" she began, just as the piece ended. We all broke into applause.

"Wonderful!" said my mother, holding up her champagne glass for theatrical value. "Sorry about the phone call. I missed the funny part you mentioned from the liner notes."

"Collin, thank you so much," I said, truly overwhelmed. "I'm blown away. That's one of the nicest presents I've ever received. Thank you."

"I also made you a CD of the piece," he said, holding up a CD that was still in the box. "Couple of my other favorites are on here, too, but I'm afraid I have to keep the oboe."

"That was awesome," Halley gasped. "I hardly ever hear oboe solos anywhere. Except, you know, on those soundtracks they play when they show penguins. You really opened my eyes. Getting those beautiful notes from such a wacky instrument!"

"Nice job, pal," said my father. "And great gift idea. I might have to steal it from you. Talk about a home run with the ladies."

"There's still one more present," said Paxton, "before the accolades are all given. It's waiting for you at home."

"Oooh," said my mother, wiggling her eyebrows at me as Paxton smiled. My father looked over, winked, and gave a thumbs-up.

"A toast to our gal Dawn," said my dad, holding up his glass, "a great gal and a great daughter." After he clinked everyone's glasses, he stood up. "Well, I've gotta go to rehearsal. Be sure and let me know if I get any calls." He got up from the table and headed out the door to his truck. "Nice performance, dude," he said to Collin as he left. "Come by some night and we'll jam."

"Let me walk out with you, I need your opinion about something," said my mother, running after him.

A short while later, when I went outside to walk Chuck, I found them leaning against the truck door, making out. When they saw me, they both got very embarrassed.

"You didn't see that," said my dad, getting into his car.

"Don't judge," said my mother after his truck pulled down the driveway. "I just wanted to see what it felt like all these years later. I needed a distraction. This has been a very rough week."

"That was so disturbing," I said to Chuck as we drove down the driveway. "You know, sometimes I think I have mixed feelings about everyone in my life except you."

"Then perhaps you'll consider that the best way to celebrate your birthday is by dumping Paxton. Bath salts? Come on."

"You're one to talk," I said. "Where's YOUR present?"

"Besides coming back?" he said. "Pull off the road right here and throw the yellow ball. It's right under the seat. I'll bring it back so enthusiastically that I will break your heart with the pure delight I take in simple-minded minutiae. Wait'll you see the look in my eyes!! It's a gift that keeps on giving."

"Okay, fair enough," I said, pulling into a large, empty supermarket parking lot. I picked up the yellow ball and heaved it across the lot. And as he ran back to me carrying it in his mouth, he delivered as promised, 100 percent.

But once he dropped the ball at my feet, he took off running across the lot. "Where you going? Get back here!" I yelled, chasing him.

"Call me at Margie's when HE's gone," he shouted back.

"No you don't," I said. "How dare you? Hey, sir? Officer? Grab that dog, please?" I yelled at a uniformed security guard.

"Does he bite?" he yelled, running to block Chuck's path.

"No," I said.

"Don't be so sure," Chuck yelled as the security guy grabbed him by the collar. I got there a second later.

"Thank you, Officer," I said to the guy, even though he wasn't a cop. "I'm stupid to have let him off the leash.

"Nice birthday present," I said to Chuck, who sat sullenly in the backseat. Neither of us said another word all night.

38
AT LONG LAST
SHEEP

By the time I got home, Paxton had left to do the midnight shift. But there was something wrapped in tissue paper sitting on my pillow. Time stopped for a second as I took in another staggering moment in the New Improved Paxton: He had given me a beautiful antique gold chain along with a handwritten note. "I thought there'd be a point tonight where we would be alone. Somehow it never happened. I bought this for you with the last of my Seattle money. Because I wanted to get you something nice for a change. It's the only way I have to show how much you mean to me. Happy birthday. Love, Paxton. P.S. Now you know why I was late with the rent."

This was not only the most emotional thing I'd seen him do, but he'd been right: It was the best present I'd ever received. I put the necklace on and felt so blessed and grateful, so loved, that I turned on Paxton's show to bask in the glorious history of late-sixties Memphis garage bands.

I felt so full of unexamined emotion. I wanted to write. So I took out my book notes and novel-writing tips. I was now two disasters over my assigned limit of "three disasters plus an ending that leads to the third disaster at the end of Act Two, forcing the beginning of Act Three that will wrap things up."

The beginning of Act Three began a couple of weeks later as a relatively calm day of walking dogs. I got a new regular client: the ironically named Regis, a three-year-old border collie who belonged to Dr. Richter's new girlfriend, Kathy Li. I had to take Regis to his sheep-herding class while his mother was having a root canal.

"I'm kind of bitter," Regis said when I asked how he was enjoying the class. "I spent the first two years of my life wondering when the sheep were going to show up? And finally they do show up and there are only three of them. And you know what? They are so fucking stupid. Why am I supposed to care where they go? Seriously. Why would anyone care?"

While Regis was in the ring, being reprimanded for his lackadaisical circling, he was screaming "Morons. Idiots! Retards!" so loudly at the sheep, I almost couldn't hear the message my mother'd left, teasing me that she had great news.

"Sav-On is interested in the Sports Tree angle," she said, looking more wild-eyed than ever, when I stopped by on my way home. "I pitched them all the sports seasons, plus the überevents like the World Series, the Playoffs, the Allstar Game, the Super Bowl, the Academy Awards. They not only went for it, they think it's even stronger because, unlike the original idea, there are no overlaps in existing product!!"

"Mom, that's amazing!" I said.

"I have a meeting with a new designer. So I was wondering if you had any other ideas I should run by him. That Resurrection of Kmart your friend mentioned — is that something the kids are into?"

"The Resurrection of Melkart? No, I don't th—"

"One second. I have to take this," she said, dashing into the next room to get the phone.

"Instincts telling you anything?" said Chuck. "Hint. Why do I let you throw things for me? Because . . . ?"

"You LET me throw things for you?" I gasped. "Because you have no prehensile thumbs?"

"No. It's an exchange of goods and ser-

316

vices," he said. "What will you get for coming up with stuff for your mom?"

"Less grief," I said. "She's my mom. It's not worth it to try and get anything from her. It doesn't work . . . I don't have the energy. What do I get from throwing things for you?"

"You get my willingness to play along with all your crazy rules. All the stupid things you care about that I don't," he said. "Ask for something in return. Or I'll take a wet tarry dump in her living room." He stared at me, unblinking, as my mother returned, ranting about shipping costs. When I didn't say anything to her, he jumped onto the sofa.

"Mom," I forced myself to say as I grabbed Chuck by the collar, "you're talking about using my ideas, correct?"

"I thought you'd be flattered," she said, suddenly wary.

"I am," I said, "but you realize that means it's now a collaboration between you and me. Right? We have to redo the original contracts."

And then, for having spoken this way, I felt a rush of nausea, vertigo, and a hint of asthma. I had to sit down.

"Silly me," said my mother. "I thought you were simply doing something nice for your mother. After all she's done for you."

I sat quietly, humiliated. "But shouldn't I be paid?" I heard someone say in my voice, using my face. "I mean, shouldn't I have a contract like you had with Ng?"

"So that's the way it is," said my mother. Her lips were compressed. I watched her face turn bright red, then purple. An expression like that required a tide of apologies, but I continued to sit quietly, staring at my lap. She squinted at me. "You think you've got me over a barrel? Well, I'm not going to be kicked around a second time. Get out."

"Okay," I said, rising. "But you can't use my ideas." I walked toward the door, then stopped and took a deep breath. "Mom, you're forgetting who you're talking to," I said. "I don't think I have you over a barrel. This is business. It's only fair that I should get paid. Isn't this how you taught me to look out for myself? Where do you think I learned all this? From you." It was completely untrue. She never taught me anything about looking out for myself. All we ever talked about was her problems. But one thing she had taught me was that flattery could disarm any moment. And my gamble paid off. A sly grin crept onto her face.

"Damned if I do and damned if I don't,

as usual," she said.

A short while later, she agreed to a revised contract.

After that, I took Chuck outside and threw the yellow ball for such a long time that for the first time ever I almost tired him out.

39
I Don't Know Who That Is

Next day, after walking Margie I picked up my phone to check my messages and realized I had four from Halley.

"Hi. It's me. I'm just wondering if you maybe heard from Kirk. He was supposed to meet me here at twelve o'clock and it's almost two now and . . . okay, talk to you later" was the first one.

"It's three-thirty and he's not answering his cell. I am starting to freak. Do you think I should call the police? Where are you? Are you okay?" was the next one. Followed by "Now I am really losing it. If you get this, can you please come over here right away?" The last one was "It's five o'clock. I don't know where anyone is. You're missing. Kirk is missing. The police are on their way. I am really fucking freaked." I called right back.

"I'm not missing," I said. "I'm at Collin's taking Margie for her quote unquote walk. Which is really more of a sit."

"Oh, thank God," she said, sounding more harried than ever. "I just spoke to the police. Kirk's not at any local hospital. They said the policy is to wait a day before filing a missing persons."

"Halley, slow down," I said. "You'll hear from him!"

"You don't understand," she said. "Kirk and I talk on the phone ten times a day. If he isn't picking up his messages, something weird happened."

"I better go over there," I said to Collin, who was working at his desk.

"Want me along for moral support?" he offered.

"You don't have to do that," I said.

"Really? Then forget I said anything," he said.

"If you want to come along, I'd love the company," I said, backpedaling. "Halley might not Life Coach me if you're there. But I don't want to take you from your work."

"Five hours of writing grant applications is plenty for one day," he said. "Not as much fun as it's cracked up to be."

"I really love that CD you made me," I said as we drove south on Pacific Coast Highway toward Halley's. "I play it a lot when I'm driving around with Chuck and the guys."

"Just the kind of venue Germaine Tailleferre was hoping for when she wrote it," he said.

Halley was pacing in front of her Winnebago with her phone when we arrived. "Something is really wrong," she said. "I called his gym, the golf course, the real estate office. His cousin hasn't heard a thing. No one has heard from him."

We all went inside and sat down in the dining room. The sound of a dog toy squeaking pierced the gloomy silence. "Sssh," I said to Chuck, who had brought along the squeaking plastic lambchop in his mouth. Halley's cell phone rang.

"I can't deal with this shit right now," she said, ignoring it. I'd never seen her not take a phone call.

"Will you take that?" she asked when it rang again. "It's Mrs. BTK. Would you please tell her I've got an emergency? I'll call later."

"Halley will call you back," I said to a fast-talking woman's voice. "Mm-hmm. . . . Whoa. That would make me feel crazy, too. But as Halley would probably say, 'What advice would you give to someone else in your shoes?' . . . Hmm. You're right, who else would be in your shoes? Look, *you* know you're not a monster. And if the people at your church are gossipy, I think Halley would tell you, 'Try another church.' Or at least, I would. Okay — go to your Yogalates class and Halley will call soon." I hung up. "She said she can't sleep because at night she starts remembering how she and Dennis used to sit down for hot cider and biscotti and then —"

"And then she turns on the TV and sees a tape of him confessing his crimes," Halley finished my sentence. "I've had that stupid conversation with her five hundred times. Enough."

The room was still, except for the piercing sounds of Chuck's squeaking lambchop. "Sssshhh," I said.

"Still sshh?" Chuck said, dropping the toy again.

"Should we drive around looking for Kirk?" was the question on the table when we became aware of the sounds of helicopters circling.

"Around here that usually means someone famous is getting married," I told Collin, stepping outside to see whose house was the focus. And when I did, I stepped out into the brightest spotlight I'd ever seen.

Like the light from a thousand flashbulbs going off in my face. It was a surreal moment of time suspended. Before anything else could register, at least ten police cars came barreling up the driveway.

"Oh God. He's dead," I heard Halley say as male voices full of adrenaline yelled, "Freeze!" And "Put your hands up!" and "Get down now!" Was I really seeing guns aimed at *me?*

Of course, we all did whatever they said.

"Is this the residence of Kurt Maron?" someone yelled. I could see an FBI ID from the corner of my eye. It was so beyond mind-boggling, I forgot to be terrified. I only worried when I heard Chuck barking inside.

"No," said Halley, facedown in the dirt. "I don't know that name." They handcuffed us all, and we sat up.

"Have you ever seen the man in this photograph?" someone asked, holding up a familiar picture of Kirk posing with his giant screwdriver. In the background, I could hear someone inside the Winnebago yelling, "Get a muzzle on that fucking dog!"

"He's a good boy!" I yelled. "Be gentle. He doesn't bite."

"Fuck! There's no one in here. Fucker was

here yesterday! Fuck! Fuck! Double fuck," I heard the guy sneer, disgusted.

40
New Cocktail Party Chatter

They put us in separate police cars and took us to the FBI headquarters on Wilshire, about an hour's drive. Turned out we had been under surveillance for the past few weeks, during which they had monitored all our calls and "vehicular activity." After we gave them permission, they checked our individual phone records. From that point on, the focus was poor Halley.

That night, we were questioned for varying amounts of time. Since he'd met Kirk only once, Collin was released pretty quickly. He could've gone home, but he sat outside and waited for me. I was detained for about an hour longer. They wanted to know if I had heard anything about an insurance scam. That was when I realized I'd been tuning out Kirk from the moment I met him, the way I used to do Mom. I had so little information, I could barely remember what that love seminar full of gardening metaphors had been about.

After they let me go, Collin and I sat together in the big dark lobby downstairs for another few hours, waiting for Halley.

"This is what you get for offering moral support," I said to him. "No good deed goes unpunished."

"I find the whole thing kinda interesting," he said, sounding a lot more chipper than I felt. "Those FBI guys were really professional. Menacing, but not too threatening. I'm set with cocktail party chat till the end of time."

Halley was interrogated for almost four hours. By the time we helped her into a taxi, she was a mess. Her eyes were swollen from crying. She was shivering and in shock. "They kept asking me about some kind of insurance scam," she said, her nose bright red, her m's all turned to b's from swollen sinuses. "This Kurt Maron guy is wanted for questioning in Virginia about the disappearance of his wife. But my Kirk didn't have a wife. This was going to be a first marriage for us both."

"Halley, you know Kirk is Kurt," I said.

"Look on the bright side," said Collin, "all they want him for so far is unlawful flight to avoid prosecution. They haven't found a body, only a murder weapon."

With that, Halley started to cry again.

"Did they tell you their theory about that?" she said, sobbing. "They think whoever killed this Kurt guy's wife used a screwdriver."

41
No Condition to Play

When we got back to the Winnebago, it was after midnight. Chuck was tied to the front bumper by his leash and not a bit happy about it.

"I'm so sorry about this," I said to him over and over.

"Okay," he said. "You owe me. Let's play ball."

When Halley saw that the inside of the Winnebago had been ransacked by the cops as they dusted for prints and searched for God knew what, she started sobbing again. I wasn't sure what to say. I had my choice of "This had to be a frame-up" and the less likely to be popular "I always thought there was something about that guy that was too good to be true."

"I'm going to reserve final judgment until Kirk and I sit down and have a talk," said Halley. "I would totally know if he was lying to me. We had a super-close connection."

"If there's one thing you should never trust again, it's your super-close connections," I said, which of course made her furious. She roared into her bedroom and slammed the door. Collin and I sat quietly at the kitchen table, listening to her exploding sobs.

"Anything I can do?" I called to her. "Hot tea? Wine?"

The bedroom door flung open. "Just make Chuck stop piling tennis balls on me," she yelled. "I'm in no mood to play. That goes double for the stupid plastic lambchop." She turned and stormed back to bed, closing the door behind her.

"How about you guys? Up for a game?" said Chuck with a mouthful of tennis ball as he exited the bedroom.

"Come here, you," I said, pulling him into my lap. "You're a good boy. But your instincts are as bad as mine."

"My instincts are flawless," he argued. "Who is the one who knew in the first three minutes that Kirk was weird?"

"You never said anything about that," I said.

"I didn't?" he said. "You're kidding! Well, I meant to."

Meanwhile, Collin and I did a Google search on Halley's computer using Kirk's real name and instantly found hundreds of pages of newspaper articles and photographs. The local Virginia newspapers had nicknamed him Mr. Fix-it because his alibi had been that he'd been up all night in the garage fixing the washer and dryer.

He had served one six-year prison term for embezzling.

"Now we know why he had so much time to take all those classes," said Collin. "Too bad the conversation never turned to license plates. We might have had a shot at figuring things out."

About an hour after we got home, we got the first phone call from the *National Enquirer,* wanting to talk to Halley. She sat frozen with anxiety. "I'm getting this creepy feeling that the world knows too much about me," she said. "I always wanted to be famous. But not like this. Will you guys stay here with me tonight? I don't want to be alone."

"I think you'd be better off at my place," said Collin. "I've got a guest room. No one will look for you there."

"What if Kirk can't find me?" said Halley. "We had a couples seminar scheduled for Saturday."

"I think you should put the relationship-counseling arm of the business on hold for the time being," said Collin.

That was when we heard the sound of twigs cracking. Chuck started to hoot. At the end of the driveway was a short blond woman in a dark leather coat holding a mic. With her was a cameraman, his lights aimed in our direction.

"I can't talk to these people," said Halley as her cell phone rang. "Jesus. It's Maura. Will you talk to her? Tell her — fuck, I don't know. Tell her to go ahead and drink."

I took the phone away from Halley and turned it off. Then we sneaked Halley into the backseat of the car, where she lay under a blanket, with Chuck sitting on top of her. As a decoy, we left the lights on in the Winnebago and the radio blasting Paxton's show.

"I hope the reporters like Mott the Hoople or they're in for a long night," I said as we drove past a second TV crew.

"Where's Mr. Fix-it?" they yelled. And "How's Halley holding up?" Other than that, they let us pass undisturbed.

When we were about two miles away and sure we were not being followed, Halley sat up.

"This is the most hideous day of my life," she said.

"Then it's all uphill from here!" I chirped.

"I think you mean *down*hill," Collin corrected.

42
HAPPY SHRIMP CHIPS

It was late when we got back to Collin's. Margie was fuming about being abandoned, so Collin gave her a can of Dinty Moore stew. Brandy, on the other hand, was sleeping soundly. She hadn't even known we were gone.

Collin pulled out the hideaway bed in the couch in his music room and made it up. I moved his music stand, keyboards, and oboes to one corner. But when it came time for me to go home, Halley wouldn't let me leave. So I called Paxton at the radio station and left him a message.

Halley and I hadn't slept in the same bed since we were in grade school. As it turned out, I hadn't missed it at all. She not only snored, she also snorted and inhaled like a pug trapped on its back. Between her epiglottal symphony and three sprawling dogs, I was still awake at 4:00 A.M. So I tried to call Paxton again.

"Why are you there?" he said, half-drunk, exhausted from a long shift. "You know, the only reason in the world that Collin butted his way into another one of your family dramas is he wants to get into your pants. You know that, right? Just ask yourself how you would feel if I was staying at Marla Civatelli's house because her family had a crisis."

"Didn't you get my message about Kirk? And the FBI?" I said. "Who's Marla Civatelli?"

"The programming coordinator at the station," he said. "She's very pretty, and she's always hanging around, offering me suggestions at the end of my shows, wanting to go for coffee. But I shine her on because I'm living with you."

"Paxton, there is nothing going on between Collin and me," I said. "And there are mitigating circumstances. I had to comfort my sister. If that upsets you, I'll come home."

"What makes you think I'm upset?" he said. "Let your new boyfriend inhale dog hair all night."

"I'm coming home right now," I said, hanging up the phone as Collin walked in from his bedroom. He was dressed in dark blue sweatpants and a gray T-shirt, and his hair was sticking straight up. His glasses were off, and his face was flushed. Between the reddish pink in his cheeks and his bewildered expression, he looked like a confused teenager. He carries himself really well, I noted. He has a nice body. Nice shoulders. A sweet face.

"Anything wrong?" he asked.

"I'm going home for a while," I said, putting on my coat.

"Now?" he said. "It's four A.M. Can I make you some coffee?"

"No, I'm fine," I said, approaching to give him a peck good-bye. But instead of a peck, I kissed him on the lips. It was only the briefest kiss, barely registering the feeling of lip surface and stubble as my lips brushed by his cheek. But the electrical wallop coming off him was so intense, neither one of us felt comfortable making eye contact afterward. I pretended not to notice anything, waving good-bye.

When I got home at 5:30, Paxton was asleep, the covers tightly wrapped around him, making him look like some kind of human jelly roll. I stood beside him a while, staring, waiting to see if he would wake up. He grumbled when I touched him gently. So I sat in the front room and stared at the bright orange sun rising over the hot pink

"Shrimp Chips" sign on the roof of the Korean market across the street. It looked strangely beautiful, like a greeting card from a holiday someone forgot to invent.

At least every thirty seconds I relived that almost-kiss.

At 7:00 A.M., the cell phone calls started from Halley again. I thought of waking Paxton, just to collect a few points for my loyalty. Instead, I tiptoed out and drove back to Collin's. And I'm glad I did. By midmorning, the shit hit the fan. And this time the fan was Halley.

43
A Slow News Day

It started with a piece on the Drudge Report, which got picked up by the *New York Post* and Yahoo!, then made its way to *Entertainment Tonight, Access Hollywood,* CNN, and Google News. Maybe because it was a slow news day, with only suicide bombings and an incoming storm update to grab viewers, but suddenly the story of a former girlfriend of Scott Peterson's who nearly married Mr. Fix-it, another suspected wife killer, really hit the spot. That she was a "Life Coach to the stars" who had been instructing people on how to have a relationship was the icing on the cake. Every reporter had some humiliating pun to make. "Life Coach/Death Coach" was a favorite.

At 9:00, Mom called to ask, "What do you think of decorations for the beginning of the TV season?"

"Mom, did you hear about Kirk?" I said.

"You mean wanting to invest in my . . . I mean our . . . tree? I told him to work up a proposal and take it to the lawyer."

"Go online and read the Drudge Report item with Kirk's picture on it," I said, feeling my time was better used trying to tether the flailing Halley to some kind of reality than detailing the shocking facts for Mom.

That morning, Halley's phone never stopped ringing.

"What do I say to all these people who want a comment?" said Halley. "What do I tell my clients? The only good thing is I am too upset to eat. I think I lost five pounds."

"What advice would you have given to one of your clients if they were in this situation?" I asked, aware that the probability of this situation recurring was minuscule.

"Well, I'd tell them to begin some kind of endorphin-producing activity like running or speed-walking. Or something emotionally cathartic like scrapbooking," she said. "I am so full of shit. Even I can't stand to hear myself talk anymore."

I had never seen her like this. Staring out of her eyes was a withered dark creature too small to drive her big skeletal system around.

"This is CNN," I said, checking the number when the phone rang.

"I can't talk to anyone," she said, hunched forward, manically doodling ever smaller concentric circles with her pen. "Can I maybe be hospitalized?"

"Look," I said, "it's like you told Mrs. BTK . . . YOU didn't do anything wrong except have bad taste. You need to do something to help yourself let go. Tell me what color candles we need to burn, and I'll go buy them."

"If I were coaching someone else, I guess I'd say, 'You made an honest mistake. It's part of being human. Own your shortcomings, incorporate them into your aura, and grow,'" said Halley. She considered this for thirty seconds. "That's not such bad advice, is it?" she said. Then she picked up the phone in a swell of new purpose and pressed star sixty-nine. When she next spoke, her voice was reenergized. "Halley Tarnauer returning . . . Larry King? Why the fuck not."

44
ARE WE ALL NOW JUST IDIOTS?

"Write about issues that keep you awake in the middle of the night" was the next exercise in my novel-writing manual. It seemed perfect because I had begun waking up at 4:00 A.M. and not being able to go back to sleep.

Things that keep me awake:
1. Paxton: A) How can I say for sure whether things are working with us when I have never seen a relationship up close that works? B) Is Chuck's advice about Paxton wisdom distilled from millions of years of Darwinian instinct? Or the voice of my own dementia packaged in a sad-eyed fuzzy form that I can tolerate? And C) Which relatively popular psychological cliché am I now? Are there even "women who love too much" anymore? Or since Dr. Phil, are we now all just idiots?

2. Mom: She totally freaked when she learned that Kirk was Mr. Fix-it. Not because of Halley, but because Kirk had presented her lawyer with an investment proposal accompanied by a check for one thousand dollars. She was certain that this paper trail was going to wreck everything. "If our product gets linked to him, we're dead," she shrieked over and over. "Nothing kills the spirit of holiday decorating faster than a grisly homicide."

3. Kirk's wife: I only found one picture of her anywhere. Who was she? Did she look like Halley? Did she have any inkling about this side of him before he attacked? Did she think she loved him? He made me a birthday dinner. I sat with him and ate the food he cooked. Was there something I should have picked up? Was Halley in danger? Was I?

4. God: The Bible says God loves man. But it doesn't say anything about Him liking us. If He did, wouldn't He have passed along certain information at critical times to at least one prophet or saint? I'm talking about the kind of information that we were going to find out anyway. Like, for example, the fact that it was bacilli, and not the Jews, that caused plague? Who in their right mind

wouldn't pass on an important fact like that to someone they liked at the time when they needed it most? The only reason I can think of for withholding those details for hundreds of years was He just doesn't like us very much.

A couple of days later, Halley's particularly effective appearance on *Larry King Live* really opened up a new set of opportunities for her. Her ease on camera, combined with her connection to so many of the famously disturbed, made her the go-to gal for simplistic panel discussions on the workings of the sociopathic mind. I came home from work early to watch the show because Halley was relying on my reinforcement to hold her ego together. I had spent the previous week helping her decide what to wear. And when I say "helping," I mean agreeing with everything she said. I nodded as she debated between duplicating what Oprah wore on the cover of *O* that month and dressing like Kelly Ripa. "Or I could go the Gretchen Wilson route — smart, sassy grassroots woman who don't take no shit," she said. In the end, she duplicated a Nancy Grace ensemble, hoping to seem the very picture of an honest businesswoman bouncing back after being bamboozled.

"Coming up next: a woman who has been in the news a lot lately. She says she has 'learned firsthand everything we need to know about sociopaths' and is here to help us learn how to spot them," said Larry King as the camera panned to Halley, looking thin and pretty. "She's counseled actress Maura Kenney, as well as the wife of the BTK killer, and she actually dated Scott Peterson. And if those aren't credentials enough, she ran a business with and almost married accused screwdriver killer Kurt Maron, also known as Mr. Fix-it. How do we spot a sociopath, Halley?"

"Send me his picture. If I fall in love with him, he's a sociopath." Halley laughed. "It's like speed-dating, only faster."

"They found Kurt Maron doing relation-ship counseling at the Esalen Institute," said Larry King. "Any comments?"

"As long as the students who use his advice are used to a dating pool full of sociopaths — for instance, politics or show business," she said brightly, "they should do fine."

"She's hot," said Paxton as we sat side by side on the floor of the Red Room, watching the broadcast. Later, I found out that when Halley was walking out to her car, she was offered a book contract from Judith Regan.

The minute the show was over, Paxton went back into the bedroom, where he had moved his desk, and closed the door. He'd become increasingly obsessed with his privacy now that Halley and Mom were always dropping by. He officially hated the apartment, calling it claustrophobic. Worst of all, he was back to insisting that the dogs sleep in the hall.

We fought about this so frequently that when I was offered a job as the overnight tech at the Animal Hospital three days a week, I said yes, even though it meant spending the night on the cot in back of the kennel from 9:00 P.M. to 6:00 A.M. It was easy work; not much happened besides demands from the patients to please take the IV out of them and throw the ball. What I liked most was that Chuck and Brandy could stay there with me. That cut down a lot of the arguing, but it was getting so I hardly saw Paxton at all. Sometimes he'd be heading for a morning shift just as I got home. Sometimes he was waking up just as I went to work. And all of this would have been fine were it not for the fact that Claire had been accepted into veterinary school and was moving up north to start a brand-new chapter of her life. Next thing I knew, Dr. Richter had somehow rehired Roxy.

I did everything I could to avoid running into her. I began skulking around, using the back entrance, making sure her car was not in the lot yet when I walked through. But like all destiny that can be stalled but not eliminated or denied, on her fourth day of work, we came face-to-face outside the restroom.

"Dawn!" she started buoyantly, as though excited to rekindle an old friendship.

"Hi," I said. When I began to walk away, she quickly changed tack.

"We have to talk," she said. "I'm so sorry about everything. I was wrong about you. I didn't understand." Her eyes began to well up with tears. "I was blind at first. And then it was too painful for me to believe," she said. "When my father changed radio stations and there was no job for Paxton at the new one, suddenly he was looking right through me. One morning, out of the blue, he announced that he was leaving. No warning. No discussion. No nada."

"But he said it was for your own good?" I offered.

"He talked to you about me?" she said, her eyes wide with astonishment.

Once the dam was broken, Roxy couldn't

hold back. She kept dashing into the dog bathing room every fifteen minutes to resume her story wherever she'd left it last. Amid her veterinary duties, and while watching me soap up dogs, she'd trudge beat by beat through painful personal stories about Paxton I didn't want to hear.

"In the beginning, we were both so thrilled about everything that was happening, we actually made plans to get married," she said as she expressed the anal glands of a shih tzu. "He actually bought me a starter ring, encrusted with diamond chips. P.S. When we broke up, I went and had it appraised. It was a piece of junk. It cost seventy-nine dollars."

A short time later, while removing stitches from the back leg of a shar-pei, she recalled how the guy who replaced her father changed the station from an alternative to a classic rock format. Paxton made a preemptive strike and quit before he was fired.

"I assumed we'd stay and he'd try to find other work. We'd been looking at houses. I didn't see any of this coming," she said while giving a bulldog his annual rabies and DHLPP shots. "I thought we were in love and planning a future." She paused, then started to cry. I put my arms around her, giving her a hug that, a few months before, would have been neck-wringing.

She followed me over to Starbucks on my break and kept right on talking. I didn't have the heart to tell her to shut up. So I listened grim-faced to Paxton stories ad nauseam. "I can't tell you how much I appreciate you talking to me about this," she said, unaware that I barely said a word. "I've never been dumped before. It really caught me off balance. I mean, originally, when I heard that he dumped you, I thought it all made sense because he and I were meant to be together. I know you two are together again now, so I hope it's cool talking to you like this. I'm sure you don't need to worry this time. Because you don't really have anything for him to use, right? Wait, I didn't mean it like that. What I meant is, I just really need your perspective. Who else can I talk to about him?"

It was stifling in Starbucks. I was breaking into a sweat. As Roxy went on and on, I leaned back on the couch and unzipped my hooded sweatshirt, pulling it off my shoulders like a shawl.

"Thank you so much for letting me unload on you," she said, sipping her third chai latte. "I am so grateful. You are a really good person, and . . . Oh my God . . ." Her face went white. "That chain you're wearing."

"Nice, huh?" I said, thinking now would not be a good time to let her know where I got it.

"I bought that for Paxton. Last month. For his birthday," she said.

45
GOD SAVE THE QUEEN

When I came home with the dogs that night, it was as if someone had taken every single thing I owned and replaced it with a slightly imperfect duplicate. Everything looked the same, but nothing seemed right.

Paxton was lying on the Murphy bed, listening to CDs.

"D'ja hear the show on Bo Diddley?" he said.

"No, I missed that," I said, sitting in our only chair. Chuck sat quietly at my feet. But Brandy, for reasons of her own, was suddenly happy to see Paxton. She jumped up on the bed and ran over to give him a kiss.

"Off," he yelled at her. "Get her off me."

"Come on, Paxton, she likes you," I said, pulling her off the bed. "She's a baby. She's been sick, and she's finally getting her energy back."

"Good. That must mean she's ready to go

home now," he said. "When's that gonna happen?"

"I haven't talked to her asshole owner in a while," I said. "I really don't want to send her back there."

"Back where?" said Brandy as I held her by her collar.

"So I don't get a say in this?" said Paxton.

A retort involving betrayal, seventy-nine-dollar wedding rings, twice-given gifts, and withheld back rent stuck in my throat. When I felt my bronchi closing, I made a cup of tea. Then I took the dogs downstairs for a walk around the block.

"You don't smell anything I should know about on his pants these days, do you?" I asked Chuck.

"Well, at the moment there are trace elements of alcohol, urine, vanilla, fructose, saltpeter, a couple kinds of oil . . . olive, eucalyptus, human. Guar gum. Whatever that is," Chuck said, "and estrogen. Mostly the lap area."

"That doesn't mean anything," I said, starting to wheeze.

"Do you have a second to talk?" I asked Paxton as he was closing his briefcase, about to head out the door to do the 10:00 P.M. show. Now dressed in his new True Religion jeans and prized original "God Save the

351

Queen" T-shirt, he sighed impatiently.

"What now?" he said.

"I just wanted to tell you how much Roxy liked this chain you bought me with the last of your Seattle money," I said.

"Where'd you see Roxy?" he said, suddenly serious.

"They hired her back at the hospital," I said.

"Really? Well, you two must have had a field day talking shit about me," he said, suspiciously. "Way to go. Nice time to fuck with my head. Right before I have to go on the air and talk to seventy-five thousand people."

I stood quietly, staring down at my crusty boots. "I thought it was kinda weird that you gave me a birthday present she bought you and said that —"

"She told you that?" He stood shaking his head in disbelief. "Whew. She is such a psycho. Now you know why I broke up with her. She's crazy. She's jealous and nuts."

"So she didn't buy you that chain you gave me?"

"Can I finish? Can I ever complete a thought without you interrupting?" he barked, then paused and glared before he continued. "She's trying to break us up. That's what's going on. *I* bought you that chain because I thought it would look great on you. Period. Roxy is a very sick, disturbed person."

As I was trying to think of a response, he angrily diverted again. "Would it be possible to put this on hold until after my show? Aren't you the chick who's worried about the rent?" Then he left, still shaking his head and muttering, "Goddamn Roxy. What a vindictive psycho bitch."

I spent the afternoon fretting about how poorly I had handled things. Maybe I shouldn't have taken any of what Roxy said seriously. After all, if you live your life basing your opinions of someone on other people's complaints, you'd soon find yourself with no members of the human race to love.

Maybe that was why God didn't like us, I thought. He was sick to death after a million years of listening to a billion souls whine about one another. Maybe even He didn't know who to believe.

Was Roxy psycho? When I replayed her performance in my head, her overwrought histrionics seemed too awkward and embarrassing to be anything but the truth.

I started out drinking hot tea as I waited for Paxton to come home. At midnight, I walked across the street to the Korean grocery and bought a small bottle of vodka. Then I made myself a much better martini than the one I'd made at Maura's the night this all started, proving that at least some progress had been made.

Turning on Paxton's show, I realized I was in the wrong mood to listen to him rhapsodize about the roots of grunge and "the original guy in the plaid flannel shirt, St. Neil Young."

When he finally came home at about 1:00 A.M. I was lying on the bed, reading. He walked in without saying a word, got himself a beer, and drank half of it in one gulp.

"Ya hear the show?" were his first words.

"No, not really," I said.

"Wanna hear it now?" he sulked.

"Sure," I said, examining the backs of my hands. They needed moisturizer.

"I have a bad feeling about all this," he said.

"About all what?" I said.

"You know about all what," he said. "And if you don't, what does that say about us?"

"Okay," I said. "This is getting too confusing. Want to know what I'm thinking? I'm not sure you like me. Maybe this is kind of cliché, but animals, well, dogs, are what I do for a living. One reason I like spending time with them so much is they seem to think people are really good. They live with us, and obey our rules, most of which make no sense to them. And the main reason they do it is because they like us. When I watch them, sometimes I'm so blown away by how enthusiastic they are about everything we do that I have to go out and buy them something squeaky or chewy. Just because I love proving to them that it's not a mistake to see the world as a great benevolent place. I hope one day to react to something with as much pure ecstasy as I see in Chuck's face every time I throw the ball. Sometimes he looks so happy, it reminds me of the way blind people smile way too big because they can't see themselves. And if none of this links to anything in you, well . . . I think you don't know who I am. And that makes me think I'm just waiting around to be surprised that you've decided it's time for you to get out of here. Again."

"Ah! Circular girl logic!" he said. "I can prove I know exactly who you are. Every time I ask you to listen to my show . . . you divert all the attention back to you. You walk the dog, you give the dog medicine, you look for the dog. You can't stand not to have all the attention."

"I've listened to most of your shows," I said. "I can hardly wait for the show about

Rosicrucian Death. What I don't understand is how you can be annoyed by a puppy. What happens if I get cancer?"

"From puppies to cancer?" he said. "There's a logical progression. You know, a lot of people think that putting animals ahead of people is a form of mental illness. A lot of very intelligent people think dogs are dirty animals with a brain the size of a walnut and a two-second attention span."

Brandy wagged her tail enthusiastically. "Dude, I tuned out for a second. Anything good going on?" she said.

"So. If you're breaking up with me because of that, then what is this really about?" he said.

I sat quietly thinking.

"You're right," I said finally. "I got carried away. You're the most important person in my life."

He got up to load the CD of his show into the boom box. "If you are ready to commit to a real future together, and it means getting rid of the dogs . . . then I guess that is something I am willing to do."

He smiled. Then he walked over to me, leaned down, and gave me a very sexy kiss. After which I did the hardest thing I've ever had to do. I took both of the dogs to the pound and left them there.

46
JUST KIDDING

Of course that's not what happened. If there was a pound where I could've taken Paxton, I would have. I'm sort of sorry there's not such a place. It would be a very good use of our taxes.

As the fight continued, I kept thinking, How long do I really want to be around a snaky, obstinate, opportunistic little prick like this?

The voice that discussed this with me in my head was using a personal pronoun. I decided it might make sense to call it my instincts.

My instincts and I told Paxton we needed some time alone to think about everything. Of course, he didn't agree, because it wasn't his idea.

"It's for your own good," I said. "You need to concentrate on your show. The dogs will just distract you."

"So this is how it's going to be?" he said.

"We just pick up and run every time anything goes wrong?"

And when I didn't speak, he followed up with "How am I supposed to pay the rent?"

"You're covered," I said. "I paid first and last month's rent up front. It's my way of thanking you for spending all your hard-earned money on a present for me." Then I packed my suitcase, took the dogs, and went back to Halley's.

Chuck was filled with so much joyful energy at our departure that his acrobatic vertical bouncing made it difficult to hook him to his leash.

Of course, as I backed the car out and realized what I had done, I panicked. "It seemed like it was just a matter of time till the other shoe dropped," I began to counter my own arguments.

"Even if he dropped his shoes all day, the guy doesn't like puppies," said Chuck. "Who doesn't like puppies? That's psychotic. In a pack, we'd kill him."

Luckily for me, the timing of my move back to the Winnebago suited Halley, who was now a mandatory guest on every crime-related discussion show on cable: on Court TV, on MSNBC, on the Discovery Channel. She loved having me around to listen as she tried out quips. "Is it funny to call him

Kirk the Ripper?" she asked me.

"Well," I said, "not Chris Rock funny. But kinda funny for Court TV."

"Oh, good," she said.

Though glib and composed on camera, she was devastated every time new information about Kirk surfaced. It was especially rough when local authorities found his wife's body hidden in the home they had shared in Virginia. Worse still, the police revealed that because she had still been alive after he'd stabbed her with the screwdriver, he'd strangled her.

With each new grisly detail, Halley's star went higher. Soon she was on TV almost daily. Before each appearance, she'd compulsively Google Kirk, fearing something would be revealed on air that she hadn't yet heard.

"Damn! His prison picture is on Smoking Gun," she said. "He even looks hot with numbers under his face. Bet it pisses Scott off. Scott loves being the cutest frosh convict."

Obsessed though she was, she was smart enough to also be keeping notes for use in a seminar she was planning called "From Singles Bars to Prison Bars: The Lie of Loving a Criminal."

"You know what's got me spooked?" she

said one night. "He used to put his hands around my throat when we made love. I told myself it was because he was so into me."

For the next few weeks, there was more family togetherness than I had ever known. In the evenings, Mom would come by, drink whiskey sours, and discuss her new holiday ideas while she awaited the debut of what she was now calling the ALL the Holidays Tree. "In the Lillian Vernon catalog, they personalize absolutely everything," she said. "So here's what I'm thinking: No one has done anything to personalize the manger scene. Say someone's a big Lakers fan. What if they could order the Three Wise Men in Lakers uniforms? Or the military! Everybody in camouflage?"

"So if someone likes ballet, they can get Mary in a tutu and Joseph in tights?" I asked when I could finally speak.

"Don't be silly. We don't have to offer that one," she said. "Go ahead and make all the fun you want. We'll see how hard you're laughing when we both cash our checks."

She was wrong. When her lawyer advised us to accept the offer that Sam's Club made to buy the ALL the Holidays Tree for $1.2 million, I did start to laugh. I laughed hard.

"The lawyer advised us to take the money and let Sam's Club handle the stress from the link to Kirk if and when it ever becomes known," said Mom. "I said amen to that. Did you hear that they found his wife's body hidden in their chimney? The only thing worse for our tree sales would be if he strangled her with a string of lights."

And then she handed me a check for $350,000.

By the end of the week, I had found an empty gas station for sale. It was on a corner lot near Alvarado and Sunset, right next door to a Sizzler. "Smells like prime rib around here," said Chuck. "Grab it." So I did.

It was one of those old A-frames with a big whitewashed billboard above the roof that used to say "Standard." Now it stood vacant, surrounded by a cyclone fence, the pumps and storage tanks gone, long grass and weeds growing through the crumbling asphalt. The price was right because it was a structure adrift between two worlds: the old, more depressed version of the neighborhood and the new upscale one in the midst of being born. Two discount gas stations across the street that were easier to approach from Sunset put the final nails in the coffin.

The first person I called to come see it was Collin. "It was probably built in the mid-sixties," he said. "That was when all this A-frame nonsense started." I followed as he walked around the lot, studying the place like it was Pompeii. "It'll be pretty easy to pull up this asphalt," he said. Then he insisted on showing me exactly how easy by getting a shovel out of the back of his car and beginning to dig. Despite his declarations, he was sweating like a guy on a road crew. Once again, I was reminded that he not only had a body underneath those ill-fitting clothes, he was in pretty good shape.

"See?" he said, breathing hard after exposing about a square foot of dirt. "Piece of cake. Or maybe a more challenging dessert. Piece of tiramisù. What color do you want to paint the exterior?"

"Well, I'm not sure. What do you think?" I said, going up to him and putting my arm through his. Side by side, we stood staring at my brand-new gasless station. The electrical current between us was so breathtaking, it was kind of embarrassing. I didn't know how to act, so I just kept standing there adrift in an erotic limbo. Luckily for me, my cell phone finally rang.

"You better take that," said Collin. "I need a break. My brain is starting to melt."

It was Halley calling with the news that Paxton had moved in with Marla Civatelli.

She'd heard it from an agitated Roxy. Apparently she had contacted Paxton after she'd learned we'd split. "You need to get rid of that necklace he gave you that she gave him," said Halley. "The toxic energy is holding you back. Go to the beach, light a white candle —"

"Halley, now that your career is launched," I said, "I hope it's okay to tell you I don't want a Life Coach anymore."

"Good girl," said Halley. "You're definitely becoming a more yellow thinker and —"

"Stop," I said. "Save it for the people who pay you."

"But as sisters, can't we be there for each other?" she asked. "It's ninety percent sure I'm going on *Oprah*."

"I'm happy to help you get ready for *Oprah*," I said. "You know what's a good idea? You should get a Life Coach."

"Hmm," she said. "I know you're kidding, but that's very good advice. A lot of Life Coaches have Life Coaches because we tune in to each other in ways normal people can't. I'm proud to see that my teachings have rubbed off in such a positive way."

Not until after the phone call ended did the new Paxton information hit.

"Marla Civatelli is a senior programmer at his station," I said to Collin, my golden moment with him now dead. "I guess he's finally got a paying job." I tried to look pleased but felt my whole infrastructure short-circuiting as I registered how quickly I'd been replaced.

"You haven't been replaced. You're just no longer useful," said Collin. "Big difference between being valued and being used." He took me by the hand and led me over to the part of the station where they used to sell soft drinks and candy bars to show me his idea for creating a dog lounging area. "Which is not to say that every filthy, bug-infested corner of the planet isn't already a perfect dog lounge," he said, "but the owners will like this one better."

When escrow closed, I still went into shock. But after that wore off, I felt a new kind of relief. Finally, a place where I was in control.

Oddly enough, that same week, Mikayla turned up at the Animal Hospital looking for me. Her stepfather had sold the condo out from under her. When I showed her the gas station, she was awestruck. "This is everything I have ever wanted," she whispered, reverently offering to work for free to pay back the four hundred dollars she owed me. I let her move into the place while we were renovating.

The following morning, on the blank and peeling billboard that used to say "Standard" just above the roofline, was painted: "Anything, anything would be better than this agony of mind, this creeping pain that gnaws and fumbles and caresses one and never hurts quite enough. — Jean-Paul Sartre."

"Well, that's uncharacteristically cheery," I said to Mikayla, noting her use of multicolored letters.

"I guess it reflects how happy I am to be living in a real gas station," she said.

Later on, when I drove to Collin's to walk Margie, it was hard to grasp the way so many things were changing. For instance, when I stepped inside the apartment, he gave me a hug. And I noticed that he smelled good. Lucky for me he was so bad at advancing that all I had to do was not retreat. I didn't want things moving too quickly.

Though it seems like time itself moves more slowly when you're in the presence of people who actually see and hear you. There's a certain weight to a moment that never comes when you feel invisible.

I guess the strangest part of the whole saga was the way that breaking up with Paxton finally taught him how to love me. Had I stayed around, I've no doubt he would have continued to find me a burden. He would have kept looking right through me, talking past me, contemplating reasons to leave.

But once I left for good, I became the greatest love that Paxton had ever known. He began to eulogize me on his radio show in such an overblown way that people kept saying cryptic things like "Do you listen to Paxton's show? . . . Good. Don't."

First of all, he changed the name of his midnight show from *Off the Grid* to *Waiting for Dawn.* Then he opened it with a techno montage of "Dawn" by Frankie Valli that merged into songs by Tony Orlando and Dawn interspersed with pieces of famous poems or songs where the word *Dawn* was mentioned, like the national anthem and the one about the dawning of the age of Aquarius. Mikayla heard him deliver more than one somber monologue about two souls united, then torn asunder, as an introduction to a block of songs of intense alternative heartbreak. I responded by making Mikayla promise to refrain from telling me any more about the show, ever again.

The day I moved into my gas station, I was filled with an oddly harmonious feeling of finally living in three dimensions. Collin had helped me clear a living area in the back corner of the station interior. We scrubbed the floor and put a bed next to the wall, behind the lube racks. Then he called and ordered drywall, promising to meet the delivery folks at 7:00 A.M.

At about 10:00 that night, I ordered takeout salads from a pizza place down the road. Mikayla was off with Otis, helping him catalog his photos of cement people.

Alone for the first time in the bowels of my future dog day care center, I got lost in a dozen books on interior design that Collin had brought from the library. I was so involved sketching plans and making lists of things to buy that it was near sunrise by the time I began to wind down. Chuck snuggled up beside me. Brandy was asleep on the other side of the room, on a blanket, her head resting on a tire. Outside, I could hear crickets. It was so late, there were no cars.

"Know what?" I said to Chuck. "Even though I still don't know if you are talking to me or I'm just talking to myself, I've decided I don't much care. Whatever's going on is fine."

"I agree completely," said Chuck.

"When you ran away, I worried you didn't know how much I love you," I said to him, stroking his head. "Now that you do, you better not be thinking of pulling any more stunts like that."

"Do you love me as much as Swentzle?" he said.

"It's not a contest, Chuck. But yes, of course I do."

"Not good enough." He scowled. "I wanna hear you say it."

"Okay, okay. I love you as much as Swentzle," I said.

"I knew I'd wear you down," he said, sounding a little smug. "So now I'll make you a promise. Remember how Swentzle just disappeared? I never will. I'm not into bullshit clichés like dying."

"You can't really make that promise," I said.

"Really?" he said. "You think I can't? Just watch me." And as he said it, a golden shimmer appeared where the horizon was supposed to be. Then a red sun pushed up, like the head of some fiery infant bulging out of the gray sea's womb, water giving birth to a dog with a mouth full of squeaking latex ball. At this celestial sign that a new day had begun, Chuck ran over and dropped that ball into my lap.

"Throw this," he said.

So I did.

ACKNOWLEDGEMENTS

I want to thank my editor, Bruce Tracy; my production editor, Beth Pearson, and my copy editor, Sona Vogel; my agent, Melanie Jackson; my friend Susan Jaffee, for the title; my brother, Glenn; and Andy Prieboy, Puppyboy, and Hedda, for all their help, in all areas, while I was writing. And, of course, thanks as always to Dawn Mazella and Halle.

ABOUT THE AUTHOR

Emmy Award–winning writer **Merrill Markoe** has authored three books of humorous essays and the novel *It's My F---ing Birthday,* and co-authored (with Andy Prieboy) the novel *The Psycho Ex Game.* She thinks www.merrillmarkoe.com will exist by the time this book is published but in the meantime an overly long biographical résumé can already be found at www.the psychoexgame.com. She lives in Los Angeles, if you can call that living.

The employees of Thorndike Press hope you have enjoyed this Large Print book. All our Thorndike and Wheeler Large Print titles are designed for easy reading, and all our books are made to last. Other Thorndike Press Large Print books are available at your library, through selected bookstores, or directly from us.

For information about titles, please call:
    (800) 223-1244

or visit our Web site at:
    www.gale.com/thorndike
    www.gale.com/wheeler

To share your comments, please write:
    Publisher
    Thorndike Press
    295 Kennedy Memorial Drive
    Waterville, ME 04901